"Why won't MyMolly marry us?"

Dulcy's voice broke—and Logan thought his heart would, too. "Is it because of me?" she asked.

"No, Dulcy," he said. "It's not because of you. Molly loves you very much. It's because of me."

"Maybe you asked her wrong."

Logan smiled grimly. "Maybe I did."

"So ask her right and then she'll marry us." Dulcy nodded her head as though encouraging him to agree with her. She was like a teacher coaching a really slow student.

"I'll try, but I can't guarantee she'll say yes. But I'll work out something so you and I can be happy. Just give me a chance, Dulcy. I'm not so bad."

The child cocked her head, assessing him, then she sighed like a grown-up and walked slowly over to lean against his knees. She patted his arm gently. "Don't be sad, Grandfather Logan, okay? I know you aren't bad." She nodded several times as though adding up a column of figures in her head.

"You found me, that's good. You gave me my Dulcy doll, that's also good. You found me again when I got lost in the airport. And you slept on the floor next to my bed so I wouldn't be scared when I woke up. That's all good." She nodded once more and smiled up at him. "Okay?"

Logan didn't think he could take much more without breaking down completely. *I can do it,* he told himself firmly. *If I have to, I can raise this child alone, but God in Heaven, I don't want to. Oh, Molly, I need you! We need you. Where are you?*

ABOUT THE AUTHOR

The Only Child—a finalist in the RWA's 1995 Golden Heart Awards—is Carolyn McSparren's first published novel. However, this talented writer has written poems and magazine articles for many years. She's always loved romantic mysteries, but not until a friend took her to a local RWA (Romance Writers of America) chapter did she begin to write romance fiction.

Carolyn has lived in Germany, France, Italy "and too many cities in the U.S. to count. In my checkered career," she says, "I've sailed boats and raised horses. I've been a horse-show momma for my daughter, who is now grown and married."

Carolyn now lives in the country outside Memphis, Tennessee, in an old house with three dogs, three cats, two horses and one husband—"not necessarily in order of importance."

THE ONLY CHILD
Carolyn McSparren

Harlequin Books

TORONTO • NEW YORK • LONDON
AMSTERDAM • PARIS • SYDNEY • HAMBURG
STOCKHOLM • ATHENS • TOKYO • MILAN
MADRID • WARSAW • BUDAPEST • AUCKLAND

ISBN 0-373-70725-8

THE ONLY CHILD

Copyright © 1997 by Carolyn McSparren.

This edition published by arrangement with Harlequin Books S.A.

® and TM are trademarks of the publisher. Trademarks indicated with
® are registered in the United States Patent and Trademark Office, the
Canadian Trade Marks Office and in other countries.

Printed in U.S.A.

For Martha Shields and Amelia Bomar, who stuck
with me from the beginning, and for Zilla Soriano,
a fine editor.

Thanks also to Alix Sullivan, a real doll lady, for sharing
her technical expertise.

CHAPTER ONE

MOLLY HALLIDAY DROVE her hands through her hair, picked up her scalpel and spoke to the grinning head on the table. "All right, Quentin Charles Dillahunt the Third, if you don't help me get your eyebrows right you're going to wind up in the slag heap."

The small bisque head leered back through empty eye sockets as Molly began to carve tiny chunks from the moist unfired clay. Feathery eyebrows emerged bit by bit.

"Where are you attaching the horns?" Sherry Carpenter asked, glancing up from the doll magazine in her lap.

Molly grinned and kept working. "The real Quentin's only four years old. What's he ever done to you?"

"Not me. He tried to bite my niece Sarah's ear off last winter. He's a little demon. You're making him look downright angelic."

"Mrs. Dillahunt, Senior, commissioned this portrait doll," she told Sherry. "Another Memphis grandparent who thinks her grandkid is an angel. Thank God, I do my commissions from photographs. I don't have to put up with Quentin in real life."

Sherry unfolded from the bentwood rocker and smoothed down her immaculate slacks. "You'd better put that thing away. Zoe and Logan MacMillan will be here any minute."

Molly checked her watch. "They're not due for twenty minutes."

"They may be early."

"Give me five minutes. I really need to finish these eyebrows. I'm a week behind on my commissions, and I don't get paid the rest of my fee until I deliver the finished doll." Her hand rested momentarily on the head and she frowned over at her friend. "Besides, how come Logan MacMillan has to approve my deal with MacMillan's? I thought Zoe ran the store."

Sherry shoved a large ginger cat off a nest of magazines on the work counter and began to organize them into a neat stack. "She does, but her father actually owns it. Usually, he simply rubber-stamps her decisions, only this time he didn't."

"Well, he should have. My dolls will sell very well in MacMillan's."

"I know that, you know that, Zoe knows that. We just have to convince Logan."

"Have to is right." Molly waved a hand at the room. "I went two thousand dollars over budget building this darned workshop. I need some more outlets for my dolls fast if I'm going to pay the bills and have enough left over for frivolous stuff like food."

"You had to build it, Molly. The dolls were taking over every flat surface in your house. Visiting you was like walking into a deli for very small cannibals." Sherry wrinkled her nose. "Not to mention the dust."

Molly bent to get a better view of Quentin's forehead. "I know, I know. I needed the workshop, I needed the showroom, I even needed the reception room. It all seemed so essential. Now I wish I'd made do with a little less space." She squinted at Quentin and ran her thumb along his cheekbone, lifting it a millimeter and rounding it off slightly. "I love making these critters, but, Lord, do I hate having to deal with professional store-buyers. Scares me to death. Thanks for giving me moral support. Now tell me a little about Mr. MacMillan."

"He used to be one of those international construction engineers—you know, build a bridge in Tanzania, a dam in Brazil, then home for a month and off to build a plant in Costa Rica."

"Somehow I can't visualize Zoe growing up in a mud hut."

Sherry laughed. "She didn't. When I met her mother, Sydney, in college I knew we were kindred spirits—anything less than a four-star hotel was roughing it. Sydney turned that old mansion into MacMillan's and converted the third floor into a chic apartment. That's where Zoe grew up. Sydney died a couple of years ago, but Logan still lives there. He's semi-retired. I guess he didn't see any reason to move."

"Is Zoe an only child?"

Sherry hesitated. "She had a younger brother named Jeremy. He was killed in an automobile accident. You were divorcing Harry about that time or you would have seen it in the papers. Big scandal. Jeremy's wife, Tiffany, was driving. They were both very, very drunk. She didn't get a scratch."

"Lord, Sherry, how awful."

"It gets worse. Tiffany was convicted of vehicular homicide, but before she could be sentenced, she ran away and took her baby with her. Sydney died about a year after that. Officially, it was emphysema. I think it was a broken heart."

"Poor Zoe. I guess you never know what kind of trouble people carry around with them." Molly opened the drawer beside her, cleaned her scalpel and put it away.

Then she picked up a smaller one and held it up to the light. "I'm glad she and Rick got married. He's a nice man."

Sherry glanced at the round kitchen clock that hung on the wall beside the door to the showroom, and laid five red-tipped fingers on Molly's arm. "Molly, you better put that head away this minute and take a look at yourself." She pulled a small mirror across the counter and positioned it in front of Molly's face.

"Oh, good grief. I look like I'm wearing a powdered wig. Why didn't you tell me my hands look like something from the mummy's curse?"

"I've been trying to spiff you up since that first day in the tenth grade when you walked into my homeroom. You're my oldest and dearest friend. I'm happy if you stay one step ahead of the fashion police."

At that moment the alarm bell from the end of the driveway sounded twice followed closely by the crunch of gravel signifying a vehicle in the parking area at the top of the hill. "Damn, they *are* early. I hate it when you're right."

She grabbed a wet towel, swathed the bisque head, stuffed it in the small refrigerator under the counter, then slid the unused scalpel back into the drawer under her worktable. She rubbed the end of her nose fiercely and unhooked her bare feet from the rungs of her stool. "For Pete's sake, Sherry, help me find my shoes!"

LOGAN MACMILLAN pulled his black BMW into the parking area beside his daughter's red Saturn, turned off the engine and listened to a silence so profound, he might have been plunged back into the Brazilian rain forest. The vegetation was different, of course, but this place felt equally isolated. They might be a thousand miles from civilization, instead of twenty-five or thirty miles from the city.

Why would this Halliday woman choose to live and work in such isolation? Despite his daughter's protest, he was glad he'd decided to come today. Zoe always accused him of not trusting her decisions, but all he wanted was to give her the benefit of his business expertise. She was developing a fine reputation as an interior designer. A wrong choice now could set her back professionally. Besides, assuming he agreed that Mrs. Halliday's dolls belonged in MacMillan's, he felt certain he could get Zoe a better deal than she could hope to negotiate on her own.

Zoe didn't wait for him. She strode down a gravel path to the left of a log house. Logan glimpsed a rectangular metal building among the pines down the hill. That must be the workshop.

"We're early," he called to his daughter's retreating back. The cool look she threw him over her shoulder told him her mood hadn't improved. Zoe had refused even to discuss their impending visit. He was going in blind and he didn't like the sensation. Still, he'd do his best to make certain she came out ahead. He owed her that. She might not believe him, but her happiness was all he cared about.

MOLLY SQUARED her shoulders, pasted what she hoped was a welcoming smile on her face and opened the door to the front room of her workshop.

"Zoe," she said. "Welcome."

Zoe leaned forward and shook Molly's hand, then stood aside. "Mrs. Halliday, this is my father. Logan MacMillan."

Molly took a deep breath to quell the butterflies in her stomach and extended her hand. He had a strong handshake, but he didn't try to break her fingers the way some men did. She could feel his long fingers winding around hers.

Then she remembered the dust on her hands. He glanced at his palm. She groaned inwardly as he frowned and rubbed his palms together. Familiar insecurity washed over her.

"Please come in, Mr. MacMillan," Molly said. She looked down to see Elvis, the ginger cat, undulate around MacMillan's ankles. She hoped the man wasn't allergic to cat hair because he was going to take plenty of it home on his slacks.

He stood a good six inches taller than Molly, but probably didn't weigh five pounds more than she did. There was not an ounce of fat on him. His face was deeply tanned and lined like a granite outcropping at the edge of the Arizona desert. His steel-gray hair was cut short. His equally steely eyes seemed to be set for long-range viewing—great vistas, massive creations of concrete. He'd have difficulty adjusting his sight to look at dolls.

He walked in warily.

"Sit down a minute, Logan," Sherry said, nodding toward the Victorian love seat to the left of the door to Molly's showroom. "You all need to get to know one another before you talk business."

He glanced at his watch. "I don't want to impose on Mrs. Halliday's time."

Zoe snorted, then she sat as far away from her father as she could. Sherry perched on a French side chair and smiled.

Molly pulled up her old rocking chair and sat with her feet curled under her. MacMillan waited politely until she was settled, then perched cautiously on the edge of the sofa as though he were afraid it might collapse under his weight.

"I must admit I'm a little confused, Mr. MacMillan," Molly said. Elvis jumped onto her lap, walked around in a circle and collapsed in a heap. She scratched his ears; he purred softly. "I've been trying for several years to find a good outlet for my dolls in town, and when Zoe said she'd like to carry them in MacMillan's I thought we had a done deal."

"Before this afternoon is over, it may well be," MacMillan told her.

Zoe moved restively on the sofa. Molly glanced at her. The young woman sat with her arms crossed tight across her chest.

Logan also looked at his daughter as he addressed Molly. "Zoe tells me that your dolls are extraordinary and would sell well at MacMillan's. I'm sure you'll convince me she's right. She generally is." He smiled a kind, sad smile that softened the hard planes of his face.

Zoe raised her eyebrows, but said nothing.

"Actually, you should thank Rick," Molly said. "He saw the dolls when he came out to do the plumbing on the workshop and dragged Zoe back to look at them."

Again he flashed her that smile. Molly felt a jolt. This guy could be really dangerous. Too attractive for his own good. Or hers.

"Tell him about the shops that carry your dolls," Sherry prompted.

"Sure." Molly ticked off her fingers. "Let's see, Andreotti in Atlanta handles my dolls, so does Minou et Cie in Brussels, and I've just started shipping to Belisarius in Los Angeles. They're all doing very well with them. MacMillan's would fit right in."

"Surely a toy store would be a more appropriate outlet. Why an interior design house?"

"These dolls aren't toys," Zoe said. "I told you that."

"Let me show you," Molly said. "Wait right here." She opened the door to the showroom, slipped through and returned a moment later carrying a life-size doll—a little girl in a pale blue party dress and Belgian lace.

Zoe turned to her father. "You see?"

Molly held the doll out to MacMillan, who raised his hands and shook his head as though she were handing him a ticking time bomb. "No thank you. I'd rather not touch it. I break things. But she's beautiful."

"Thank you. She's a portrait doll."

"What are portrait dolls?"

"People commission me to sculpt dolls that look like their children or grandchildren. They tell me it's better than a regular portrait or even a statue. Some of them, like this one, are life-size."

"And expensive?"

"Up to six or seven thousand dollars."

"You can actually sell dolls for that kind of money?" MacMillan asked, and ran a hand along his jaw. "I don't know enough to make an educated decision."

Zoe stood up abruptly. "But I do. That's the point, isn't it? In addition to the portrait dolls, Mrs. Halliday also designs and sculpts her own. And she makes beautiful copies of antique dolls. I know we could sell them in MacMillan's." She turned to Molly. "Thank you, Mrs. Halliday. I have another meeting at the shop. My father can conclude the negotiations. Supposedly that's what he came for. Nice to see you, Mrs. Carpenter." She walked to the front door and opened it.

"Zoe," Logan called after her.

She kept going. She didn't quite slam the door after herself, but she certainly closed it with a snap.

"Should I go after her?" Molly said.

Logan sat back on the couch and shook his head. "Sorry about that. Zoe resents what she perceives as my interference, but with an investment of this magnitude..."

"Investment?" Molly said. "You're getting the dolls on consignment, didn't Zoe explain that?"

"Consignment? Zoe neglected to mention that. I assumed she was buying them wholesale." He realized with a sinking sensation that Zoe had deliberately set him up. "I'm sorry, Mrs. Halliday. I misunderstood." He stood and began to move toward the door.

"Whoa! Not so fast." Molly laughed. She had to do something to lighten the atmosphere. "You came to see dolls, and by gosh, you're stuck with them. Come on, Mr. MacMillan, you are going to see enough dolls to last you a lifetime."

Sherry tucked her hand under MacMillan's arm. "Don't worry, Logan, unlike real children, they don't bite."

Molly opened the French doors at the back of the room and turned on the lights. She and Sherry hung back. MacMillan stood transfixed in the doorway.

Dolls in satin and lace rode in wicker carriages and antique sleighs; Native American dolls in beaded buckskin sat astride miniature ponies; Irish colleens in tartan shawls swung milk pails; baby dolls slept in bassinets; on a center table smaller dolls played jacks or snuggled under receiving blankets. Around the perimeter of the room, waist-high Victorian ladies nodded to nearly life-size portrait dolls of toddlers and young children dressed in everything from Belgian lace to jeans and cowboy boots.

MacMillan began to work his way methodically around the room as though he were in a museum. He kept his hands carefully clasped behind him. Molly understood. For a man who broke things, the showroom was a disaster waiting to happen.

"How's the experiment with the vinyl going?" Sherry whispered.

Molly held up crossed fingers. "Great. I've cast a couple of my favorites and one of the big toy companies is definitely interested in mass-producing them. I never planned to go commercial, but the money's too good to pass up."

"Which ones did you pick?"

"The Jeannette doll—you've already got one of her. Then a new one I don't think you've seen. The Dulcy doll is the one right in front of Mr. MacMillan."

Sherry gasped and stared at MacMillan's broad back.

Molly saw him stiffen like a bird dog on point.

Suddenly, he reached forward and grabbed the very doll she'd been talking about by its arm. He whirled to face them. As the doll swung, its right leg hit the edge of the table and shattered. Shards of bisque rained onto the table and floor. Without a word, MacMillan grasped the doll around its body and held it up so that both women could look into its face. Sherry moaned softly, "It can't be."

Molly felt her scalp tighten. MacMillan's face was stony, his eyes hard and flat.

He threw the doll onto the table so hard that the crown of its head shattered. Two gray eyeballs flew out and rolled across the tile floor. Without a word he pushed past the two women, through the reception room and out the front door. They heard his footsteps as he ran up the path, heard his car door open then slam, the engine roar into life, and a moment later the gate alarm pealed as he drove into the road and away.

As the sound died, Molly reached out and picked up the broken doll from the table. She cradled it in her arms and turned to Sherry. "What on earth just happened here?"

Sherry sagged against the doorjamb as though her legs wouldn't support her. "Molly, have you made any other dolls using that mold?"

"I told you, that's one of the two I cast in vinyl."

"Where is the other one?"

"In the workroom. I haven't finished painting her face yet."

"Go get her. Bring her here."

Molly opened her mouth as if to argue. Then shrugged and went out.

A moment later, Molly returned from the workshop carrying a large doll loosely wrapped in brown paper. She unwrapped it and laid it naked on the table.

Sherry gasped. "Oh, Lord, it's uncanny!"

"For Pete's sake, Sherry, what?"

"Remember I told you that Logan's daughter-in-law took her baby and disappeared? The little girl was named Dulcy."

"Poor MacMillan! But I don't think he heard me say her name. You and I were both whispering. And surely just a name wouldn't be enough to set him off like that."

Sherry looked into Molly's eyes. "Molly, that doll you call the Dulcy doll—that's the spitting image of Logan's Dulcy, the way she'd look now."

Molly felt the hackles rise on the back of her neck. "No way."

But Sherry wasn't listening to her. She was off in some reverie of her own. "Rick and Zoe loved that child so much. Why didn't they recognize the doll, too? I did."

"They didn't see her is why," Molly said practically. "I was using my bathroom sink to cast the vinyl head while Rick finished plumbing the workshop. The Dulcy doll was there so I could refer to her if I needed to. I just got her dressed and back down to the workshop today." She shook her head. "Specially for MacMillan and Zoe. My timing is as flawless as ever."

"My God, just think how awful it would be if they saw a thousand of her sitting around in some toy store next Christmas!"

"Wouldn't happen. These two are perfect likenesses, but if the company mass-produces them, I'll give them a more generic prototype. The new doll won't look like the little girl who disappeared."

"Molly—she did more than disappear. Dulcy MacMillan has been dead for two years."

Molly stared at Sherry.

"That's impossible! She was alive and well a year ago when I modeled the doll."

LOGAN MACMILLAN CAME to his senses five miles down the country road, barely in time to avoid a head-on collision with a pickup truck. He braked, swerved and wound up on the verge of a six-foot ditch. The other driver honked in irritation.

After his breathing returned to normal, Logan turned off the engine, climbed out of the car and slammed the door behind him. He picked up a softball-size stone from the shoulder and threw it underhand as hard and as far as he could. It splashed in a cow pond fifty feet away.

Funny that he could still pitch. The last time he pitched to Jeremy, his son was ten. Logan had been home between jobs for a full four months that time.

He wiped his muddy hands down the sides of his jacket and grimaced. He'd always been so certain that sooner or later he and Jeremy would be able to spend time together, to catch up on all those years they'd been apart. How wrong he'd been.

He needed to hit something, so he punched the BMW with both fists hard enough to leave a dent. Pain radiated to his shoulders. His car insurance would probably skyrocket. The hell with it. He was beginning to feel a little better.

He tore open his tie, and yanked at his collar until the button popped.

Suddenly, his adrenaline bottomed out. He walked around to the driver's side, slid in and turned on the ignition, then the heater. He had been in shock before and knew he was close again. As warm air flooded from the vents, he closed his eyes and fought for control. Much as he longed to put Molly Halliday and her dolls out of his mind he couldn't. He'd have to drive back, apologize, pay for the doll and find out how she came to create such a bizarre likeness.

He didn't believe it was a coincidence that the doll named Dulcy was an exact likeness to the image the computer had made of how his granddaughter would have looked.

If she had lived.

CHAPTER TWO

MOLLY STOOD under a steaming shower, scrubbed her hair and body, then let the water course over her shoulders until it started to chill. She could feel the tension in her knotted muscles begin to ease. All in all, this had been some afternoon. What had started out as a simple showing for Zoe MacMillan had deteriorated into a Greek tragedy with Zoe's father, Logan, as the tragic hero. Molly didn't understand what had happened, but she planned to, for her own peace of mind, if for no other reason. She toweled her hair, and because she still had to feed the animals in the chill evening September air, blew it dry—something she seldom took the time to do.

She pulled on a pair of clean jeans and a teal blue turtleneck sweater, dug her windbreaker out from under a pile of flea-market clothes from which she intended to make dresses for her newest dolls and went out to the barn where Eeyore, the Sicilian donkey, and Maxie, her granddaughter's pony, waited impatiently for her.

She dumped sweet feed in Eeyore's and Maxie's buckets, then tossed them a couple of flakes of hay. She scooped up corn to throw to the five geese that clambered honking out of the pond when they saw her coming and waddled toward her at breakneck speed, their necks stretched out so far, it was a wonder they didn't tip over.

She flung the corn as far from her as she could. If she dropped it at her feet, they'd crash into her like bumper cars.

Absentmindedly, she put the feed away, hung up the scoop and strolled back to the house to fix herself a sandwich.

In the kitchen she sniffed basil and fresh mint from the pots on the windowsill. The wet-concrete odor of damp bisque was finally gone from the house together with the last of the dust. Her ex-husband, Harry, had hated the mess. In fact, he'd probably divorced her because of the dolls.

Molly poured herself a glass of iced tea and twisted a sprig of mint into it, enjoying the quiet. Sherry often teased her about being a hermit, but Molly did not regret for one moment spending most of her divorce settlement to buy her woods and pasture, to build her log house and barn. She never wanted to go to another fancy corporate function again, if she lived to be a hundred.

How could she ever have guessed when she let Sherry con her into taking that first doll-making class that she would find her life's work? She was content for the first time in her life, and never lonely. Sherry dropped in four or five times a week. Molly's clients loved coming out to see her. Her daughter, Anne, brought her granddaughter, Elizabeth, by nearly every day after school to ride her pony. Molly still missed her volunteer work at the Abused Children's Center, but there wasn't time, not if she expected to make a living. Funny that she'd started volunteering because Harry said she had to do something charitable to make him look good at his firm.

Molly sipped her tea slowly, so lost in her thoughts that when the doorbell sounded, she jumped a foot. Nobody came up her driveway unannounced. Although a person could walk through the woods to the house and bypass the gate alarm, dense underbrush and snakes tended to discourage walkers.

No, it was more likely that a car had driven up while she'd been in the barn.

The doorbell pealed again. She peeked through the front curtains and saw a black BMW. Then she saw MacMillan on the front porch. She felt a stab of alarm. Should she open the door to him?

"Mrs. Halliday," a deep voice spoke through the door. "I must see you." It wasn't so much a request as a command.

Molly sighed. Get the confrontation over with. Maybe she could get an explanation as well.

She opened the door and snapped, "Didn't you do enough damage on your first raid?" Then, seeing his face, she reached out to him quickly. "You look as though you've been rode hard and put away wet," she said. "You need a drink."

"Excuse me?" he asked. He seemed to be having trouble focusing his eyes.

He was no longer immaculate. Besides the bisque dust, there was mud on his jacket, his tie was loose, his shirt gaped open at the neck. His hair stood on end as though he'd been driving his hands through it, and his skin had a gray caste that his tan couldn't quite hide.

"Come into the kitchen," Molly said, and took his arm. "You need a glass of orange juice, my friend, and you need it quickly." She shoved him onto a stool, poured a glass of orange juice and ordered, "Drink it before you pass out."

He peered into the jelly glass as though it held arsenic.

"Do it. It won't bite you."

He took a sip, then drank greedily.

"More?"

"Thank you, no."

"Iced tea then? Or Scotch?"

"Nothing, thank you." He set the empty glass down carefully. The bar stool put him for the first time almost at eye level with Molly in a room still flooded with western light from the setting sun. He took his first real look at her.

How could he have missed seeing her clearly before? The shock of recognition of her sheer femaleness startled him. He stood and strode back to the relative sanctuary of the front hall.

Molly followed him.

At the door he turned and took his checkbook from his inside jacket pocket. "I've come to pay for the doll."

"I planned to bill you."

"How much?"

"Fifteen hundred dollars will do. Use my desk." She pointed at an aged plantation desk inside the living room.

He sat down, wrote the check and handed it to her.

She stuck it into her jeans without looking at it. "Sherry told me what happened. You must understand something, Mr. MacMillan. I am a craftswoman, pure and simple. I'm certainly not clairvoyant. In fact, I do not have a bit of ESP in my entire body."

This time he did look up, and straight into those amazing blue eyes. They were full of intelligence and compassion. He kept his voice even. "The doll—"

"Please, let me finish. Sherry told me your granddaughter died two years ago. I'm sorry, that is simply not possible."

This was the last thing Logan expected to hear. He was stunned and then anger began to take over. What right had this madwoman with the teal blue eyes to tell him his granddaughter had not died? He felt his heart begin to speed up. "I assure you, Mrs. Halliday, I have seen her death certificate."

"I don't care if you had all nine justices of the Supreme Court testifying to you," she said. "I don't make things—children—up. And I certainly don't pull the names of dead grandchildren out of the air. I name all my dolls. It's standard in the industry. It's easier to keep them straight that way and the customers like it."

"So?"

"So, that doll, the one you smashed this afternoon...I didn't pull her name out of a hat, either." Molly sat on a wing chair across from him.

It was as though a ghost had stepped into the room. He looked at the woman before him, noticing that she met his gaze head-on.

He stood up. "Mrs. Halliday, this is obviously some sort of confidence game. I won't tolerate it."

"Oh, for Pete's sake, sit down before you fall down. Hear me out. Do it. There. That's better."

"Very well, I will hear you out, but I assure you—"

"Look, when I designed the Dulcy doll—"

"Stop calling her that!" he shouted.

The anguish in his voice took Molly's breath. "Mr. MacMillan, Logan," she said gently. "That's her name. It has always been her name, ever since I saw her and decided to model her."

She watched his hands curl into fists and hoped he didn't plan to hit her, but she stood her ground. "I said I saw her and I meant it. Obviously I also heard her name. I told you, I don't make up children in my mind and then model them. Within the last year, I saw that little girl and heard someone call her Dulcy. Who could forget a name like that?"

"Even if I believed you, what proof have you? Do you take pictures?"

Molly shook her head. "Only when I'm working on commission. Let's face it, most children look a good deal alike. Shortly after my divorce four years ago I decided I wanted to devote my life to creating dolls, and in the beginning I tried to find a mold that had the same expression and bone structure as the child I was working on, then I either added or subtracted material to make the doll as much like the child as possible. I still use that technique sometimes, but after a while it didn't satisfy me. I took some sculpture classes and began to sculpt my own molds. The Dulcy doll is my fourth attempt at creating a portrait from scratch, and the only one I'm really proud of!"

"That doesn't explain..."

"I know. It's a rather long-winded way to the point, which is that I know Dulcy's face intimately. In my mind I've touched the curve of her cheek, the angle of her eye socket. And I know the Dulcy doll is a perfect reproduction of the child I saw. I have a photographic memory for faces. I may not know where I met you or under what circumstances, but I remember your face. In Dulcy's case, I remember the name, too. Usually I don't."

"For the sake of argument, let's say that you did see Dulcy somewhere in Memphis, heard someone call her name. She was not quite two when Tiffany ran away with her three years ago."

Molly relaxed. At least MacMillan was prepared to talk rationally to her now.

"I'm sorry, but I can't project change on the faces I see. I couldn't sculpt the way you looked at twenty or the way you'll look at ninety. The Dulcy I saw was that age, that shape, that size and called by that name. How many

Dulcys do you think there are in the United States, Mr....Logan? A few thousand? There is something I don't understand, by the way. If you haven't seen your granddaughter since before she was two, why are you so sure that the child I sculpted looks the way she would look?"

"Computer simulation." Logan leaned forward. "How much did Sherry tell you?"

"She filled me in on as much as she knows."

"She knows most of it. I guess I owe you an explanation for the rest."

Molly realized that even that small an admission had cost him dearly. It was clear that he wasn't used to accounting to anyone.

"When my daughter-in-law, Tiffany, ran away with Dulcy, she was out on bond awaiting sentencing for vehicular homicide. She was probably facing a sentence of five to eight years in prison. Even with good behavior, she'd have served two years, maybe more."

"Sherry told me about your son's death."

A flash of pain crossed MacMillan's face, but he continued stoically. "My son, Jeremy, wasn't the only one killed in the wreck. Edward Valdez, a cardiologist, was changing a flat tire when Tiffany hit his car. His family is rich and prominent. They demanded the prosecutor go for the maximum sentence possible. No plea bargains, no lesser charge, no probation or credit for jail time served. They wanted Tiffany's blood. They would have gotten it."

"Please, I know this is hard for you..." Molly reached a hand out to touch him. He drew back as though any physical contact would shatter his iron control.

"I have told the story many times since Jeremy was killed, Mrs. Halliday."

"Doesn't make it any easier."

"In an odd way it does. While I'm talking, I can almost convince myself that the entire thing happened to someone else. It's only afterward that the full force of Jeremy's death hits me again. Do you have children, Mrs. Halliday?"

Molly nodded. "A daughter, a son-in-law and a granddaughter. I'd go nuts if anything happened to any of them."

"Unfortunately, I've remained sane. Madness might be easier. Did Sherry tell you that Jeremy was an alcoholic?"

Molly nodded and felt a chill as she looked into his eyes, as flat and bleak as an Arctic ice floe.

"My granddaughter, Dulcy, was not even two," he continued. "Tiffany's mother is dead, her father has remarried and lives in Spain. At the trial, her lawyer argued that since Tiffany grew up with a drunken mother and an absentee father..." He stopped speaking a moment and closed his eyes. "An absentee father," he repeated, "she was not responsible. The jury looked at the size of her trust fund and were not impressed by his argument."

Molly wondered whose side Logan had been on. Most men would feel vengeful for the loss of an only son. She couldn't tell from that careful voice, that stony face, what Logan felt about his daughter-in-law.

"My wife, Sydney, and I were the obvious ones to take custody of Dulcy," he went on. "Tiffany signed the custody papers willingly. We made plans to help her get her life back on track after she was paroled."

"Then why did she run away?"

MacMillan sighed. "I can only guess. I think she couldn't bear to face us or prison or the world or perhaps most of all, her own guilt. She was used to running away from problems that she couldn't buy her way out of.''

''But she didn't leave Dulcy behind.''

''No.''

''You never suspected she planned to leave?''

He shook his head. ''She was very careful. All the time we were worrying about how she would survive her prison sentence, she was setting up the mechanism to disappear. She was to be sentenced on Monday. On Friday afternoon, Zoe was baby-sitting Dulcy at the store. When Tiffany came to pick her up, she'd been drinking again, and she and Zoe really got into it. Zoe didn't want to let her have Dulcy, but couldn't really stop her. In the end, Rick drove Dulcy and Tiffany home in Tiffany's car while Zoe followed in theirs. Tiffany swore she wouldn't drink or drive anymore that night. Zoe and Rick had to be content with that. It was the last time any of us saw either Tiffany or Dulcy. When she didn't show up in court on Monday, the judge issued a warrant for her arrest, but she and Dulcy had simply vanished into thin air.''

''The police couldn't find her?''

''They came up empty. We found she'd raided her trust fund, so she had plenty of cash with her. The private detective we hired traced her partway. He's the one who discovered that Dulcy—'' MacMillan's voice broke. He cleared his throat and continued in that same cool way he had before.

This time Molly wasn't fooled. He wasn't cool. He was being torn apart inside. She knew she couldn't offer him sympathy. He'd hate it.

''Why do you think the child is dead?''

"I don't *think* Dulcy is dead. I *know* she's dead, dammit! Do you think that if I thought there was the slightest chance Dulcy was alive, I wouldn't be combing the country—no—combing the planet, to find her?"

Molly raised her hands. "Okay, let's leave that for a minute."

He looked at her appraisingly. "You haven't asked the usual question."

"Which is?"

"Why Tiffany took the child when Dulcy would be better off with us."

"I can guess the answer to that one already."

"Because you're a mother?"

"No, I used to volunteer at the university center for disturbed and abused children."

Logan sat up very straight and said, "Dulcy wasn't abused."

"Not in the usual sense. But I've seen drunken mothers, drugged out on crack, hooking, with AIDS and TB. They love their children and will kill to keep them, even if they're doing massive and irreparable harm to those children in the process."

"It's difficult for me to excuse a parent who would knowingly do something against a child's best interests. Jeremy and Tiffany must have known what their alcoholism would do to Dulcy. They never managed to stop drinking even after Dulcy was born."

"It seldom stopped the mothers at the center, either. Alcoholism is a disease, Logan, but it's not like the mumps. You don't get over it after a week of bed rest. It takes strength and a good support system. From what you tell me, Tiffany didn't have either."

"We were her support system, or wanted to be. Unfortunately, we weren't enough." He took a deep breath and stared at Molly as though seeing her for the first time. "You are a remarkable woman, Mrs. Halliday. I admit I underestimated you. Frankly, a woman who spends her days making dolls..."

"Let me finish for you. I make dolls, I hide in the woods, I live in a log cabin..."

"Hardly a cabin."

"Not a suburban ranch, either. Come on, admit it, you thought you were meeting Beatrix Potter."

"Actually, you have a great deal in common. I seem to remember she retired to a farm."

Molly laughed, then said, "But she never worked again." She shrugged and grinned at him. "Hey, I'm divorced, middle-aged and my only talent is my dolls. I didn't choose harsh reality, it chose me. Now, tell me why you think Dulcy is dead."

"The private detective we hired discovered that Dulcy had died of viral spinal meningitis at a small hospital in the Midwest. He brought us her death certificate."

"You flew there? Saw the body?"

Logan shook his head. "My wife was in intensive care by that time. I didn't even tell her. What was the point? Besides, the whole thing had happened three months earlier. Someone—I can only assume Tiffany—had abandoned Dulcy at the local clinic. They tried to save her, but it was too late. They tried to trace her parents, but eventually they gave up and buried her there."

"What made your detective think that was Dulcy?"

He shrugged. "He said he showed her picture to the nurses who had worked to save her. They identified the picture. It was Dulcy, all right."

"I see."

"They were certain. They had no reason to lie."

"Nor do I."

He leaned back and closed his eyes. The lamplight carved his face into its essential planes. Looking at him, afraid to speak for fear of disturbing his small moment of repose, Molly longed to model that face. Every ounce of grief and loss were carved into him. He had a massive head, and the short gray hair revealed the fine sculpting of his skull. His was a face constructed of angular planes—the angle of bone strong over the eyes, the high sharp cheekbones, the eagle's nose, and finally, the strong jaw.

He sighed, shook his head and opened his eyes.

Molly felt the shock of his gaze deep inside her. Unfortunately for her peace of mind, the shock went to a part of her body she had thought long dormant. She was reacting to him the way a woman reacts to a man. Not possible. She didn't even like him. The day her divorce was final, she stepped out of the sexual arena without a moment's regret. The last thing she wanted was to climb back into the ring.

Not that it would be possible with someone like Logan. He was probably no more than two or three years older than she. Middle-aged men went for twenty-year-old trophies.

Now, one glance from those gray eyes of his sent awakening shivers straight through her body and straight as an arrow to her groin.

Hoping that he couldn't detect the blush she felt spreading up her face in the lamplight, she found herself babbling. "You said you saw a death certificate. What name did it have?"

"Jane Doe. But the picture, Mrs. Halliday. They identified the picture."

"Logan, I'm going to ask you something you are not going to like. Please don't get angry."

"I'm too tired to get angry."

"Do you trust that private investigator?"

He drew himself up in the chair. "Mrs. Halliday, I have no reason to doubt the man. First, why would he end a lucrative contract? I had every intention of pursuing Tiffany until I either went bankrupt or found my granddaughter."

"Yes," Molly conceded. "There is that."

"Second, he has a good reputation. My lawyer recommended him. He has been successful in several other cases. I checked his clients. They were satisfied."

"Better and better. Still, either there was some mix-up about the picture and the identification, or something's going on we're not aware of."

"I doubt whether the entire staff of a hospital would lie. What would be the reason? Some sort of misguided loyalty to a criminal?"

"We don't know who made the mistake. Another thing that puzzles me is how Sherry was able to recognize that doll as Dulcy."

"She and my wife worked together to decorate Sherry and her husband, Leo's latest house. She saw a great deal of Dulcy when she was a baby, and she's been a good friend ever since. She's seen all the computer enhancements the detective produced. She'd have known Dulcy's face at almost the same moment I did. What I don't know is why she didn't recognize the doll earlier." He considered. "Or why Rick and Zoe didn't."

"I just put her out today when I knew you were coming." She sighed. "Ironic. I really rushed so that she'd be there especially for you." She leaned back and closed her own eyes, trying to recall where she had seen the child, remembering instead only the child herself. She wasn't certain she should tell Logan about the picture in her head.

He seemed able to read her mind. "If you saw this child, tell me where, how, what she looked like."

Molly opened her eyes, looked at him and made her decision. "She was the saddest, gravest little girl I have ever seen in my life."

He sucked in his breath. He gripped the arms of the chair as though he'd like to rend the leather with his bare hands. "Sad how?"

Molly closed her eyes again. This time she saw more. "It was in a park somewhere. I remember there were lots of children swinging, sliding, one of those little merry-go-round things, I think. A friend of mine and I were on a bus tour with a bunch of other local people on our way to Aspen and Vail. We must have stopped there to picnic. This child was sitting alone on the grass. She had a book in her hand—not a children's book. It was thick and there were no pictures on the cover."

MacMillan snorted. "Come now, she would hardly have been reading a book."

"Why not? Children learn to read early these days. Maybe there were pictures inside. She wasn't smiling. She looked up at me, right into my eyes. I wanted to stoop down and hug her, but something warned me she wouldn't allow that." She looked up at him. "That's when I heard someone call out 'Dulcy' and she closed the book, stood up, brushed off her jeans and walked away. She didn't run, she walked, quite calmly, the way an adult walks to a business meeting. She wasn't like any child I've ever seen. So self-contained. I knew I had to try to capture that self-possession."

"Where was this?"

Molly threw up her hands in frustration. "I simply can't remember."

"And I'm supposed to take your word for all this over a licensed private investigator's?"

"Look, let me go through my photographs from my trips. Maybe something will click." She hesitated a moment. "You never tried to find your daughter-in-law after the detective said Dulcy was dead?"

"No." His voice was flat, hard. "She made her choice. I stood by her throughout her trial even though she killed my boy. Zoe has never forgiven me for that. But when I found out she'd abandoned Dulcy to die..." He cleared his throat. "Frankly, I don't give a damn what happens to her."

"But if Dulcy is still alive and with her?"

"If—and I still think it unlikely—there was a mix-up or a cover-up, then I will hunt them down and bring my granddaughter home. Tiffany can go to Outer Mongolia for all I care."

Molly saw the muscles along his jaw tighten until they stood out like steel cables. She shivered. This man would make a dangerous enemy.

"Will you tell me something?" she asked. "I can understand that you were startled when you picked up the doll, but frankly, I thought you overreacted big time. It's only a doll."

"Only a doll?" He stared at her in genuine surprise. "It was a corpse!"

"But..."

"I felt as though you were playing some sort of sick joke at her—my—expense. I see now that wasn't true. Please accept my apologies. I don't usually fly off the handle like that."

"Apology accepted. Listen, maybe the child who died looked enough like Dulcy so that the hospital staff made an honest mistake."

Logan shook his head. "Forgive me. I stopped hoping a long time ago."

"Don't let yourself hope then. But for pity's sake, check it out."

"I plan to. If Dulcy is alive, I must find her and bring her home. But I'm not sure how much more disappointment I can take."

Looking into his eyes, Molly realized how difficult it must be for such a man to reveal this sign of weakness, not only to a woman but a comparative stranger. She felt sympathy for him in the same moment she knew how deeply he would resent her expressing it.

Molly sighed. She couldn't leave this problem alone any more than she could abandon this strange, lonely man. "I think the first thing to do is talk to your detective. See if you still believe him. Maybe take Rick and Zoe with you."

"I don't plan to tell Zoe any of this until I'm certain the child is alive and we have some hope of finding her."

"Then I'll go with you." There. The die was cast, the words were spoken. She could only hope he'd refuse her offer. But he didn't—not exactly.

"I can't ask you to—"

Just then, the driveway alarm sounded. Logan MacMillan started as though she'd stuck him with a pin.

A moment later, Molly went to the front door and opened it.

"Gram, I know it's late, but I had to say good-night to Maxie." A coltish prepubescent girl with chestnut hair straight down her back flew into the room, followed by an exasperated woman who might have been Molly twenty years earlier. The child stopped when she saw Molly was not alone.

"Sorry, Mom. We were in the neighborhood. I tried to stop her," the woman said, and grinned.

"No sweat. Anne Crown, this is Logan MacMillan. Logan, my daughter." She smiled at the child. "And this is my granddaughter, Elizabeth."

Logan, who'd stood when Anne and Elizabeth came in, nodded.

"Hello," Anne said. "Hope we're not interrupting anything."

"Hi," Elizabeth said, then turning to Molly, "Got any carrots in the fridge?"

"Yes. Don't forget Eeyore," Molly called after the child, already disappearing into the kitchen. They heard the refrigerator open and a moment later shut. "And don't slam the—"

The back door slammed.

"Please sit down, Mr. MacMillan," Anne said. "We can only stay a minute. I have to get home to fix dinner." She glanced at her watch. "Phil will probably have to go back to the office. It's the end of the quarter. No rest for the poor tax accountant." She shrugged. "I had to pick Elizabeth up at the Fitzgeralds'. Anytime we're close to Mom's, Elizabeth insists on stopping by."

"The attraction is Maxie, her pony, not me." Molly laughed. Looking at Logan, she realized he had retreated into his shell.

The back door slammed once more. "Okay, old mom. Maxie pig and Eeyore pig are stuffed. We can go home now. I've got tons of homework."

"You spending the night Friday?" Molly asked Elizabeth as she followed the pair to the door.

"What're you offering?" the girl said. "Pizza, maybe? A movie?"

"I was thinking more along the lines of brussels sprouts and barn-cleaning."

"Yech!" Elizabeth made a face. "Can I bring Karen?"

"Sure. Maybe pizza. Maybe popcorn. Definitely barn-cleaning."

"Deal. 'Bye, Gram." The child leaned over and kissed Molly. Anne raised her eyes to heaven and waved good-bye as she followed her daughter to the car. Molly stood in the door and watched them until she heard the drive-way alarm go off as they turned onto the road. Then she came back into the living room.

"I must be going, as well," Logan said. "I've taken up entirely too much of your time." He stood by the window. Molly realized he'd watched the pair into their car and down the road.

"Don't be ridiculous. We've barely started. I've got a couple of steaks in the refrigerator. I'll whip up a salad. Stay."

"I couldn't."

Molly had visions of a turtle pulling back into his shell. "Why? Because it's on the spur of the moment? You're a vegetarian? You really do have plans? What?"

Logan stammered, "I...uh." He looked across at Molly in the doorway, her hands on her ample hips, her feet wide apart, peering at him with those marvelous eyes as though she could see right into his soul. She didn't seem pleased at what she saw.

He thought of the cold chicken he'd planned to pick up on his way home, the silent kitchen in which he'd eat it, the lonely empty apartment, the broad empty bed. "All right."

"Good. Want a drink? I don't, but my friends do."

"I don't drink."

"Okay, how about a soda?"

He nodded.

"Come into the kitchen while I fix the salad."

"Your granddaughter is very beautiful."

Molly snorted. "She's nothing of the sort, but she's going to be. She inherited Anne's brains and her father's metabolism."

"You seem very comfortable with each other."

"She doesn't say ma'am or sir, if that's what you mean. I want real respect, thank you, not the fake kind. She respects what I do. It's going to be tough to lose her in a couple of years."

Logan sat up. "What do you mean, lose her?"

Molly turned away from the refrigerator, a head of romaine lettuce in her hand. She said seriously, "Because sometime between now and age fourteen she will turn away from me for a few years. If I'm lucky and live long enough, I should get her back around twenty. We have entirely too good a relationship, so I'll be one of the people she'll have to rebel against if she's going to grow up. Painful for everybody, of course, but teenagers are certifiably loony, anyway. The trick is to get them to adulthood without a pregnancy or a police record and definitely in one piece." She glanced at Logan and gasped. "Oh, God, that was a stupid thing to say. I am so sorry. Please forgive me."

"Perfectly true. Unfortunately, I discovered too late that a parent actually has to be on site to accomplish that."

Molly obviously had no idea what he meant, and he wasn't ready to explain.

He watched her move easily and competently around the kitchen. She radiated warmth and a kind of inner composure that he didn't think he'd ever encountered before. Suddenly a wave of panic swept over him. She touched him. Made him feel. He didn't dare feel anything. If he allowed one crack in the protective shield he'd built around himself, all the pain might come crashing in.

"I'm sorry," he said quickly. "I've remembered I have an engagement. I must leave. I apologize." He strode to the front door.

Molly stared after him, heard the door slam, the car start, and a moment later the alarm sound. She looked down at the lettuce in her hand and shook her head.

"That man is definitely a menace," she muttered.

CHAPTER THREE

LOGAN STRUCK the heavy bag again and again. He felt
each blow all the way to his shoulder, but he kept punch-
ing. Barely protected by light boxing gloves, his hands
still ached from hitting the BMW. Sweat poured down his
face, slid over his naked shoulders and chest down to the
waistband of his sweat pants. The thrumming rhythm of
the bag echoed off the attic walls.

He saw the face of George Youngman on the bag every
time he hit it. He'd trusted the private detective. If the
man had lied or screwed up, Logan intended to make him
very sorry.

Eventually, his bursting lungs drove him to his knees.
He rolled over on the mat and listened to his heart thud
against his rib cage. Stretching out, he waited for his
pulse to slow down.

Overhead in the wooden rafters a fat spider scuttled
across its web.

Each night when he came up here from his apartment
to use Jeremy's exercise equipment, he felt close to his
dead son. The place needed a good cleaning, but he liked
it as it was, spiders and all.

His pulse rate slowed and stabilized quickly. He was in
good physical shape for a man his age.

He stuck his left boxing glove in his right armpit to pull
it off, then pulled the other off and dropped both on the
mat beside him. His emotional shape was something else.

He felt older than the pyramids and more battered than the Sphinx.

He rolled over, pulled Jeremy's rowing machine to him, climbed in and began to row. He had to exhaust himself totally or he'd never sleep.

The cordless telephone on the floor beside him buzzed. He reached over and picked it up.

"Where have you been?"

"Zoe." Wearily, Logan acknowledged the anger in his daughter's voice. "Here. At least since about six."

"Why didn't you call me? I've been worried sick!"

"Why?"

"Sherry called looking for you and said there'd been some kind of a mess at Molly Halliday's after I left. What was she talking about?"

Silently, Logan cursed Sherry. He hadn't planned to explain anything to Zoe. "Nothing. A minor mix-up."

"You broke something, didn't you?"

"As a matter of fact . . ."

"Oh, Lord! Do we still get the dolls?"

"Why didn't you tell me they were going to be on consignment?"

There was a silence at the other end of the line. "Would it have made a difference?"

"Of course it would, Zoe. I went there to get you a better deal. You know I don't interfere with the store."

"Oh, right."

Logan sighed. He couldn't ever get through to Zoe. "Let's talk about it tomorrow, shall we? I'm sorry I worried you."

The phone slammed down. Logan listened to the dial tone.

She never called him by any name. She spoke of him to other people as "my father," but when she spoke to him directly he was never "Daddy" or "Dad" or even "Father."

She was right to blame him for all the mistakes he'd made, all the years when he'd dropped in on his family's lives and dropped out again. But he had truly believed he was doing the best thing for them all. Good intentions didn't count with Zoe.

At least Zoe had her plumber. Rick was a full-time husband to Zoe. He didn't go running off to the Arctic Circle to work on a pipeline. Logan and Rick might not be on the same wavelength, but he could see why Zoe would choose a man like Rick after a lifetime spent with an absentee father.

He began to row again. His legs and arms hurt, his back ached, but he didn't stop. He knew how tired he had to be to sleep. He hadn't reached that point yet.

He was glad he'd walked out on Molly Halliday. Her eyes had a way of seeing into him that zeroed in on his pain.

Then he remembered her soft full mouth. A mouth made for deep, gentle kisses. Her breasts seemed created to pillow a man's head.

His loins tightened. If one meeting with Molly could awaken longings in him that he had denied for years, she was very dangerous. She could infiltrate the protective wall he'd painstakingly constructed around his emotions.

He thought about the easy way she acted with her daughter and granddaughter. They treated one another casually, certain of the love they shared.

God, how he envied her!

"YOU DEMONIC LITTLE troll, I could just murder Sherry for bringing that man out here!" Molly jabbed at Quentin Dillahunt's right eyebrow with a viciousness it didn't deserve. She knew if she didn't calm down she'd ruin the portrait and have to start from scratch. She didn't have time.

"I keep seeing you with Sherry's horns on you, you little beast." She smoothed her thumb across Quentin's pate as though the horns had begun to grow. She wasn't really mad at Quentin or Sherry. She was mad at Logan. Whether she liked it or not, the moment he destroyed the Dulcy doll he became entwined in her life. She didn't want anybody entwined anywhere, drat it!

Of course he had to find out the truth about Dulcy; he had to find the child—or try to find her—if she was still alive. The thought of a little girl dragging around the country behind an alcoholic felon of a mother was more than Molly could bear.

Maybe she had opened Pandora's box. But like Pandora, she'd managed to keep hope alive for Logan. That ought to be worth something. He'd been living without hope for a very long time.

She laid down the scalpel before she did irreversible damage. Logan had paid for the broken doll; maybe she should simply walk away and forget the whole thing.

Except that she wasn't built that way. She had to know about Dulcy. Unfortunately, that meant she had to deal with Logan again, and that she had to go outside her little compound into his world of society women and powerful men, a world she'd thankfully left behind when she and Harry divorced.

Did she have the nerve to go back out there without her status as a craftswoman to protect her? She dealt with wealthy and powerful clients every time she sold a doll. Those clients knew she was a recluse, and they loved it. The last magazine interview about her dolls had gone on and on about her log house, her menagerie, and the fact that she hadn't put on a skirt in three years. She had to admit the paragraph about her "unabashedly gray hair" and her "crinkly" blue eyes had made her want to reach for the Clairol and the telephone number of the nearest plastic surgeon.

But she'd gotten over it.

Then why did it bother her that Logan MacMillan probably saw her the same way. Why should she give a tinker's damn what he thought of her? Why should it be important that he see the woman she really was?

The damned man was too sexy for his own good.

Sherry should have warned her. Molly took a deep swig of her diet cola, looked into Quentin's piggy-little eye sockets, and saw instead the sad gray eyes of Logan MacMillan staring back at her.

The man was strung so tight that if you poked him right he'd probably fly apart. Molly was not in the rescue business. True, he'd had more than his share of sorrow, but that didn't give him the right to show up behind her eyelids every time she blinked.

Molly sighed, wrapped Quentin's head in a damp towel and slid it into the refrigerator under her work counter. She'd have to refire the piece in the morning, but she hadn't messed it up yet. She cleaned her tools carefully and arranged everything neatly in the cabinets beside her.

She locked the workshop behind her and walked up the brick path toward the back door of her cabin.

If Dulcy MacMillan was still alive, Molly had to help Logan bring her home. Only Dulcy mattered. Any developing feelings Molly might have for Logan must be squelched before they made her miserable.

She went at once to her junk closet and began to pull out cardboard boxes stuffed with souvenirs and photographs from her trips. They weren't marked by date—that would be too organized—but maybe she could find a picture that would jog her memory. She had to remember where she'd seen that child!

"MRS. HALLIDAY. I'm so glad you came." Zoe Jackson set a small celadon vase down on a Federal end table and met Molly three steps inside the front door of Mac-Millan's.

Molly shifted her heavy leather handbag to her other shoulder and smiled.

"My father said there was a problem yesterday. He broke something?"

"No problem. He paid for it—a lot, I'm afraid."

"You're still going to let us carry your dolls, aren't you?" Zoe pointed to a tall Welsh dresser against the far wall. "I thought I'd clear off all that Chinese-export stuff and set up a display area on the shelves for the smaller dolls, with the larger dolls in buggies and strollers on the floor."

"That would be perfect." Molly followed her. "We didn't actually settle anything yesterday, but I think you made your point before you left."

Zoe sighed. "I know. I behaved badly. I'm sorry. It's just that sometimes I feel as though my father treats me like I'm about six years old."

Molly laughed. "My father tried to balance my checkbook for me until the day he died. Fathers are like that."

Zoe smiled politely. "At any rate, I know we'll sell lots of dolls for you and get you plenty of portrait orders. Did you and my father manage to discuss how much commission MacMillan's would charge on the orders we acquire for you?"

"Afraid not. Don't worry about it, Zoe, we'll work something out. How's that precious Rick of yours?"

This time the smile was radiant. "He's not quite so precious at home, you know."

"One of my mother's friends once told me that given the choice of a twenty-carat diamond or her own personal plumber, she'd opt for the plumber every time. You're lucky to have married one."

"You know that old story about shoemaker's children never having shoes? It goes double for plumber's wives. The hot-water faucet in our bathroom has been dripping for weeks. Rick keeps promising to fix it, but he never does."

Without Logan around, Zoe reverted to her normally pleasant self. Molly had always thought she was high-strung and nervous, but now that she knew she'd lost a mother, a brother and a niece, that was understandable. "Is your father here? I really came to see him."

Zoe's face clouded. "Oh, yes. The negotiations."

"Nothing like that," Molly assured her. "Just something that came up last night."

Zoe obviously wanted to ask more questions, but she didn't. "He still lives upstairs. Funny, I was raised in that apartment, and now I don't feel comfortable even going up in the elevator. This is my bailiwick." She spread a hand at the opulence around her. "Shall I buzz him for you?"

"Please."

"Have a look around. You haven't been in before, have you? I should have invited you when Rick brought me out to see your dolls."

Molly watched Zoe move among the showcases with grace. She must take after her mother. Tall, slim, casually elegant, she looked every inch a successful businesswoman. She must be over thirty. She wore a simple navy suit that probably cost more than Molly's entire wardrobe. No jewelry. Not even earrings. It was as though she didn't want to distract the customers from the luxurious surroundings.

Molly didn't think she needed to worry. A czar in full coronation garb couldn't distract from a store like MacMillan's. Molly felt as though she'd strayed into Ali Baba's treasure cave. The shop was awash in Scalamandré silks and what her mother called antique "sit-arounds," as well as furniture made of wood so old and so beautiful that Molly longed to pet the chairs like cats. Everything was displayed in a sort of higgledy-piggledy ebullience that looked casual but undoubtedly wasn't.

In her freshly pressed dress jeans and polished L.L. Bean topsiders, Molly felt a familiar sense of panic. She glanced at the other customers. At least no one realized she longed to run out the front door. She picked up a small triangular damask pillow and promptly dropped it when she saw the price tag.

Zoe came back looking puzzled and curious. "My father says would you please go up. The elevator's by the back door." She pointed and watched until the door slid shut on Molly.

When the door opened onto the MacMillan living room, the first thing Molly noticed was the number of throw pillows. No doubt Sydney MacMillan paid wholesale prices, but she'd still piled them three deep on every piece of ornate French furniture in the room.

Logan held the elevator door open for her. He was dressed casually but immaculately in slacks and a sweater. He smelled as though he'd just gotten out of the shower, and his gray hair was still damp. "I wasn't expecting you," he said.

Molly came close to pushing the button and letting the elevator doors shut on her again. She must have been out of her mind to come. "I-I'm sorry," she stammered.

"No, I meant I'm glad you came. When I left so rudely last night . . ."

"Please. It's all right."

"Come in. I won't bite." He smiled. "I've got coffee if you're interested."

"No, thank you." She stood in front of the elevator, poised for flight. "Last night I went through all my old photos. I found something I thought you should see."

"Show me."

Molly dug into her capacious handbag, pulled out a folio of photos, flipped it open and handed it to Logan. "Take it to the light. Ignore all the people in the foreground. They were on the tour with me. Look at the background. I imagine someone can blow it up if you'd like."

Even at ten in the morning there was almost no light filtering into the living room through the heavy gold damask drapes drawn across the windows. Logan pushed them aside and raised a cloud of dust. The room—revealed in the sudden light—seemed like a disused movie set or a posh suite in a bankrupt hotel.

He stared at the picture. "Dear God, that's Tiffany. I'm sure of it." He glanced at Molly. "But I don't see a child."

"Try the next one."

Logan flipped to the next photo. He went very still. "That hair," he whispered. "I can't see the face clearly, but Dulcy's hair was just this color. And curly like this."

"It's an odd strawberry blond. I think that's one of the things that caught my eye when I saw her. So it really is Dulcy?"

He shook his head as though to clear it. He couldn't take his eyes off the photo. Molly saw that his hands were shaking slightly. She wanted to reach out to him, but instead she clutched her handbag even tighter. After a moment he steadied himself. "I still can't believe it."

"It's a start, at any rate. Do you have those computer enhancements?"

"Yes. In my office."

Molly followed him down a long hall papered in gold silk damask and into a small room at the back of the house that was bathed in light from a bank of windows across the back wall.

This must be where Logan really lived. The door was held open by an irregular chunk of concrete. A two-foot section of steel I-beam stood on end to form a side table beside a brown leather chair with the dye worn off arms and seat.

There were three steel file cabinets, a battered steel desk, shelves stuffed with books, a blue umbrella rack full of rolled up blueprints. On the walls were framed photographs of dams and bridges in various stages of construction. A large computer sat on a credenza. Everything seemed immaculate and orderly but chosen for serviceability rather than show.

"Please have a seat." Logan pointed at the leather chair and went directly to the file cabinets. He dropped the photos on the desk and searched rapidly through the files in the top drawer. There was an urgency about him now. He pulled out a thick file and dropped it in Molly's lap. Then he sat in his desk chair and stared at the two photos again, squinting to see the background. "The computer enhancements are at the back of that file."

Molly found them. Her eyes widened. "It *was* Dulcy I saw!"

He glanced up sharply. "You say that as though you weren't sure before."

"Of course I was sure. I just wasn't sure-sure."

Logan flipped the photos to look at the backs. "Do you know where you took these? Don't you write dates and places on your photos?"

"The ones before that are from Oklahoma City, the ones following are from Denver. I checked my itinerary. We stopped for lunch along the way in Moundhill, Kansas."

MacMillan's jaw dropped. "Where?"

Molly repeated the name, then asked, "Why? What's the problem?"

"Moundhill, Kansas. That's where Dulcy's buried."

CHAPTER FOUR

AT ELEVEN-THIRTY that morning, Molly and Logan walked into George Youngman's office unannounced. Youngman showed only a moment of surprise, then he became all smiles. Molly could see why Logan trusted him. The private detective had guileless blue eyes and a generous mouth. He stood five feet seven, and was built in a series of soft globes like the Michelin Man, yet gave the impression of muscles lurking beneath the paunch. His firm handshake didn't last a second too long. His office was large and comfortably furnished. On the wall behind his desk were gold-framed photographs of Youngman shaking hands with high-ranking policemen and prominent lawyers.

Logan introduced Molly and held her chair for her. Youngman sat behind his oversize desk in his oversize leather desk chair.

"I was surprised when I got your call, Mr. Mac-Millan, after all this time," Youngman said. "Something I can do for you or the little lady?" He shot his immaculate white shirt cuffs. They were monogrammed with an elaborate "GY." Molly revised her first assessment. She instinctively distrusted men who wore monograms.

"I need to review a few things about my case," Logan said.

Youngman leaned forward. Molly saw his hands tighten suddenly on his desk mat. The small tufts of brown hair on his knuckles seemed to stand up like the ruff of a dog that senses danger. "You got some new information on your daughter-in-law? Something you want me to run down for you?"

Logan shook his head. "Not precisely. Refresh my memory, Mr. Youngman. Who told you that my grand-daughter Dulcy had died?"

This time there was no mistaking Youngman's reaction. He sat back in his chair and drew his hands quickly into his lap. He answered carefully, as though he'd been expecting the question or something like it for a long time. "As far as I can remember, and it's been a while, I got a call from an informant in Kansas about the kid being dead." The detective nodded, then said, "Yeah. That was it. An informant." He shrugged. "By that time the mother was long gone." He clicked his tongue against his teeth. "Tough break."

"Refresh my memory, Mr. Youngman, just how did the person who called know you were looking for Dulcy?" Logan smiled gently. Molly could tell he had also noticed the detective's response.

"I guess it was from some of those fliers I distributed to police departments, Mr. MacMillan. Why?"

"And the people at the hospital definitely identified the child as Dulcy?" Molly asked.

"Yes, ma'am, absolutely."

"Were you paid to say Dulcy was dead?" Molly asked.

Youngman turned to Logan. "What the hell's this all about?"

Molly answered before Logan could speak, "I saw Dulcy MacMillan alive and well long after you told Mr.

MacMillan she was dead, Mr. Youngman," she said. "Her mother was with her."

"You can't have!" Youngman squawked and shoved his chair back so hard it crashed into the wall behind him. He jumped up and held on to the chair, his fingers working against the leather.

"Sit down, please, Mr. Youngman," Logan said sternly.

"You must have realized that someone who knew her might see her alive one day," Molly said.

"I don't have to listen to this!" Youngman darted around the corner of the desk.

"Yes, you do." Logan blocked his way, his quiet voice forcing the man back. "My granddaughter is alive, isn't she?"

"No!" Youngman snarled. He made a futile attempt to push by Logan, thought better of it and moved to the other side of the desk where Logan couldn't reach him so easily. He began to deflate. "At least I don't think she is." He raised his hand as though to ward off a blow. "Swear to God, Mr. MacMillan, your daughter-in-law told me Dulcy was dead." Youngman frowned at Molly. "Heck, she is dead. You saw some other kid who looked like her."

Logan ignored Youngman's last statement. "Tiffany paid you to lie to me."

Youngman shook his head. "No way. You got to believe me. All she did was tell me which nurse to show the picture to. If the kid's alive, I got conned same as you did."

"That nurse. What was her name?" Logan asked. His voice was dangerously quiet.

Youngman's eyes shifted and he gulped. The fleshy rolls that covered his Adam's apple quivered. "I don't remember."

"You have the files. Look it up!" Logan snapped.

Youngman shook his head. "I dump all my inactive files after a year, unless it's something about pending litigation." He swung a hand at the file cabinets in the corner of the room and said plaintively, "I run out of space, as it is."

"Why didn't you give me the nurse's name at the time? And why did Tiffany call you, not me or my daughter?" Logan asked.

Sweat gleamed on Youngman's upper lip. His head swiveled from Molly to Logan. "She said somebody told her you'd hired me. Said you was one of them sex abusers. After the kid's money. She didn't want to talk to you." Youngman hunched his shoulders. "She was crying and screaming fit to burst. Said Dulcy was dead. Told me to go on out to Moundhill and show that nurse the kid's picture. Told me a bunch of other stuff, too, about how much better off Dulcy was dead than with you and your family. How you'd paid off the lawyers to get custody of her for her money."

"And you believed her?" Molly snapped.

"I don't see what was in it for you, Youngman," Logan said, "unless Tiffany paid you more than I could. You had a good thing going with me. Even if the dead child had been Dulcy, you'd have done better to string me along a while longer, wouldn't you?"

Youngman drew himself up. "I am an honest man, Mr. MacMillan. I wouldn't take advantage of anybody like that."

Logan shook his head. "So you took the word of a convicted felon that her child was dead and got the hospital to corroborate her story. All because you're an honest man.''

''She's the kid's mother.''

''Where is Tiffany now, Youngman?''

''I don't know, swear to God! You told me to drop it after that! You said you didn't care if Tiffany got away once you found out Dulcy was dead. You said that.''

Logan stood and reached a hand down to Molly. ''Yes, I said that.''

''Did you tell the police about her call?'' Molly asked.

Youngman gulped. ''Well, no. Wouldn't do any good. She'd 'a been long gone before they got there.''

Logan took Molly's arm. ''I have to get out of here now.'' He glared at Youngman. ''I have to call my lawyer, the man who sent me to you. He needs to know what a consummate professional he recommended.''

''I didn't do anything wrong!'' Youngman squawked.

''Except to keep facts from a client and conceal the whereabouts of a convicted felon.''

Youngman called after them. ''I could make it up to you. I could maybe trace the kid for you now.''

Logan spun round. ''So you admit you know she's alive?''

Youngman took a couple of steps backward. ''I don't admit nothing. But if she is, I mean, I'm good at finding lost kids.''

Molly knew it was time to get Logan out of there. ''Thank you, Mr. Youngman,'' she said. ''I don't believe we need your services.'' Then she grabbed Logan and dragged him out of the office.

Molly took the keys from Logan's hand without a protest from him. His face looked like thunder. If he planned to take out his anger on something, she didn't want him using a couple of tons of BMW to do it with.

She climbed into the driver's seat and waited for him to get in beside her, then pulled out into traffic.

"I owe you an apology," he said after half-a-dozen blocks. He sounded rational. Bad sign.

They were passing Overton Park. Molly swung in and stopped beside the fourth fairway of the golf course. Logan stared straight ahead, his jaw set, his eyes seemingly focused on some faraway object.

Molly studied his profile. "Logan," she said, "let's talk about what happened. You seem to be taking things so calmly."

Logan shook his head like a punch-drunk boxer. "I'm anything but calm. I feel so damned guilty."

"Whatever for?"

"Tiffany read me perfectly. She must have realized instinctively that I would have no problem believing she could leave her sick child to die alone. She counted on me to call off the search once I thought Dulcy was dead." He ran his hand over his hair and closed his eyes. "I've been refusing to admit even to myself how angry I was at Tiffany when Jeremy was killed."

Molly laid her hand on his arm. She could feel his muscles bunched tightly under the wool of his jacket. "Of course you were angry. You can't help your feelings, Logan. But, cut yourself a little slack. You stood by her, tried to help her."

"She must have seen how I felt, how Zoe felt. Being around us must have been like heaping salt on a wound."

"Are you excusing what she did?"

He shook his head. "Not for a minute. But I'm beginning to understand her reasons for running away." He placed his hand over Molly's and turned to her with a faint smile on his face. "All that matters at the moment is that I believe you. The child you saw, the child you modeled, was Dulcy." He stared at her in awe. "If it hadn't been for you and that doll, I might never have known that my granddaughter is still alive. Tiffany would have gotten away with it because I allowed a fake death certificate, a sketchy description of a dead child and a detective I knew nothing about to convince me of a lie."

"Come on, Logan. Youngman's story was plausible. He had the child's death certificate and the identification of a nurse at the hospital where she supposedly died. As you said, he had no reason to lie to you about Dulcy's death. You were paying him a bunch of money to keep looking for her—money that he'd lose the minute you called him off. Besides, your son had just been killed, your daughter-in-law had disappeared with your grand-baby and your wife was dying. You shouldn't feel guilty."

"Zoe wouldn't agree with you."

"Zoe would be wrong."

"She's been furious with me because I didn't go to Moundhill and bring that child's body home to be buried beside Jeremy and Sydney in the family plot. We've had more than one argument over it."

"Why didn't you?"

"If one really does believe in an afterlife, a soul, then the child wasn't there anyway. Dulcy left the moment she died. I didn't see any sense in disturbing her poor remains just to bury her in another grave in another cemetery."

"I agree completely. So when are you going to tell Zoe?"

"Good God! I can't tell her. What if I can't find them? What if something's happened since you saw them?" He looked hard at Molly. "I can't get Zoe's hopes up. She's suffered enough already."

"She has a right to know, Logan! She's part of this."

"No!"

Molly threw up her hands in frustration. "You're going to do it all on your own and present her with a resurrected niece?"

"Better than letting her hope and then dashing her hopes all over again." He shook his head. "I have to protect her."

"I think you should tell her. If you don't, I promise it will come back to haunt you, whether we find Dulcy or not."

"No. The decision is mine alone and it's final."

She stared into his eyes for a long moment. She wished she could convince him that Zoe was a grown woman. To treat her like daddy's little girl was the worst kind of condescension. Molly hesitated, then relented. "Oh, all right."

"Bless you." Impulsively he put his arm around her shoulder and squeezed. She was as startled as if he'd sprouted wings.

And even more startled by her own reaction. She hadn't been this close to a man in more than three years. Logan's arm felt taut around her shoulders. He smelled wonderful, like autumn leaves and ginger. Every endorphin in her body snapped to attention. Was she so starved for affection that a hug from an attractive man stirred her so completely?

Blushing, she thrust away from him, praying he had not sensed her reaction. She took a moment to fiddle with the keys until she had her breathing under control again.

As she turned on the engine, he laughed. She'd never heard him laugh—not a real laugh, at any rate. "Suddenly, I'm ravenous."

Molly looked down at the serviceable steel watch on her wrist. "No wonder. It's past noon."

"Let's have lunch at the museum restaurant. It's close, the food is good and it's quiet."

"I don't know. I'm not really dressed for the Brush and Quill."

"Nonsense."

As the hostess showed them to a table five minutes later, one of a group of elegantly dressed women at a nearby table waved and called to Logan. He smiled and waved back.

"Go on over and talk to her," Molly whispered.

He shook his head and sat opposite her. "One of Sydney's friends. I barely know her."

"Good customer of MacMillan's?"

"I have no idea. I told you, the shop is Zoe's territory."

"Well, at the moment she's looking at me as though I were an armadillo. Hadn't you better go speak to her?"

"No. We have to plan our campaign. I cannot—will not—trust another private detective to do the job. I've got to find Dulcy myself."

"You can have whatever help I can give."

"We'd best start with what we know."

"Or what we don't," Molly said. "You said Tiffany's scheme wouldn't have worked unless you'd been willing to believe she'd abandon a sick child. It took more than that. There is a real little girl in Jane Doe's grave in Kansas, a child the same age and with the same coloring as Dulcy. How did Tiffany find out about her?"

"She must have seen the child, maybe known the parents, or been around the hospital where she died."

Molly nodded. "She didn't call Youngman until months after the child died. Why did she wait so long?"

"Maybe she didn't find out about the other child's death right away. Or maybe it took that long to make her plans. She may have started trying to find a way to get Youngman off her trail the minute she found I'd hired him. The other little girl's death must have seemed like the perfect opportunity to do just that.''

"If you bought the story, she was free and clear, and if you didn't, what had she lost?" Molly said. "She'd just have to disappear again.''

"We know she was living in Moundhill, maybe she hung around the Moundhill hospital,'' Logan said. "Perhaps she was a patient there.''

"Maybe Dulcy was a patient there,'' Molly said quietly.

Logan stared at her in alarm.

She reached across the table toward him. "It's possible. But we know she was alive and well long after that. I saw her, remember?''

Logan said with growing excitement, "She might still be living there.''

Molly took a deep breath. Logan wasn't going to like her next words. "Did you ever think that maybe she's made a new life for herself in Moundhill? Settled down. Married, even.''

"I hadn't considered that.''

"Consider it, then,'' Molly said. "What if you find Tiffany is sober, Dulcy is living happily with a new step-father in a middle-class ranch house in Moundhill and going to Brownies every Thursday? Do you call the po-lice, break up the family? Send Tiffany to jail? Drag Dulcy kicking and screaming back to Memphis to live with a man she likely doesn't remember?''

"Dulcy belongs with me. I will be a good father to her.''

"Logan, you're her grandfather. It's not the same thing. You've been a father. The job descriptions are different."

"No, I haven't been a father."

"But Zoe and Jeremy..."

"They're my biological children, all right, but I was never a father to them. I was gone for months at a time. Sydney had all the problems of being a single mother and none of the benefits. Well, almost all the problems. We had plenty of money—overseas jobs pay very well and there are no expenses to speak of. We decided the money was worth the long absences." He threw down his napkin. "By the time I realized how wrong we were, Zoe hated my guts and Jeremy was a practicing alcoholic at sixteen."

"Zoe loves you."

He snorted. "She blames me for Jeremy's drinking, his delinquency, his marriage, his death and for Dulcy's death, as well. I used to think she married Rick just to spite me because he was a plumber without a college education."

"If she did, she lucked out. Rick is a saint."

He grimaced. "I must admit he's been there for her."

Molly could fill in the unspoken corollary. Rick was there when Logan hadn't been. Maybe that was the key to Logan's coolness toward his son-in-law. Rick made it all look so easy, while Logan struggled to rebuild his damaged relationship with Zoe.

Still, understanding Logan's pain didn't mean she had to agree with him. "So all this is not about Dulcy, it's about you," she snapped. "You want to prove to Zoe and to yourself that you can be a father. Of all the selfish, idiotic..." She pushed her chair back. "I'm not hungry. I'll catch a cab."

. He caught up with her at the foot of the museum steps and grabbed her arm. "Wait, dammit! Listen to me. You're wrong. It's not about me. Tiffany's life will be hell until she comes home to face what she did. No way can it be good for Dulcy. When we find Tiffany, I'll help her any way I can, but I will take custody of Dulcy and raise her with love. Molly, you've got to help me. I don't have anyone else. Please."

"What do you want me to do?"

"Fly to Moundhill with me."

"I don't think . . ."

"Listen to me, please." He kept his hand on her arm and walked her to the BMW. He held the door and she got in against her better judgment. He climbed in the other side and faced her without turning on the engine. "You've worked with abused children, you know the system."

"So?"

"What's going to happen if I find Tiffany and Dulcy in Moundhill? Let's assume that instead of a decent life, they're living in squalor. Whatever money Tiffany took from her trust fund must have run out long ago and there was no way she could get more. Maybe she paid it all to Youngman. She may be slinging hash or clerking at the grocery store—or worse. She wasn't only into alcohol, Molly, she was into cocaine. Even Zoe doesn't know that."

"Oh, dear." That changed things. Molly knew from the seminars she'd sat in on for her volunteer work what addiction to cocaine could do to women. They didn't hesitate to sell their bodies and their children's bodies when their need for the drug became too much to handle.

"Even Jeremy's death didn't stop her drinking or do-ing drugs," Logan continued.

"Why did she take Dulcy along? It would have been easier for her to disappear alone."

"Maybe she loves Dulcy the way a child loves a favor-ite toy. Maybe she took Dulcy to punish us, Zoe and Sydney and me." He ran his hand down his face. "I don't know anymore. Not after today."

"I still don't see how I can help. If you find Dulcy, surely they'll give her to you."

"Say I waltz in to the local police station with my or-der of custody executed before Sydney died. They'll pick up Tiffany for extradition. Youngman was right. Tif-fany may well tell them I'm a pedophile and after the child's money. In today's climate, they may believe her. Dulcy could wind up in foster care."

"But I'm not a lawyer or a psychologist. I make dolls, period. And I've known you less than twenty-four hours during which you have acted about as stable as pluto-nium."

"Touché. You, however, have 'mother' written across your forehead in letters the size of a marquee."

"Oh, thank you so much. Just what every woman wants to hear."

"Even though I've known you such a short time, I would trust you with my life, and what's more, with my granddaughter's life. Besides, you can identify her. I haven't seen her since before she was two. You've got to come with me. And without letting anyone know where you're going or why."

CHAPTER FIVE

"IT'S BEEN NEARLY eight hours since I left you. I need you to tell me you'll go with me to Kansas so that I can make reservations." Logan was breathing hard. He cradled the phone against his shoulder and ran the towel over his sweating face and chest.

"I only said I'd think it over," Molly said over the line. "I didn't agree to anything."

"Look, let me come out to your house right now. We can talk about it all night if that's what it takes to persuade you."

"No." She sat down on her bed. "I'm practically ready for bed."

"So much the better." He chuckled.

She tried to chuckle back, but to her ears, it sounded as if she'd just choked on a peach pit.

"All right, how about I take you to breakfast?" he offered. "I've already got a call in to my travel agent. It's not that easy to get to Moundhill by plane. We'll have to fly into Wichita and rent a car."

"Logan, talk sense. I have animals to feed, a half-dozen commissions that I'm behind on, Quentin Dillahunt's evil little head hardening in my refrigerator, and I am terrified of airplanes. Isn't there somebody else you can take?"

"Nobody else has laid eyes on Dulcy. Sleep on it, please. I'll see you at nine o'clock tomorrow morning."

He sighed. "Please come with me. In just two days you have become more important to me than you can possibly imagine. I need you. Don't desert me now."

Molly sat on her bed and listened to the dial tone. She'd lied to Logan. She wasn't ready for bed. She still wore her jeans, though her feet were bare. She wandered into the kitchen. Elvis, ever-vigilant for a handout, trotted after her with his tail in the air. She opened the refrigerator, found a diet cola, and on impulse pulled out the meat drawer.

She'd give Logan breakfast here. He probably ate healthy junk, but if she did decide to go with him, she needed to finish the country ham before she left. She checked the freezer. Biscuits. There were always plenty of eggs. One overdose of cholesterol was unlikely to do irreparable harm to their arteries, and country ham beat bran flakes any day of the week.

Not that he needed the extra energy. He'd become a different person since he'd found a direction, a focus, something to do. He'd turned into a cross between a dynamo and one of his blasted bulldozers. At the moment, she felt like a very small sapling standing directly in his path. He was going to mow her down any minute. He was obviously used to calling all the shots and making all the decisions. If this was the way he treated Zoe, no wonder they had problems.

She knew darned well all his sexy innuendos were nothing but cheerful banter, but they really affected her. She shook herself and reached for Elvis. He eluded her and scampered down the hall. "Fickle cat!" she snapped.

She called Sherry and poured out the whole story to her. "And the worst of it is, he refuses even to discuss the possibility with Zoe and Rick that Dulcy is alive," Molly said. "He treats her like a child."

"He's being an overprotective daddy," Sherry said. "And, he's never really gotten to know Rick. Do you know a plumber who doesn't work twelve hours a day, six days a week? And Logan still goes gallivanting off for months at a stretch. Their orbits don't match." Sherry paused for a moment before going on, "Neither do their views of the world. I think Zoe may keep her two men apart a bit as well without realizing it. She demands Rick's complete loyalty. I don't think she'd be too happy if Rick and Logan suddenly started going fishing together."

"Maybe they should. Rick is the dearest, sweetest, most sensible man I know."

Sherry laughed. "He also has a scruffy beard and wears jeans to work. When Logan's home, he prefers three-piece suits and red power ties. Besides, Rick became the most important person in Zoe's life just when Logan wanted to become a full-time father to her. Bad timing."

Molly snorted. "I refuse to get involved in any more dysfunctional families. It's taken me years to get over my own." She hesitated. "On the other hand, Logan may act like a field marshal, but he's so damned sad. I hate to abandon him."

Sherry laughed. "That's my Molly—half of you wants to hide in your cave and make dolls, the other half keeps turning into Joan of Arc."

"And look what happened to *her*."

WHILE SHE WAITED for Logan to show up for breakfast, Molly called her daughter. "Anne, I'm going out of town," Molly said. "I'll have to renege on Elizabeth's sleep-over Friday. Can the two of you look after the animals for a few days?"

"Where are you going? Why? How long?" Anne asked. Then she caught her breath. "Mother, are you involved with that gray fox?"

Molly heard the verbal quotation marks around that word *involved*. "Even if I were, and I'm not, I'm a grown woman. I'm sorry, Anne, I can't tell you any more. I promise I'll keep in touch."

Anne sighed. "Mom, you know we'll look after the animals. It's time Elizabeth started getting Maxie ready for the Thanksgiving horse show anyway. I'll even make Phil take off on Saturday afternoon and come watch her ride." She hesitated.

Molly, who was used to her daughter's silences, waited for her to continue.

"It's just that Phil and I worry about you, Mom. You're out there all alone. The world's not safe and neither are the people in it—not even the handsome foxes. I love you too much to want to see you hurt again. Sometimes I worry that you don't think things out too clearly."

"Thank you, darling, for your vote of confidence," Molly said. "But I'm tougher than you think and not nearly so naive. I can look after every part of my self, including my heart. Don't worry. I'll keep in touch while I'm gone and tell you everything when I get home. I'll call Elizabeth this afternoon to apologize for finking out on her sleep-over." She hesitated, then blurted out, "I love you all. I'm so glad I have you."

"Mom? Are you all right? You never talk like that."

"Maybe I should. 'Bye, darling."

She hung up to Anne's drawn-out "Mooooother" on the line.

Next, she called Sherry to report her decision to go with Logan.

"My God, Molly," Sherry said. "You're not seriously flying off into the wilds of Kansas with Logan MacMillan." Sherry's laughter echoed down the wires. Then her voice turned deadly serious. "Do you truly think you can find that child?"

"We have to try. The difficulty is that we're a pair of rank amateurs. Frankly, I don't have the foggiest notion where to start."

"I wouldn't either. But I'll say some prayers for you. Trust you to wind up going searching with an incredibly attractive man. Nothing like that ever happens to me."

"When has it ever happened to me before? Besides, we'll probably hate one another cordially by the end of the first day. Logan MacMillan isn't my type," Molly lied glibly, wishing it were true.

"Then you are deaf, dumb and blind."

"What's more to the point, I am definitely not his type."

"I wouldn't be too sure of that."

Molly stretched her bare feet in front of her and ran her hand through her hair again. "Okay, you said you'd known Sydney since college. Do I remind you of her?"

Sherry chuckled. "Not in the least. Sydney cared more for externals and appearances than any human being I have ever met. She knew darned well Tiffany was a hellraiser, but all she could see was her future daughter-in-law's social standing and a wedding with twelve bridesmaids. Boy, did she get a rude awakening. Besides, Sydney was what the movie magazines used to call 'divinely thin.'"

"That let's me out. I have good reason to know that men Logan's age go for women Anne's age. He'll probably treat me like a sister, or worse yet, an aunt. Frankly,

I'm surprised some rich young widow hasn't snapped him up before now.''

''Logan keeps them at arm's length. He is courtly, charming, available for dinner parties when he's in town, pleasant and detached. I think he doesn't want to risk losing anyone else of value to him, so he simply refuses to care for anybody again. Of course, that old Byronic 'secret pain that only you, fair love, can assuage' is a downright killer with the ladies. I've considered seducing him myself.''

''Leo would kill you.''

''Only if he found out. Unfortunately, I haven't the skill for double-dealing that most women have.''

''Meaning?''

''I'd louse up my stories and get caught. Easier to stay faithful. Of course, you don't have a heavy husband waiting in the wings with a shotgun. You and he are both unattached. Enjoy.''

''Thanks for the insight, Sherry.''

''One more thing, Molly, don't forget that Tiffany is a convicted felon who killed two people. She wants that child with her desperately. She's dangerous.''

Molly hung up the phone thoughtfully. She still had half an hour before she expected Logan. Breakfast was well in hand. She pulled on a windbreaker over her black turtleneck and walked down to the workshop. Elvis padded along behind her.

Once inside, Molly pulled out Quentin's head and began to add soft bisque to his chin. She worked silently for twenty minutes until she heard the gate alarm. She covered the head, put it back into the refrigerator, closed the shop and walked up the hill to meet Logan.

He was dressed for business. ''Good morning,'' he said formally.

Every time Molly left him a trifle loosened up, he reappeared as distant and formal as ever. He was like some kind of plastic that had a memory—melt it, bend it, curl it into a ball, it sprang right back to its original rigidity.

"Can you handle cholesterol?" she asked.

He smiled. "Upon occasion."

"Good, because we've got country ham and hot biscuits for breakfast."

LOGAN DRANK his coffee and watched Molly straighten the kitchen. He'd enjoyed breakfast. Molly had kept up a cheerful line of patter about her small farm and the animals. It all served, as he supposed it was meant to do, to keep his mind off the task at hand.

The food had been good, but eating with Molly gave it an even better flavor. She had served the meal on bright yellow Italian pottery. Watching her as she moved easily among the pots and pans, he thought her the most appealing woman he had ever met.

With a sudden startling jolt of insight, he realized he had an appetite for her, a simple physical hunger. He wanted to nibble her all over, taste her, feel the texture of her skin and curl her crisp hair around his fingers. He jerked himself from his reverie. "What?" he asked.

"I said, have you told Zoe we're leaving tomorrow?"

"I told her I was leaving. I did not mention you."

"Logan..."

"I'm not protecting your honor. I'm guarding my privacy. And I'm protecting Zoe against disappointment."

"I don't agree, but it's your decision."

"You see, Dulcy was much more to Zoe than simply her brother Jeremy's child. She and Rick can't seem to conceive—no reason that the doctors can find, but they've been trying for years without success. I think Zoe was jealous of the ease with which Tiffany got pregnant."

"I can understand that. Sherry Carpenter loves me dearly, but she can't help begrudging me Anne and Elizabeth."

"It goes even deeper with Zoe. After Dulcy was born, Tiffany decided to go back to school to finish her degree. She didn't want to be bothered with a baby. She dropped Dulcy off at the shop nearly every morning. Sydney was too ill to look after her, so we set up a kind of nursery in the workroom at the back, and Zoe took over Dulcy. She was everyone's pet, but she was Zoe's special love."

"Then surely she'd be overjoyed to think that Dulcy might be alive."

He shook his head. "I can't raise her hopes. We may not find Dulcy. Perhaps she *is* dead."

"I'm sorry, Logan, but we can't put that toothpaste back into that particular tube."

"I know that," Logan said. "I'll pick you up Thursday afternoon about two. We'll get a rental car in Wichita, spend the night there and drive to Moundhill first thing Friday morning. Doctors often take long weekends. I don't want to miss seeing the staff at that hospital." He glanced over at Molly. "I've reserved two hotel rooms in Wichita for Thursday night."

Molly let out her breath. Good. "Can't we leave here early Friday morning?"

"No air connections. Molly, we haven't discussed money."

"Yes, we have. You said you'd pay all the expenses."

"And I will. But you'll be missing at least a weekend's work, possibly more if we have to trace Tiffany beyond Moundhill."

"I hadn't planned to be away more than a couple of days. I can catch up when I get home."

"I shouldn't need you any longer than that." Logan knew he was lying. He needed Molly beside him every step of this journey, and that included helping him get reacquainted with his grandchild. But he wasn't about to tell her that until she was a long way from home. Then he trusted her maternal instincts would take over.

"Zoe still wants your dolls for MacMillan's." He smiled. "I agree with her. The store can arrange contracts for your portrait dolls, but that's not enough to pay you for coming with me. The usual industry-consulting fee is five hundred a day. That's fifteen hundred dollars if you get home Sunday evening."

"Wow! I'm in the wrong business!" Molly laughed. "But you and I may be at each other's throats by dinnertime Friday."

"We may also not get home on Sunday. Can we say fifteen hundred plus expenses for the trip?"

"No, we cannot!" Molly said. "That's like signing a blank check! I'm not spending the next six months traipsing all over the western hemisphere with you. Look. There's a fancy new kiln I'm dying for and can't afford. You buy it for me and promise me I'll be home before the end of next week. Deal?"

"Deal." He offered his hand. If he needed her longer than that, he'd renegotiate.

Molly took his hand and felt the same electricity she always felt when he touched her. So long as Logan considered their arrangement purely business, she'd be safer from her feelings.

"Now, get out of here," she said. "I've got to finish most of Quentin Dillahunt's head before Friday." Molly watched him walk to his BMW, hands thrust into his pockets. She could have sworn she heard him whistling. *Lord,* she prayed, *let us find that child quickly. He can't take much more disappointment.*

And I can't spend much more time with him without falling in love with him. Damn!

CHAPTER SIX

MOLLY GRIPPED the arms of her seat, closed her eyes and prayed as the engines revved and the plane raced down the runway. She kept her eyes shut tight until she heard the clunk of the retracting wheels and knew that they were safely in the air. The plane banked sharply and she gasped. Her eyes flew open.

She hated takeoffs almost as much as she hated landings. She glanced at Logan, completely relaxed in the seat next to hers. She willed her fingers to release their grip on the armrest, willed her spine to flex.

He covered her hand with his. Her nerves heightened the jolt of electricity. It was as though she'd stepped onto the third rail of the subway.

"Sorry, Molly, when you said you hated to fly, I didn't understand how much."

She smiled wanly. "I'm fine, really."

"Why did you insist on bringing that doll with us?" Logan pointed toward the front of the cabin. The box containing the vinyl Dulcy doll could not be squeezed into the overhead bins, so it stood in the front closet with the hanging bags.

"She's better than a photograph. Besides, maybe when we do find Dulcy, the doll can help establish a connection with her, if we go about it the right way."

Logan shook his head dubiously. "That doll makes me uncomfortable. It's like carrying an effigy."

The plane chose that moment to lurch violently. Molly caught her breath and clenched her fists in her lap. After a moment the plane smoothed out. She exhaled and glanced at Logan. He showed no reaction. "You're used to this, aren't you?"

He laughed. "Actually, I'm more used to open-cockpit two-seaters."

Molly shuddered. "Have you ever crashed?"

"Not yet."

"Oh, God."

"I'm sorry. I was kidding. It's bluebird weather all the way. We'll be there in no time." He loosened his seat belt. "Sherry says you travel a good deal. Don't you fly?"

"I swore after my divorce I'd fly only if I were going across a major ocean—a small ocean wouldn't qualify." She shrugged. "I had to fly to all Harry's conventions and meetings."

"Why not stay home?"

"He wouldn't let me. Part of my job was schmoozing at all the parties. I was very good at it, but I was terrified somebody would catch on to how miserably out-of-place I felt and send me home in disgrace."

"You couldn't be out-of-place on the moon."

"Huh. I haven't put on a skirt or played hostess since my divorce." She felt her hand begin to relax as though some of Logan's calmness was passing from his hand into hers.

"Sydney loved to fly to places like Barbados and Mustique," Logan said. "Unfortunately, I worked in places like Sidi-bel-Abbès and Zamboanga."

"If you hated your job, why did you stick with it all those years?" Molly asked.

He turned to her, a startled expression on his face. "Have I given you that impression? I loved my job,

Molly. At least most of the time. I hated being away from my family, not seeing my children grow up, and yes, I hated the damned dirt and lousy living conditions, but there's nothing to equal building a dam so that people who've never had power can see at night, or building a plant that will put starving people to work so they can feed their families. I've lived places most people only dream about. Someday I'd like to show them to you."

Molly gulped. He spoke as though they had a future together. She laughed shakily. "I'm terrified in a 747. I'd pass out in a two-seater." She turned to look at him. "Besides, if we find Dulcy, you're going to be a full-time father."

"I want Dulcy to see more than one small corner of the world, Molly."

"But would you take her off to live in the jungle?"

"Of course not. But I intend to continue short-term consulting."

Molly noted that he no longer spoke of *if* they found Dulcy, but when. She prayed he would not be disappointed.

"No," he said as he moved his seat back and closed his eyes. "I'm going to be a full-time father whatever part of the globe I wind up in. Count on it."

"I WARNED YOU I don't wear skirts," she said later as she and Logan returned to their hotel rooms after dinner. She looked down at her navy slacks and red cowl-neck sweater. "I hope I didn't embarrass you."

"I'd enjoy walking into a restaurant with you if you were wearing bib overalls and hip boots."

Molly flushed beet-red. "At least I fit in with the other cowboys."

"By no stretch of anyone's imagination could you be confused with a boy anything." Logan chuckled. "You'd look female in body armor and a motorcycle helmet."

Molly struggled to get her door unlocked quickly. She knew the back of her neck was as red as her sweater, and she was terrified that Logan was going to make a pass. "What time do you want to start out tomorrow?"

Logan shrugged. "Say, nine o'clock? It's about an hour and a half drive from Wichita to Moundhill. I'll order breakfast for both of us at eight-thirty in my room."

Molly relaxed and turned to face him. He didn't intend to make a pass. She wasn't certain whether she felt relief or exasperation. It would have been nice if he'd shown some interest in her as a woman. Still, she was better off this way. She might have thrown herself into his arms and made an idiot of herself. She sighed.

Logan reached out and laid his hand against her cheek, his long fingers softly moving an errant curl away from her forehead. She froze. He just stood looking down at her from sad gray eyes. "Thank you, Molly Halliday." He opened her door and walked away to his own room.

Molly knew she should be exhausted, but she was too keyed-up to sleep. She still felt the touch of Logan's hand on her face. She settled down in the chair by the window and opened her new murder mystery—the one she'd been too nervous to read on the plane. She glanced out the window and was surprised to see Logan stroll out the front door of the hotel, turn left and stride off as though he were going to a race. She'd assumed he was going straight to his room and to bed.

She looked at her watch. It was only nine-thirty. If he planned to go to a bar for a drink there was certainly no reason he should include her. She was only a glorified employee. Still, she felt a wave of annoyance. Maybe he planned to pick up some young tootsie. Could be he did that every evening. What did she really know about him, after all? She ignored the flash of jealousy and tried to concentrate on her book, but her eyes kept straying to that window.

Ten minutes later, Logan showed up again, this time coming from the other direction and still moving fast.

She relaxed. It was only an evening walk. Of course, most people didn't clock eight-minute miles on their walks. The man was definitely an overachiever. She concentrated on her book. After a short while, she realized she'd read the same page four times, and the words were beginning to blur. The book slipped flat in her lap; her head lolled back against the headrest of the chair. Just five minutes, then she'd get to bed. She was worn-out from the plane ride. Amazing how exhausting terror could be. Just five minutes.

She woke with a start and a sharp pain in her neck from the back of the chair. She glanced down at her watch to see that she'd been asleep over half an hour. She rubbed her neck, yawned, closed the book and pulled herself up. As she did, she saw Logan come around again.

For pity's sake, how many times did he intend to walk around the same block? Tomorrow was bound to be a long, hard day. Logan was doing the driving to Moundhill. He needed his rest.

She knew she should mind her own business, but she simply couldn't. There was something compulsive about the way he walked. She pulled on her windbreaker, checked to see that she still had her room key in her pocket and let herself out into the hall.

On Logan's next round, he found her perched on the low stone wall across from the entrance of the hotel.

"Hi, sailor," she said.

He didn't look all that pleased to see her, and for a moment, her nerve nearly deserted her.

"You're going to catch cold sitting there with nothing on but that jacket," he said.

"And you're going to catch pneumonia. Look at you, it's fifty degrees out here, and you're sweating like a hog in August. How long do you plan to go on with this hamster routine?"

"Not that it's any of your business, but until I'm tired enough to fall asleep."

"Want some company?"

He glanced down at her legs. "You couldn't keep up with me."

"Hey, I can try." She pushed off from the wall.

"Fine." He strode down the driveway.

Molly regretted her gesture before they reached the street. He was right. His legs were a good six inches longer than hers, and he was used to moving fast. She generally meandered along, smelling the roses. This man might only be going around the block, but he walked as though all the demons in hell were nipping at his heels. She trotted behind him. Before they turned the first corner, she was puffing.

"Dammit, slow down!" she called after his retreating figure.

"You wanted to come," he said, but he stopped to wait for her. When he turned to her this time, however, he was grinning.

She came up to him and bent to put her hands on her knees. "You did that on purpose."

"Uh-huh."

"Look, I'm all for exercise, but I'm about two heart-beats away from atrial fibrillation here. Can't we just have a pleasant evening's stroll without trying out for the Olympic race-walking team?"

He laughed. "Sorry, Molly. Come on. We can even stroll arm in arm if you like."

"I don't actually need you to hold me up, thank you," she said.

He moved off sedately. She fell into step beside him.

After her breathing returned to normal, she asked, "How long do you usually do this?"

"I told you, until I'm sufficiently tired out to sleep. I have gym equipment at home. That's what I normally use to wear myself out."

"But that's crazy. That's no way to wind down. You're just keying yourself up more. Your adrenaline must be pumping a mile a minute. No wonder you never get any sleep."

"You're an expert, I presume?"

"No, I'm a mother." A few minutes later, as they passed the front door of the hotel, she took his arm. "Come on. We've got a long day tomorrow and I don't want you falling asleep at the wheel."

"I'm nowhere near ready to sleep. Just go to bed, Molly, and leave me to it. I know how tired I have to be before I can get any rest."

"No way. Come upstairs with me and let me apply the Halliday system for instant relaxation. My daughter used to give me fits about going to sleep when she was a child. I got to be an expert. It was that or entertain her half the night and have her fall asleep in English class the next day."

"It won't work, Molly. I've tried everything except sleeping pills. I won't resort to them."

"Mr. Macho?" she called over her shoulder.

As he stepped into the elevator behind her and punched the button for the second floor, he said seriously, "No. I saw what sleeping pills did to Sydney that last year. I'd rather stay awake."

"Sorry, Logan. I should have guessed. Come on." She stepped out of the elevator and walked to her room. He took the key from her hand and opened her door.

As she crossed the threshold, it suddenly hit her that all this could very well be open to misinterpretation. Her entire body went hot with embarrassment. She was doing everything except painting a sign across her chest that said Open For Business. Any man under the age of ninety might well misconstrue the signals.

She turned to him and said, "Um, maybe this wasn't such a great idea."

He closed the door behind him and leaned on it, looking at her steadily. His face was serious, and she felt her own flush. She took a deep breath. She'd gotten herself into this; now she intended to get herself out.

"Okay," she said. "Here's the plan." She walked over to the basket of tea bags and coffee packets set out beside the electric teapot in preparation for early-morning coffee. She hunted through and found the two she was looking for. "I thought I remembered some hot chocolate." She handed him the electric teapot. "Go run some water in this."

"Hot chocolate?"

"Well, hot milk is better, but this will have to do."

He took the pot with a wry grin and walked into the bathroom. She heard the water run in the sink and leaned against the side table. What on earth had possessed her to invite the man into her room? She reached over and clicked open her side of the connecting door between their two rooms. She prayed he had left his open, as well. When he came back, she'd make him a cup of hot chocolate and shove him through that door into his room with admonitions about long hot baths. Then she'd try to get some sleep, herself.

"Here you go. Hot water." He reached under the table and plugged in the pot. Instead of moving away from her, however, he stood much too close and smiled at her.

This whole thing was getting out of hand, she thought. He was enjoying himself enormously at her expense. She didn't think he was seriously contemplating anything beyond that, but that was enough. She felt a flare of anger and backed up until she felt the arm of the chair behind her.

She took hold of the back of the chair and tried to keep her voice as schoolmarmish as possible. "Actually, if you really want to sleep, you could order up hot milk and a turkey-and-onion sandwich from room service."

"What for? We just had dinner a couple of hours ago."

"Tryptophan. Guaranteed to make you sleepy. Turkey and onions are loaded with it. Why do you think men always go to sleep after Thanksgiving dinner?"

"I thought it was to get out of doing the dishes," Logan said. He hadn't moved and he was still watching her with that lopsided grin on his face.

"Well, it's not." The teapot began to whistle. "It's chemistry."

"So many important things are." He pulled the plug from the wall, prepared the hot chocolate and handed Molly her cup. "To you." He raised his cup and sipped it. Molly took a gulp of hers and burned the roof of her mouth so badly her eyes stung.

"What next?" Logan said as he set his cup, still three-quarters full, on the table beside him. "Onion sandwiches, turkey, warm milk, or in this case, hot chocolate. Surely you didn't feed Anne onion sandwiches at bedtime."

"Of course not. Don't be silly. I used to sing to her."

"Are you going to sit beside my bed and sing to me?" He clicked his tongue. "Sorry to say I forgot my teddy bear, but you could always deputize."

"You're enjoying this, aren't you?" she said sulkily.

"Absolutely. It's a whole new side of you, Molly."

"Oh, go to bed."

He walked over to her. "You know," he said casually, "there's an entirely different school of thought on relaxation techniques in the interest of a good night's sleep."

"And that is?"

He reached down and lifted her chin. "Maybe some day I'll discuss it with you." He leaned down and touched his lips to hers, softly, gently. She caught her breath. She felt as though she'd just been smacked in the stomach with a cattle prod. She wondered if her hair were standing on end.

"Good night, Molly," he said softly.

Then he was gone, out the front door to the hall.

Molly gulped and raced across the room to throw the latch on the connecting door between their rooms. She'd die if he opened his and found she'd left hers unlocked.

She fell back on her bed without even taking off her shoes. Good grief! He must think she was the world's most totally naive idiot. He was undoubtedly laughing at her fit to beat the band.

She sighed. At least he *could* laugh. Maybe she'd missed her calling. She'd get new cards made up that said, "Molly Halliday, Comic Relief."

Logan was the first man to kiss her since Harry's last corporate Christmas party, when one of the young lawyers got blind drunk and made a pass at her in the file room. She certainly had not reacted to that kiss the way she reacted to Logan's. Even on her honeymoon, she didn't remember one kiss that ever boiled the blood in her veins the way Logan's kiss had.

For the past three years, she'd denied she had any physical or emotional needs left.

Wrong. Logan had triggered all the right physical responses. She'd once heard one of Harry's more loathsome colleagues talk about his mistress as a "juicy middle-aged divorcee." She'd despised the man and hated the phrase, but looking down at her body, her breasts engorged and her nipples standing straight up through the cotton fabric like Tartar helmets, she had to admit she fit the bill.

What on earth was she going to do about it?

LOGAN CLOSED the door of his room behind him and looked at the connecting door between his room and Molly's. He had an almost unbearable desire to open his side and see whether hers was locked or not, but after that kiss, if he opened her door, she might just brain him with a lamp. His body was heavy, aroused, stirred with the kind of passion he hadn't experienced in years.

He kicked off his shoes, sank back on his bed and locked his hands behind his head on the thick pillows. How long had it been since he'd experienced desire?

Jeremy's death had turned him into ice. The painful experiences since had added layer upon layer until he was one big glacier. Apparently, the molecules of hot male blood still flowed in his veins, and Molly was a blowtorch. She was melting him. He was beginning to feel again.

Feel. That was the operative word. He'd nearly died once in Alaska when he'd been caught out in a sudden blizzard and lost his way. His hands, feet and face bloomed with frostbite when they found him. He was numb until he warmed up, then, God, the pain! It had been as though someone had lit gasoline and shot it into his circulatory system. He longed to embrace Molly's warmth, to allow her to thaw out his heart, but he feared the pain he'd have to endure in the process.

He chuckled. She brought laughter with her, all right. And beauty. Not many women could look so desirable when they were out of breath, but then most women didn't have Molly's lovely bosom. He hadn't planned to kiss her, but all that hot chocolate and turkey stuff had been so prim and proper, he had to get through to her somehow.

He caught his breath. Sherry said Molly had her share of hurt, too. He'd have to go slowly.

He never wanted to hurt her. He needed her too badly.

CHAPTER SEVEN

DR. MARGUERITE LARSEN, hospital administrator of the tiny Moundhill hospital, was probably Molly's age, but to Molly's somewhat envious eye, was doing a much better job of concealing it.

On the wall behind the doctor—prominently displayed among the awards and framed certificates—was a large colored photograph of Dr. Larsen with a man and woman Anne's age. In the picture, Dr. Larsen knelt in the grass with her arms around three boys who ranged in age from preschool to midteen.

"Thank you for seeing us," Logan said as he and Molly sat in front of the broad mahogany desk. The doctor nodded.

"As I explained over the telephone," Logan continued, "I've dealt with enough hospitals to know that the word uppermost in your mind anytime someone asks any questions about the hospital is *litigation.*"

Dr. Larsen's shoulders tightened visibly. "Is that why you're here? To sue the hospital?"

Logan shook his head. "Not at all. From everything we know about the case we're asking about, the hospital staff behaved in an exemplary manner. In any case, I'm not a lawyer. I'm a grandfather."

Dr. Larsen's shoulders did not relax. "Perhaps you'd better tell me just what we're talking about, Mr. Mac-Millan."

Logan looked over at Molly and took a deep breath. "Two years ago, an abandoned child died in this hospital of viral spinal meningitis. That child was later identified as my grandchild, Dulcy MacMillan. We now have reason to believe the child who died was someone else and that Dulcy is still alive. Dulcy was taken by her mother. We're looking for them both."

"If the child who died was not your granddaughter, Mr. MacMillan, I don't see what assistance I can give you."

"We have evidence that my daughter-in-law knew of the death of the child and set up the false identification. It's possible she was an employee of this hospital at the time the child died."

"I don't know how she could have found out about the child's death from some other source. Or perhaps she or this—Dulcy?—was a patient here at the time the other child died."

"That could be."

"What do you want from me?" the doctor asked.

"We have to start somewhere. We'd like to show pictures of both my grandchild and her mother to you and your staff to see if you recognize either of them."

"That can be done, although the staff has recently undergone some major changes. I've only been here six months, myself."

"We would also like to see the records of the hospital staff employed at that time, and the records of the girl who was identified as Dulcy."

"That, I'm afraid, is not possible. Our records are confidential."

"My lawyer assures me that records of deceased patients become a matter of public record and can be obtained. So do death certificates. You can show us those

records at least. We need your cooperation. We don't
have time to waste. The child who died was abandoned
by her parents. Surely the police were called at the time
to try to locate them. There must have been an investi-
gation."

Apparently, the word *police* was more poisonous to Dr.
Larsen than *litigation*. The woman drew herself up and
folded her arms tightly across her chest. She glanced from
Logan to Molly as though trying to figure out precisely
where Molly fit in.

Molly smiled and tried to look nonthreatening.

"My daughter-in-law is a convicted felon, Doctor,"
Logan said. "Any law enforcement officer who stops her
for running a stop sign can detain her. The state of Tennessee will extradite. If my granddaughter is still alive and
with her, then they are both on the run. The child is being raised in an atmosphere of isolation and uncertainty.
Surely any humane person would want to help as much
and as quickly as possible. That's all we're asking for—
your help and the help of your hospital staff."

"But this woman is the child's mother, after all."

Logan reached into his coat pocket and brought out a
folded legal document backed by a blue cover. He handed
it to the doctor. "This gives me legal custody of Dulcy.
The judge would not have signed it if he'd felt Dulcy belonged with her mother."

"Please, Doctor," Molly said, then gestured toward
the framed photograph on the wall, hoping she was
guessing right. "You're a grandmother. Surely you understand how badly we need to get Dulcy safely back to
the people who love her."

The doctor stared at Molly narrowly for a moment,
then sighed and leaned back in her leather chair. "All
right. Let me offer a compromise. I'll check the records

to find out who the floor nurse was when the Jane Doe was admitted. I'll get the dead child's records brought up. We're still not computerized, I'm afraid." She laughed shortly. "If either the nurses or the doctors who worked on the case are still employed here, I see nothing wrong with letting you talk to them or anyone else who may have been involved. I can't give you the child's file, but I can have relevant parts of it copied for you if necessary."

"That's better than nothing," Logan said. "I would prefer to look for any information myself, but I'll have to trust you."

"What do you hope to gain?"

"Further confirmation that the child who died was not my granddaughter. And possibly, a lead to her mother."

"But the woman could simply have been visiting a patient here during the time the child was dying."

"But how would she have found out about the child? She'd have had to go wandering around in Pediatric Intensive Care looking for possible candidates." Logan shook his head. "No, I think it's more likely that she worked around the hospital in some capacity. That way, she'd have known about the child."

"Did she have medical experience?"

"Not to my knowledge," Logan said.

"Okay, so she might have been on the clerical staff or in housekeeping."

"Yes," Logan said. "She might still work here. We know she was still living in Moundhill a year ago."

Dr. Larsen bit her lip, considered a moment, then made her decision. "We certainly don't want convicted felons working for the hospital, Mr. MacMillan. May I see a picture of your daughter-in-law?"

Logan pulled out his wallet and extracted one of several photographs. "I brought as many as I had."

Dr. Larsen looked at the picture. "I can tell you she doesn't work here now. I know everyone on staff."

Logan's face fell.

"Do you have a picture of your granddaughter?"

"Only as a baby."

"I think I can do better than that," Molly said. "Logan, I'm going to bring in the Dulcy doll."

"I'M SORRY." The tall Native American nurse thrust her hands deep into the pockets of her lab coat. She stared down at the photograph of Tiffany MacMillan and shook her head. "I feel as though I've seen this woman somewhere." She reached for the picture. "But I can't tell you for certain it was in this hospital."

"Please look again, Ms. Herdshorses," Logan said.

"No. It just won't come to me. I'm terribly sorry, Mr. MacMillan," Eleanor Herdshorses handed the picture back. "I remember that little girl as though it were yesterday, but I never saw this woman around her. Somebody brought the child into the emergency room and just left her there, lying on one of the benches. I don't know how long she'd been there before she was noticed. For a small hospital we're pretty busy, and of course so many poor people use the emergency room as a primary-care facility. Insurance pays for the emergency room, so people wait until they are desperately ill, then come here." She sighed deeply. There were dark circles under her eyes.

She rotated her shoulders as though to ease the muscles, then she continued. "The little girl was nearly comatose right from the beginning." She opened the file she held in her other hand. "A hundred and six temperature—viral meningitis. The doctor in the emergency room diagnosed it. By then she was already far enough along so that her back was starting to bow. Terrible. Brain swelling. Kidneys shut down. She died twenty-four hours later. We tried everything, but there wasn't much we could do except watch and try to make her as comfortable as we could."

"Didn't anyone try to trace the parents?" Molly asked. She thought of how she would feel if Elizabeth faced a terrible death, alone and abandoned. She swallowed and tried to keep her voice level. "Surely they came back or at least called?"

"If so, there's no record of it. I'm sorry. I wish I could help."

"How about afterward? The man who came to identify her?"

"What man?" Mrs. Herdshorses asked.

"A Mr. Youngman. Didn't he talk to you about two months afterward?"

"Not me. Maybe the doctor or one of the other floor nurses talked to him."

"Could we speak to them, please?" Molly asked.

Mrs. Herdshorses shook her head. "I'm the only one left who was here then. We have a high turnover. Nearly everyone wants to move to a larger hospital."

Molly nodded, picked up the box she had set on the chair behind her and carefully unwrapped the Dulcy doll. "Can you tell me, was this the child who died?"

"Ooh!" Eleanor Herdshorses reached for the doll with the same lust Sherry Carpenter and Zoe MacMillan both showed when presented with one of Molly's dolls. Her tired eyes glowed. "Isn't she beautiful?" She held the doll as tenderly as a baby, looking down into her eyes and smoothing her hair. She looked up at Molly. "Is this supposed to be the Jane Doe?"

Molly nodded.

"Well, she's not. The child who died—I can remember that child's face every time I close my eyes. That poor little tyke. But—" she shook her head and handed the doll gently back to Molly "—this is not the same child. That one had red hair, all right, but not like this. This is a real strawberry blond."

Logan closed his eyes a moment and expelled all the breath from his lungs in one long sigh. Molly reached out to touch his arm; he covered it with his other hand. After a moment, he opened his eyes. "You're sure the dead child didn't look like this?"

"Positive. I wish I could be more help."

"You'll never know how much help you've been," he told her.

"Look, you look like you could use a coffee or something," the nurse said. "Go on down to the cafeteria. I'll show that woman's picture around up here. I've got a break in ten minutes. I'll bring it down to you."

"Thank you."

Ten minutes later, Nurse Herdshorses waved from across the half-empty cafeteria and came over to them, the picture of Tiffany in her hand. "Couple of people said she looked familiar, but nobody knew who she was. I'm sorry." She laid the picture on the table beside Logan's coffee cup. "Look, I've got a buddy in the sheriff's substation. Name's Jerry Wolfpaw. I called him. He'll be there until seven if you want to go by to talk to him."

"Thank you so much." Molly reached out and touched the nurse's arm. "Can't we get you something?"

"Thanks, but no. I've got a kid just down from a tonsillectomy. I ought to be getting back. I don't really have time for breaks. Good luck." She turned and glided out of the cafeteria, one hand kneading the muscles in the small of her back.

"God forbid Elizabeth should ever get sick, but if she does, I hope there's somebody like that around for her," Molly said.

"Amen to that," Logan said. He smiled and reached over to lay his hand on hers. Molly felt her own hand respond to the touch of him with that same electricity shoot right to her armpit. She looked up quickly to see whether or not he felt it too, but he merely looked tired and dispirited.

"Molly, I had some crazy idea we'd find her here. Stupid. Nothing's that easy. At least we've finally got incontrovertible proof that the child who died was not Dulcy." He ran his other hand down his face "But we shouldn't forget that somebody's little girl died alone two years ago. Before we leave town, I want to find a florist. Whoever she was, she deserves flowers on her grave."

Molly felt hot tears start. She just let them spill down her cheeks.

"Honey, you want some more iced tea? You okay?" The waitress loomed over the table. "Hey, when'd she do her hair that color?"

"I beg your pardon?" Molly looked up into the face of the waitress, a large worn woman whose overpermed gray hair blended into her wrinkled face without a solid line of demarcation.

"Her." The waitress gestured toward the picture. "Looks real good on her though, dudn't it?"

"You know this woman?" Logan snapped.

"Well, sure, honey. Worked here. Cashier. Didn't stay long, though. Just up and disappeared. Boy, was my manager pissed."

Logan stood. "Please sit down a moment, Miss...."

"Verlene, honey. And I couldn't. My manager would *really* be pissed if I sat down with the paying customers."

"Don't worry," Logan said, "I'll square it with your manager. Tell me everything you can remember about her. We're trying to find her."

"Oh. Well, sure, if you'll take care of it if I get in trouble." The woman sat, carefully easing her bulk down into the seat. She rubbed her right instep. "Oooh, that feels good. I been on my feet since breakfast."

"About this woman," Molly asked.

"Sure. Terry something—Rogers or...I know, Rigby. That's it. Terry Rigby." She leaned over close to Molly. "Only reason my manager hired her was she had you know..." She pantomimed a huge pair of breasts.

"She was a cashier?"

"Yeah. She started out waitressing, but my manager, well, he thought she'd maybe be available. Didn't have on no wedding ring or nothing." She snickered maliciously. "'Course, I knew she had a baby."

"How?" Logan asked.

"'Cause she asked me did I know anybody could look after her little girl while she was at work is why."

"You say she left?"

"Yeah. I always did think she was after drugs. You wouldn't think it in a small town like this, but we got us a real drug problem. Always making up to the doctors. Folks think you can get drugs in a hospital." Verlene clicked her tongue. "Heck fire, way they keep those things locked up, easier to get 'em out of the po-lice department."

"What made you think she wanted drugs?" Molly asked.

Verlene shrugged. "Something about her eyes. Half the time she come to work—late, like as not—them eyes would be real red and beady. Always having headaches and things. And mean-mouth? Lord, always acting snippy like she was too good to be working here. Had to be something. Stands to reason, don't it? Who'd work here if they didn't have to? Besides, her shoes was too good." She turned to Molly. "You know?"

Molly nodded. She did indeed know. Even Verlene would be able to tell that Ferragamos or Donna Karan didn't come from the local dollar store. A woman who wore designer shoes had to have some ulterior motive to work in a place like this.

"Verlene, you got customers."

The man who came to the table was a five-and-a-half-foot symphony in plaid polyester. Even his hair looked like a cheap wig.

"We asked Verlene to help us, Mr. . . ."

"Travis Pokerandt." He looked at Logan's proffered hand for a moment as though wondering whether or not to accept it, but in the end, he did. Verlene stomped off. Pokerandt took her place.

"Yeah, I hired her," he said after Logan showed him the picture. "Fired her butt, too. Always late. Hungover half the time. Had a mouth on her, too. Why you looking for her?"

Logan explained.

"I don't owe her one little thing," Pokerandt said. "You want what I got, you can have it."

Twenty minutes later, Logan and Molly left with a positive ID of Tiffany MacMillan as Terry Rigby, with her new social security number, and with the address listed on her employment application.

The apartment listed as her address had been jerry-built in the late sixties. It wasn't so much on the wrong side of the tracks as right on them. Only a narrow strip of gravel separated the nearest apartment from the rails. The vibrations over the years had caused long cracks to open in the concrete, and the iron bolts that held the outside staircases to the side of the building wobbled dangerously as Logan and Molly climbed them in search of the resident manager.

What little grass there was in the courtyard had already turned mud-brown. A few scraggy shrubs struggled dispiritedly against the incessant wind.

"Lit out in the middle of the night. Just took off like that," Mrs. Havermeyer, the manager, told them. "Owed me two months' rent." Her eyes narrowed. "You being family and all, you can pay me."

Logan declined.

Mrs. Havermeyer slammed her door in their faces.

Back in the car, Logan turned to Molly. "Okay, Molly, do we try the law?"

"What have we got to lose?"

Silently they drove to the sheriff's substation to find Deputy Wolfpaw.

"I'll update the NCIC—that's the National Crime Information Computer—that Terry Rigby is Tiffany MacMillan, but she may have established a dozen other identities by now. If she could figure out how to set up this one, she could do it over. At least if she's on the NCIC, every police force knows that if they pick her up and hold her, the Memphis police will be willing to extradite. That's not much help. Folks, I hate to say this, but you need some professional help."

"Absolutely not!" Logan snapped.

"You got something against private investigators?" Wolfpaw asked, turning to eye Logan curiously.

"I assumed you did. Don't policemen resent the interference of the non-police?"

"Mr. MacMillan, almost every job a PI does is for a defense lawyer. Frankly, if some PI can come up with concrete evidence I've arrested the wrong man, I damned well want to know about it before I get the guy convicted and sent to prison. The answer is no, I don't resent PIs. At least not the reputable ones."

"Ah. That's the problem. How do you tell the difference?" Logan breathed.

Wolfpaw leaned forward, looking closely at Logan. "There are sleaze-buckets in every profession. There are bad cops, too. You act like you ran into one of the crooks, am I right?"

"I employed a man who came highly recommended from someone whose judgment I will never trust again. The man hired convinced me the child who died here was my granddaughter. It now seems he didn't even talk to the nurse in charge of the case."

"You never checked up on him?"

"I had no reason to doubt him. Besides, my wife was dying, my son had just died, my daughter-in-law had absconded. I was not in the best mental shape myself at the time."

"Yeah. Look, there are plenty of good PIs all over. We got an agency here in town, even."

"In the middle of Kansas?" Logan sounded incredulous.

"Sure. 'Bout your age. Retired FBI man. Works with his wife. They go all over the world for their clients. You'd like them. Watson and Watson they call themselves. I can vouch for them, and me you can trust. Want me to call them for you?''

''I hardly think that—''

Molly interrupted. ''Yes, please, Deputy Wolfpaw. It's five o'clock, but if they could see us this afternoon, we'd appreciate it.''

''Molly!'' Logan said warningly.

''Logan, he's right. We need professional help. We know the name Tiffany was using, but do you have any idea how to make that work for us? Well, do you?''

Logan looked at her hard, then sighed. ''No, you're right. Call them.''

''What harm can it do? If we dislike them or distrust them or they can't see us, what have we lost?''

CHAPTER EIGHT

TWENTY MINUTES LATER, Molly and Logan drove across a cattle guard into a pasture behind a heavy stand of evergreens situated to break the northwest wind sweeping down the prairie. They were less than ten miles outside of Moundhill, but for the last ten minutes they had been in real farm country. Late black-eyed Susans bloomed throughout the pasture and ran along the fencerows.

"This is not my idea of a detective agency," Molly said as they pulled up in front of a large, white, modern house with many windows in high gables. "Maybe this is the wrong address."

"According to Wolfpaw, these people are not your usual detectives," Logan replied.

As they hesitated in the car, the Chinese-red front door opened. A tiny woman came out onto the porch and waved to them.

"Come on in," she called. "Tom and I have been waiting for you ever since we got your call." She was hardly more than five feet tall, and although Molly guessed she was well past sixty, her nut-brown face was largely unlined and she moved like a teenager. Her blond hair was streaked with gray and cut very short.

The man behind her was Logan's height but thick-bodied. He had warm eyes and a slow smile that Molly instantly found comforting.

Nell Watson ushered them into the house and to seats in the living room. She sat across from Molly.

"Wolfpaw told us your story," Tom said from the doorway. "While we're talking, can I get you something to drink? Scotch? Soda? Coffee?"

Logan shook his head. "Nothing, thanks."

"Okay, if you're sure," Tom said to Logan. "Now tell me what you have to go on. Tiffany's new name? Her fake social security number?"

Logan nodded.

"Let me have them," he said.

Logan reached into his inside jacket pocket, found a slip of paper and handed it to Tom.

He glanced at it. "Fine. I'll be back as soon as I've checked this out." He disappeared down a hall. They heard a door slam.

"Now," Nell said, "You'll stay for dinner. I won't take no for an answer. Do you mind coming to the kitchen with me while I fix it?"

"We don't want to trouble you," Molly said.

"It's no trouble." Nell led the way to a big open country kitchen with a glassed-in dining area beyond. She opened a drawer and pulled out place mats and napkins. "Molly, do you mind taking the salad out of the refrigerator? The potatoes are already in the oven. And I'll stick the steaks on the grill. You just sit and watch. You look as though you could use some peace and quiet."

Logan agreed. Although Molly seemed to have gotten her second wind from Nell Watson, he felt tired in his bones and more discouraged than he dared admit.

He wondered what Tom Watson was up to and where he was. He became aware that the two women sounded as though they were chatting to each other a long way from him rather than in the same room. He couldn't focus on their words. They seemed to have established an easy companionship almost at once.

Men—at least men he knew—did not function in that way even with friends, and certainly never with strangers like the Watsons. There was always an undertone of jockeying for position, for power, a searching out and probing of even the dearest companion's defenses. He remembered being wary all his life. Wary in business, even wary with Sydney—first to win her, and then to keep her happy. Molly hammered away at that wariness, those defenses, without even being aware that she did it.

He wanted her desperately. Something in her called to him as no woman ever had.

As he watched Molly place the salad bowl on the table, he wondered whether what he felt when he looked at her could be love.

If so, it was a new experience. The curve of her cheek, the quirk at the corner of her mouth, the way she drove her hands through her hair had become incredibly dear to him. He wanted to make love to her, certainly, but almost more than that he wanted to hold her so close to him that she blended into his very soul.

"Okay, we've got something."

Logan started. He had been concentrating so hard on Molly, he had not heard Tom come back into the room.

"What did you find out?" Molly asked.

"There's a Terry Rigby with the same social security number who had an apartment in Laramie, Wyoming, up to a month ago. Her lease isn't up, so she should still be there. What's more—" he paused for effect "—she writes checks at the Laramie Tots and Tykes Shop."

"Yes!" Molly shouted. She ran to Logan, and threw her arms around him.

Logan stood and hugged her back hard, his mind racing. He asked Tom, "How did you find her so quickly?"

"It's really very simple," Nell said. "Tom ran her social security number through our database."

"I thought that was illegal," Molly said.

Nell laughed. "The government's computer is definitely off limits. There are a number of private investigators making macramé pot hangers in Uncle Samuel's guest houses who forgot that. But there are private databases that gather information and publish it to reputable private investigators like us."

"We subscribe to a database that captures numbers from credit checks, leases, mortgages, every way they can," Tom said.

"So she's in Laramie now?" Logan asked.

Tom shrugged. "It runs about ten days behind, so theoretically she could be in Timbuktu by now, but at least you're closer than you were."

"And she still has Dulcy with her," Molly said.

"So it would seem."

"When do we leave?" Nell asked.

"I beg your pardon?" Logan asked.

"Oh. I am sorry," Nell said. "You haven't even hired us yet."

"Of course I'll pay you for everything you've done so far, but beyond that, no, at this point I don't plan to hire you for anything further."

"You want to go yourself," Tom said matter-of-factly. "Don't blame you."

"We've come this far, and thanks to you we have someplace to go from here."

"First thing tomorrow morning," Nell said, "we'll call our travel agent in Wichita for you. He'll be glad to make your plane reservations. Frankly, I'm glad you don't want us to go with you, or even, for that matter, instead of you." She leaned against her husband's shoulder. "It's nice to be able to stay at home occasionally. But if at any point you do decide you need us in Laramie, please don't hesitate to call. We'll try to come as quickly as we can."

"Thanks."

"It's not going to be that easy to fly to Laramie," Nell said. "You'll probably have to drive back to Wichita, fly to Denver and take a feeder airline to Laramie."

Molly cleared her throat. "How big is a feeder airline?"

Logan glanced at her, then looked more closely. Her face was set and white; a pulse jumped convulsively at the base of her throat. Her hands chafed together in her lap as though she needed to warm them.

"You know, a commuter plane," Nell said.

Molly nodded.

Logan wanted badly to get to Laramie as quickly as possible. How could he convince Molly that she was safer in an airplane than on the highway?

She sat silent, accepting the inevitable. Apparently, she was prepared to do just that, no matter how miserable it made her.

"No," he said, not realizing he intended to speak until the word left his mouth. "We'll drive."

He saw Molly's shoulders release their tension. She closed her eyes and let her breath out in a rush. He wanted to put his arm around her, tell her it was all right.

Tom started to say something, but Nell put a hand on his arm. Logan realized she'd picked up on Molly's terror and guessed the reason for it. "Probably just as quick, really," Nell said. "You'd spend half the day waiting in airports and not get there until tomorrow night anyway." She smiled dazzlingly at Logan. "It makes sense to drive."

"We'll leave early."

"I have a good feeling you'll find her. Now let's eat," Nell said.

After dinner, Tom took Logan out to the office to show him the computer setup.

Nell took the plates from Molly and rinsed them in the sink. After a moment, she asked, "You're worried about him, aren't you?"

"I'm not sure what you mean."

Nell leaned both hands on the sink and turned to Molly. "Tom and I have worked dozens of these cases." She opened the dishwasher and began to stack the plates. "We nearly always find the child we're hunting for."

Molly sighed. "Then you know what we're up against. Logan doesn't have a clue."

"How do you?"

"I worked with abused children as a volunteer, even considered going back to school for a degree in psychological counseling before the dolls took over my life. As a matter of fact, when I started making dolls, I thought I might be able to reach some of the children with them."

"Let's go sit in the living room where we can be comfortable."

Molly sank onto the overstuffed blue leather couch. As the down cushions deflated under her, she felt as though someone were letting the air out of her body, as well. "Logan remembers a cuddly baby. Dulcy's nearly five now, and has probably been alone with her mother for the last three years."

Nell folded her legs under her, tailor-fashion. "Surely the child's been to day care or a play group. She must have had other children to mix with."

"Tiffany probably wouldn't dare let anyone get close. And they obviously lived in squalor. You should have seen that apartment in Moundhill. It was dreadful."

"But she had money from her trust fund."

"Not so you'd notice it." Molly shook her head. "How do I tell Logan Dulcy could have broken bones or bruises because momma's boyfriends slap her when she cries? He has no idea how easily shaking a child can cause brain damage. Can he take the scars of old cigarette burns or scalding water?" She dropped her head into her hands. "Can he take AIDS?"

Nell put her hand on Molly's shoulder. "Oh, I pray it's not as bad as that."

Molly's face was bleak and tears welled in her eyes. "I've seen them, Nell." Molly spread her arms and opened her hands. "I've held them while they cowered or tried to bite me. And sometimes they stammer or they don't speak at all."

Nell shivered. "Tiffany couldn't. . ."

"Tiffany probably wouldn't mean to hurt Dulcy. From what little I know of her, I'm sure she's done her best, but addiction is a tough master. These kids turn into little adults. They're the responsible ones. They have to be the parents, and the more they fail, the worse they feel." Molly's voice went high like a child's. "Who's coming home tonight? Sweet Mommy? Drunk Mommy? Mean Mommy? Mommy's trick or Mommy's pusher or Mommy's pimp?" Molly hugged herself and her voice turned flat and hard. "Then there's the anger," she continued. "Children are never allowed anger—not even righteous indignation, and believe me, these children are entitled to that. One little girl I worked with had four separate personalities to deal with her problems."

She leaned back against the sofa and closed her eyes. "How can I prepare Logan? He's expecting a precious angel to climb onto his knee and talk baby talk. He's probably going to get a complicated little disaster who needs intensive therapy and may never be completely well."

"He was wiser than he knew to bring you with him," Nell said softly.

Molly raised her head and brushed the tears away from her cheekbones. "I'm the naive one. Until Tom found her in Laramie, I never really believed we'd succeed."

"You sound as though she and Logan are both your responsibility."

"I know they're not. Logan and I met less than a week ago. But he's living a fantasy that being a father to Dulcy will redeem him."

"Tiffany will take care of his fantasy. I expect she'll fight him like a wolverine." Nell leaned over and grasped Molly's arm. "You're more involved than you think. You've dropped everything to traipse around Kansas looking for Dulcy. Now, granted, Logan had a great deal to do with that, but I don't believe that's all there is to it. This child and her story have wormed their way under your skin, Molly Halliday, and you're stuck with her and her grandfather, whether you like it or not."

Tom and Logan came into the room.

"Listen, it's after ten," Nell said. "You're too tired to drive to the motel even if there's a vacancy. Besides, we need to figure out just what you're going to do when you leave here. Of course you'll stay the night. We have tons of room. Tom, please help Logan get the bags in. Our extra bedrooms are all made up, so you can choose whatever sleeping arrangements you like."

Molly gulped. She hoped no one noticed.

Nell eyed her. She shooed the men out the front door to the rental car, then turned to Molly. "It's obvious you two are crazy about each other. Why don't you stop pussyfooting around and hop into bed while you're still young enough to enjoy it?"

CHAPTER NINE

FAT WHITE FLAKES began to drift down the windshield before Molly and Logan reached Denver in late afternoon. The sullen sky darkened quickly. "This isn't supposed to happen," Molly said, looking out at the snow. "I didn't think it ever snowed this early."

"Won't last. Don't worry. We can still get to Laramie tonight." Logan inched the rental car forward and stopped behind the car in front. "What now?" He flicked on hazard lights to alert the car following him and jumped out of the car.

He slipped and fell on his backside in the slush. He struggled to his feet, cursing.

A Colorado state trooper walked up to the car. "Sorry, folks, big rig blocking the road up ahead. Bad accident. Road's closed."

"What the hell are we supposed to do? We can't turn around and head back to Denver," Logan said.

"There's an exit about fifty yards ahead. Plenty of motels around Fort Collins. Suggest you check into one and bed down. It's going to get real bad tonight, but it's supposed to clear by morning." He tipped his hat. "Ma'am," he said to Molly. Then he walked on down the line, bringing his message to the cars behind them.

"Hell!" Logan snarled as he slid in behind the wheel and started the engine again. "If we hadn't stopped for dinner, we would have been ahead of that truck."

"Or under it."

"Huh," Logan said.

Over the next twenty minutes, they inched forward until they reached the exit that took them to a two-lane road. The roadway was growing slicker by the minute.

Molly, a Southerner to her toenails, gripped the armrest beside her, peered at the ditches that ran along each side of the road and thanked God that Logan had experience driving in bad weather.

Neon motel signs flickered by, but Logan didn't even slow down. Soon there were fewer and fewer signs of life. Molly longed to stop, but she felt responsible for landing them in this mess. They should have flown to Laramie. She kept her mouth shut.

The snow turned to sleet and freezing rain that whipped against the windshield like shotgun pellets. Ice piled up in the corners of the windshield so that only the arcs cleared by the wipers remained clear. Logan hunched forward over the steering wheel and slowed little by little until they were creeping along at no more than twenty miles an hour. Molly was glad when darkness fell. At least she had no way of telling whether they drove between flat fields or over the top of mountains, or how far down they would plummet if they spun off the road. She didn't speak.

"Damnation," Logan snapped as the taillights of a car rose up no more than ten feet in front of him. Molly caught her breath. Logan touched his brakes. The car fishtailed, and for a moment Molly was sure Logan had lost control. She whimpered and tried not to scream.

After the car settled, he glanced over at her. "Flying couldn't be worse than this."

"You can't open the door and step out of a plane."

"Well, you can, but it's not advisable. In any case, I think we'll have to stop. Snow I can handle, but this is ice."

Molly breathed a sigh of relief.

"The problem is, where. I thought that patrolman said there were motels all over."

"Maybe we can't see them through the sleet."

"Or maybe they're all filled up and have turned off their vacancy signs," Logan answered. "Aha. Up ahead. See? Looks like civilization. We may have to spend all night sitting in a coffee shop."

"I don't care, just so long as it's warm and out of this mess."

Logan pulled off carefully onto a brightly lit parking lot.

"Oh, dear," Molly said, peering out her window. The motel looked like something left over from the days of Bonnie and Clyde. Several individual bungalows rose out of the gloom, and in the center was a slightly larger building with a sign that blinked Acancy in sad red neon.

"Stay here," he said. In five minutes he skated his way back to the car.

Molly held her breath. She didn't think she could take another minute of driving through this weather. Even sleeping in the car would be preferable. "Please, God," she prayed, "let them have room for us."

Logan opened the car door and slid inside, running his hand over his head to dislodge a crown of ice crystals. "Got the last room. We'll have to share. It's not the Ritz, Molly, but it looks clean. Your choice. Stay or go on?"

"Stay, please."

Two minutes later, as he brought in the bags, he found Molly staring forlornly at the lone double bed. The mattress sloped down from each side to a canyon in the center.

"I have a suspicion this place generally rents by the hour," Logan said as he stamped the snow and mud from his loafers and dropped the suitcases beside the door.

"It's fine," Molly said in a small voice. She made no move to sit on the bed.

Logan opened the door to the tiny bathroom. The lock didn't work. Obviously it had worked at one time because someone had put a fist through the thin plywood door beside the doorknob. The hole had been patched with duct tape.

Despite the run-down appearance of the place, the towels were shiningly white, the sheets crisp and freshly ironed; there was plenty of toilet paper. There was, however, only one thin plaid blanket covering the bed and only two flaccid pillows. Logan flipped on the heating unit under the window; a blast of blessedly warm air fanned out into the room, accompanied by a whir like bat wings.

Molly leaned against the door and massaged the back of her neck.

"I'm sorry," she said softly. "We should have flown to Laramie."

He pulled off his soggy gloves and dropped them on the floor beside the bed. A small voice in his subconscious agreed with her. They'd have been safely in Laramie long before this freak storm hit if only Molly hadn't been afraid to fly. He glanced at her. She had not moved from the doorway. Her face was white. There were dark circles under her fine blue eyes, which threatened to brim over with unshed tears.

Damn him for a fool! He'd pushed her too long, too hard, he'd frightened her and put her in danger. She owed him nothing. She didn't even have to be here. She'd hung on gallantly, never questioned him, while he ignored her physical needs in his determination to reach Laramie at all costs. She shouldn't apologize because she was afraid of flying. He didn't deserve an apology; he deserved a kick in the pants.

He wrapped his arms around her and pulled her against him, resting his chin on the top of her head. "We'd have spent tonight propped on chairs in the Denver airport, Molly. At least here we have a bed." He glanced down at the sagging mattress. "Well, something like a bed at any rate." He pulled her down on the end of the bed beside him and began to chortle under his breath. He knew she could feel his body shake. She pulled away and turned to gaze up in his face suspiciously.

He began to laugh in earnest. "I've had better accommodations on Hudson Bay surrounded by polar bears."

"If I hadn't been so terrified . . ."

"At least this way I could feel we were getting somewhere. If that trooper was right, the roads will clear early. We can be in Laramie by afternoon." He looked around the room. "I'm the one who should apologize. This is hardly the place any decent man would bring his woman."

Molly stiffened. She pulled away and stood up. "Hadn't we better call Anne and Zoe to tell them where we are?"

"Why?" He sat on the edge of the bed and began to pull off his muddy loafers. "Besides, you see a telephone in here?" He swept a hand at the room.

Molly hugged herself. "There must be a pay phone by the office, surely."

"Don't worry, Molly, we'll call tomorrow. I'm too wet, too tired and too damned exasperated to drag out in that blizzard, and I'm not about to let you do it."

"I beg your pardon?" She turned toward him.

"I said I'm not going back out there and neither are you."

Bingo. Apparently, he'd landed on Molly's hottest button. She wasn't the kind of woman to take orders from anyone. She reached for her parka, her purse and the door handle just as he surged off the bed.

"It's like glass out there," he told her. "You'll break your fool neck. Don't be ridiculous!"

"Don't tell me what to do, Logan MacMillan. I am not *your* woman. I am not now and have never been a possession of yours." She wheeled and stumbled over the suitcases. The back of her head cracked smartly against the doorjamb. She saw stars.

He reached her in an instant. "Molly, are you hurt?" His hand moved to the back of her head, his fingers probing through her hair.

She opened her eyes not on stars but on Logan's gray eyes, his strong face, his body against her. She tried to step back and stumbled again.

"Whoa, there. Are you determined to commit suicide?" Logan grabbed her around the waist and hauled her away from the suitcases and back toward the bed.

She wriggled, avoided his eyes, her body rigid.

"Hey!" he said, annoyed. She stole a quick glance at him from under her lashes and away again instantly, but not before he caught the blush spreading from her neck to her forehead. Through her open parka he felt her nipples swollen and hard against his chest. "Well, damn," he said. Then he kissed her.

His hot mouth demanded response, demanded that she open to him. This wasn't any butterfly kiss over hot chocolate. He kissed her hard enough so that she felt her teeth against her upper lip. His tongue darted in to find the roof of her mouth and paint her with flame.

Molly struggled against him and her passion for only a moment. Then her tongue answered his, her hands found his back, slid up his spine, climbed the rope-hard muscles along his ribs.

They tumbled onto the bed locked together mouth to mouth, body to body. How could they have come so far so fast?

Molly knew that if she committed this absolute folly, she probably ought to be committed to the nearest insane asylum. Then came madness.

Clothes became obstacles. Molly and Logan ripped, unzipped, unsnapped, unbuckled and pulled over their heads. Logan unfastened Molly's bra one-handed with as much skill as he'd used at seventeen. He flung it across the room and hooked his fingers into the waistband of her cotton panties. He functioned by feel because his mouth was fully engaged in kissing her and his tongue in drinking deep of the peach-ripe nectar of her mouth.

At last skin touched skin.

Molly forgot to worry about the state of her body.

Logan felt his body respond as she touched him. He wanted her. He'd wanted her all his life, this wild, sweet, brave woman who poured her strength and life into him with every breath she took.

This wasn't a match to a fire—more like a short fuse to a keg of dynamite.

It didn't matter that the bed sank in the middle and felt as lumpy as a moon crater. He found the soft sweet darkness between her thighs and she welcomed the hot sweet hardness of him within her. She met him thrust for thrust, finally bracing her hands against the bedposts and wrapping her legs around his hips to hold him tighter inside her.

At last she cried out and arched her back against him, her eyes half-shut and glazed with pleasure. A moment later he joined her.

Molly cradled him in her arms as he lay spent, still buried in her.

"Oh Lord," she whispered.

Logan raised himself on his forearms to smile down into her face. Only a fine rim of dark blue showed around her dark pupils. Her mouth looked full and soft and bruised. "This was ordained from the moment you got mud all over my hands at your front door."

"It wasn't mud."

He brushed her hair back from her ear. "Close enough. But I wanted you, anyway. Took me a while to admit it. Maybe five minutes."

Molly laughed. "I thought you were probably a jerk, but one of your crooked smiles and I was lost."

"Why didn't you say something? Do something?" He moved beside her and cradled her against his chest.

She raised onto her elbow. "Because I never learned how to make the first move. I was scared, if you want to know the truth. Scared you'd laugh at me or look down that long nose of yours at me and be very, very polite. Anyway, I knew it was the wrong thing to do," she said seriously.

"How wrong? We're adults. We've no one to answer to but ourselves. We're not likely to give each other any diseases—my God, Molly, can you get pregnant?"

She giggled. "No, my dear, I cannot." Suddenly she felt middle-aged. "I am too old and sere for that."

" 'Nor spring nor summer beauty hath such grace as I have seen in one autumnal face.' "

"Isn't that by John Donne?"

"As I recall, the lady he wrote it about was somebody's mother," Logan said. "You are beautiful now in a way I suspect you were not at twenty. There's all that warmth and wisdom in your eyes."

"And all those lines around them."

"Nonsense. You are the most beautiful woman I have ever seen."

"And you are a liar and a flatterer. But who cares?" She snuggled against him. "I'm cold."

"We'll have to move so I can pull this poor excuse for a blanket over us."

He longed to explore her body with his hands and tongue. He wanted to memorize her like a road map so that he could find his way home again to her center in the dark. At the moment, however, all he had strength for was sleep. He drifted drowsily as she leaned over and kissed him softly. He held her against him and drank in the scent of her hair as it tickled his nostrils. He sighed deeply. Tonight at least he wouldn't have to walk until he dropped. He'd had the best kind of exercise there could be. He dropped into sleep with the peaceful sense that for the first time in years he wasn't utterly and completely alone.

Outside, the last flake hit the pavement, the wind sighed away in disgust and the snowplows began to open the highways to the disembodied strains of Clint Black and Billy Ray Cyrus.

A HUNDRED AND FIFTY miles away a small girl with strawberry blond hair woke in a dark and unfamiliar room. She lay very still for a moment, trying to remember the name of the woman who had brought her here.

She thought once of her mommy, then thrust the image away from her. She had long since learned not to cry. Carefully, so as not to wake the other sleeping children in the room, she crept out of the small bed and pulled the thin blanket and pillow after her. She wriggled along the floor until she had disappeared completely under the bed, then she pulled the bedclothes after her. She curled into the tightest ball she could, wrapped her arms around her pillow and pulled the blanket around her like a shroud. Maybe if she was lucky, they wouldn't find her.

CHAPTER TEN

ZOE JACKSON HUNG UP the telephone and turned to Rick. "You will not believe this. That was my father. He and Molly Halliday spent last night in a sleazy motel in the middle of a snowstorm."

Rick dropped the Sunday sports section onto the bed beside him. "Good for him."

"Have you lost your mind? He could have a heart attack or run off the road or something."

"I'd swear I heard just a touch of jealousy there."

Zoe glared at him. "Jealous? Of Molly Halliday?" She swung off the bed. A coffee carafe with two mugs sat on the chestnut desk under the window. She poured herself a cup of coffee, turned to Rick and raised her eyebrows.

He shook his head. "I've hit my caffeine limit already. Come on, baby, we've been over this before. You know he's sorry you grew up without him." He reached toward her, but she sidestepped him smartly and went to stare out the bedroom window.

"Oh, sure," she said. "You don't know what it was like growing up in that mausoleum above the store. By the time I met you, I had moved out into my own apartment and Mother was sick." She picked up a pencil off the desk and began to doodle on the telephone pad.

"When we were kids, Jeremy had his trains and his gym equipment in the attic. I never had a sanctuary. I lived in a decorator's idea of the perfect little girl's room with immaculate toys on immaculate shelves." The pencil point snapped. Zoe tossed it up and dropped it into the wastebasket. "My mother used to bring her best clients upstairs to show off the place at a moment's notice, so everything had to be perfect all the time," she said bitterly. "My immaculate clothes came out of an immaculate closet in an immaculate room."

She turned to Rick and gestured at the closed door of their bedroom. "My door stayed open all the time, did you know that? Unless my father was home, of course. He's always been a great one for closing doors. Mother wanted to know what I was doing in there every minute."

"Didn't Jeremy live in the perfect little boy's room?"

Zoe sat in the desk chair and propped her bare feet on the side of the bed. "He slept in one, but he lived upstairs in the attic. Mother's emphysema kept her from climbing stairs. That's why we put in the elevator from the store to the apartment. Besides, she didn't understand boys so she just let him do anything he wanted."

Rick reached over and began to massage her feet. She gave a soft little moan, leaned against the chair and closed her eyes. She seemed a long way away.

"Mother knew all about girls—or thought she did. I was the one who was supposed to go to the University of Mississippi, pledge the best sorority, come out with all the other little debutantes and have a wedding with twelve bridesmaids when I married a tall, handsome neurosurgeon. Then I'd buy a house in Chickasaw Gardens and have two point three children."

He laughed. "So you ran off with me in an old Volkswagen beetle."

"Only decent decision I've ever made. Ooh, don't stop, that feels wonderful."

"Not just to spite your mother?"

Zoe sat up and dove across the bed into his arms. "No, dearest, darling Rick. Without you I'd be on Valium and have zippers in my wrists."

Rick sighed, held her and nuzzled her thick dark hair.

Her voice was muffled against his chest. "Mother was sure Tiffany would be the perfect wife. Look how she turned out."

"You turned out pretty good."

"I don't think Mother would agree with you." She pulled away from him and wandered back to the window. He watched her silently.

She moved the curtain aside. The air conditioner hummed. The day was bright and nearly as hot as August. Zoe shook her head. "Hard to believe it's snowing where my father is."

"Before she died, your mother must have realized how wrong she'd been about Tiffany."

Zoe shrugged. "She never thought her own values were wrong, only that she picked wrong. Not the same thing."

She leaned her head against the window. Tears squeezed out from under her eyelashes. "My father always thought we were the perfect family because Mother worked so hard when he was home to convince him that we didn't need him. She wanted him to feel left out because it gave her control over him, over all of us. She resented the hell out of him for leaving for months at a time, even though she was the one who made him go. When he came home, she resented him because his very presence made demands on her."

"That makes no sense."

"You didn't know my mother. She always tried to convince my father we were the Cleavers. Only we didn't need Ward."

"That must have made him feel real good about coming home."

"She had a point." Zoe turned back to him and perched on the windowsill. "He took over the minute he walked in the door. He wanted to make the decisions even though most of the time he didn't know the background."

"Hey, I don't blame the guy for trying to feel needed."

Zoe raised her head and glared at him. "Needed? Mother needed him for one thing—money."

"How about sex?"

Zoe snorted. "It messed up her makeup."

MOLLY WOKE to a predawn silence so deep the room might have been at the bottom of Carlsbad Caverns. She lay against Logan's naked back.

She was a real live mistress! Amazing. Maybe Logan would get up and act as though nothing had happened. Could she bear that?

Without warning, Logan rolled over and captured her in his arms. "That wasn't all me last night, was it? What I wanted?"

"What we wanted. I just didn't have nerve enough to let you know."

"You're not sorry?"

"Not a bit."

He nuzzled her neck. "I wish with all my heart we could stay here in this god-awful room and make love until neither of us has the strength to leave it." He sat up. "But we can't."

She touched his shoulder. "I know, my dear."

He swung out of bed. "We've wasted enough time." He heard her gasp and took her in his arms. "I didn't mean that the way it sounded, Molly."

She snuggled. "You're sure about that?"

He caressed her hair. "I long to pillow on your soft warm body and kiss your wide sweet mouth... but..."

"Right. It's a long drive to Laramie. However, if I don't get my wide mouth around a hot cup of coffee and a logger's breakfast, I won't make it past Cheyenne."

Logan laughed. "I thought that was thunder I heard, now I realize it's just your stomach rumbling."

"There's bound to be enough hot water for two showers if we're quick. Don't move until I'm dressed." Molly kissed him lightly and climbed out of the warmth of his arms. She yipped as her feet hit the floor then realized he'd pushed the blanket aside.

"If we share one shower, we won't have to be so quick," he said.

THE SNOW had vanished; water dripped from eaves, and there were two neat furrows of dry roadway where cars had already worn away the ice. They made good time once they got back onto the interstate.

Past Cheyenne the fierce winds had driven the snow hard against the fences along each side of the road. The upland meadows beyond were brown but free of snow.

"What do we do if Tiffany's not in Laramie?" Molly asked quietly.

"I don't know. Put Tom and Nell Watson on her trail, I suppose." He looked away from the highway for a moment and touched her knee. "Whatever happens, I can't regret the journey. It's brought me you. That's quite enough for one lifetime. Perhaps it's foolish to ask the gods for more."

"You don't mean that."

"No, I don't." He laughed, but there was no mirth in the laughter. "I haven't ever thought further than the quest. Part of being male, I guess. Now it's finally gotten through to me that there is a good chance we'll get to Laramie and actually find both Tiffany and Dulcy.''

Now was the time to talk about what they might find. Molly dreaded it.

"I know Dulcy probably doesn't even know she has a grandfather," he said. "Do children that age wonder where they came from?"

"Yes," Molly replied, "but they don't press the issue until they get into school and see the way their friends live. Then they begin to wonder why they're on the run and alone."

"You asked me once what I'd do if Tiffany had remarried, turned her life around," Logan said.

"Yes, and it made you furious."

"I want what's best for Dulcy. Besides, Tiffany's facing prison and the child needs a father."

Molly glanced at him. "You're not her father."

He made a small sound of disapproval in the back of his throat.

"Things may be bad. Can you handle that?" Molly asked. She hoped he wouldn't ask her definition of bad.

"I don't intend to handle things by myself. I want to find her, get her home and bring in some professionals to help me with her."

"She's going to need love from everyone around her. That and consistency. Have you thought about Zoe and Rick?"

Logan snorted. "Zoe means well, but she doesn't know anything about raising children."

"Do you?"

"At least I've had two. I plan to learn from my mistakes." He took his hand off her knee. "Besides, I don't intend to cut her or Rick out. They're her uncle and aunt.

But the major decisions should be mine.'' He pointed at a signpost. ''Well, Molly, we have just passed the borders of Laramie. It is, as they say on television, showtime.''

''Do you intend simply to drive up to her apartment building, assuming we can find it, ring the doorbell, and when she opens the door say, 'Give us your child'?''

Logan pulled into a service station without speaking. He filled up the tank, waited for Molly to return from the bathroom and drove off, all without answering her question.

''The apartment building is three blocks from the university. I asked directions,'' Logan said.

Molly saw tension in his hands on the wheel, his narrowed eyes, the vein throbbing in his temple. ''Logan, it's Sunday, you know.''

''I'm aware of that. If Tiffany has a regular job, she could be at home.''

Molly's stomach was doing flips. She was scared. The woman could meet them at the door with a rifle.

They might walk in on Tiffany, glimpse Dulcy, then be forced to sit by while she fled again and took the child with her.

''Are you sure you don't want to wait for the police?'' Molly asked.

''Yes, dammit. I don't want to bring the officials in until we know what we're up against. If we can persuade Tiffany to come home with Dulcy, then we may be able to avoid unpleasantness. After all, she can't like living on the run, either. She was used to luxury.''

''It's your call.''

''It is indeed.''

They found the apartments on a side street. They were close kin to the apartments in Kansas. Logan turned off the ignition and sat staring straight ahead. Molly watched the throbbing vein in his temple, saw the rise and fall of his chest, the sweat along his upper lip.

"Dear God," he whispered, "let me do the right thing." He turned to Molly and smiled, a soft, tender, sad little smile. "Kiss me, my love. I need your sweet strength."

She kissed him gently, softly and without passion. He held her hand hard for a moment.

"Come with me."

Molly followed him up the front walk and up the stairs toward the second floor.

Logan squared his shoulders and knocked on the door of apartment 2B. Inside they could hear the thump of rock music. Molly stood slightly behind Logan. Her heart was thumping, too.

The door opened. "Yeah?"

The man—boy, really—who opened the door had a hammer in one hand and a long-neck beer in the other. He was tall, thin, Nordic blond, and wore jeans and cowboy boots.

"Excuse me, I'm looking for Tiff... Terry Rigby."

The boy shook his head. "Nobody here by that name, man." Behind him, Molly saw packing boxes. She stepped forward.

"Oh, are you just moving in?" she asked brightly.

"Yeah." He moved aside. A dark girl looked up from a box of books, smiled briefly, then bent to her task.

"Do you know where the last tenant went?" Logan asked.

The boy shook his head. "No, man, sorry. You could try the manager." He stepped out long enough to point to his left. "Down there."

"When did you move in?" Molly asked.

"Got most of the stuff in this afternoon."

Molly looked at Logan, realized he wanted to continue the conversation and touched his arm. "Sorry to have bothered you. We'll check the manager." She pulled Logan away. Geared up emotionally for confrontation, he was clearly deflated by the anticlimax. Neither spoke until the door to the manager's apartment opened.

The motherly woman who stood there was Molly's age and Molly's size. Behind her on a brown vinyl couch a fiftyish man in jeans that gaped over his belly sat staring fixedly at "60 Minutes" on the television set.

"Excuse me," Logan said, stepping into the room. The man on the couch looked at them for a moment without interest, then turned back to the set. "I'm trying to locate the woman who had apartment 2B. Do you have a forwarding address?"

The woman froze, the man's head snapped around from the set to stare at him. The temperature in the room seemed to drop as suddenly as though someone had switched on a refrigeration unit.

"You'd better come on in." The woman said, "You family?"

Had Tiffany left again owing back rent? Done something else illegal? Molly held her breath.

"She is my daughter-in-law," Logan said. "The little girl is my granddaughter."

"Oh, Lordy," the woman whispered, her eyes round. The man on the couch stared fixedly at Molly and Logan.

Molly put her hand on Logan's arm.

"Was she expectin' you? Come up to visit?"

"Not exactly. No. Please, Mrs . . . ?"

"Oh, Maybelle Washington. This is my husband, Joe. Joe, where are your manners? Don't you know to get up when a lady enters the room?"

Joe's vacant eyes moved from Logan's face to Molly's. He stayed seated.

"Mrs. Washington, when did they leave?" Logan asked. "Do you know where they went? It's important I find them quickly."

"I just don't know how to say this. We didn't know about family and all. No way to, was there?"

"Please, Mrs. Washington," Molly asked.

Maybelle Washington shook her head. "No good way to say this. She's dead."

CHAPTER ELEVEN

"DEAD? Who's dead?" Logan asked.

"Why, your daughter-in-law. Here, you better sit down. Joe, you move over on that sofa right this minute. Mister, can I get you a beer or something?"

"What happened? Are you sure? When?"

"Let's see. Thursday, it was. Had to break in and all." Maybelle shook her head. "Accident, the cops said, Mr...?"

"MacMillan. Logan MacMillan. And this is Mrs. Halliday."

"How do." Maybelle smiled at Molly, then turned back to Logan. "I got to say, Mr. MacMillan, she had her a bad problem with alcohol." She dropped her voice. "Ain't all, either. Mixing alcohol with something else."

"The child, Mrs. Washington," Molly begged. "What about the child?"

"Now, ain't that sad! The police come and took her. Didn't cry or nothing. Wouldn't you think a kid's just lost her momma would cry? Real brave she was."

"Took her where?"

"Lordy, I don't know. Didn't have much stuff, Mr. MacMillan. I just put what little there was down in the storage room against the rent she owed me." Her eyes lit up. "Two months' back rent it was. Plus, I had to have the place cleaned and fumigated. Say, you didn't tell that nice young couple a woman died in there, did you?"

"I assure you we did not. We didn't know."

"Well, of course not. What am I supposed to do with her stuff?"

"What sort of stuff?" Molly asked.

"Kids clothes, books, a couple of toys. Her clothes. Didn't have much, like I told you."

Logan was obviously champing at the bit to be gone. "Do you have a name? Someone you know who took Dulcy?"

"Dulcy. Ain't that the sweetest thing. So that's her name! Well, I never."

"Please, Mrs. Washington, where did they take her?"

"How would I know? Police just put her into a police car and drove off is all I know. Now about that rent . . ."

Logan surged to his feet and pulled Molly after him. "We'll be back, Mrs. Washington. In the meantime, I have to find my grandchild."

NOBODY AT the police station knew where Dulcy was. Logan spent fifteen minutes persuading the desk sergeant to call the homicide detective who'd been notified after Tiffany's body was discovered.

Twenty minutes after that call, Logan and Molly drove up to a neat ranch house. Logan took his briefcase from the back seat.

A man close to Logan's age opened the door of the house. The smell of steaks wafted through the house.

"We didn't want to interrupt your dinner, Lieutenant Holman," Logan said as he shook hands. "It's good of you to see us on Sunday. It's an emergency. We have to find my grandchild."

"That's okay. Sit, please. We've finished dinner. That's the leftovers."

Molly's empty stomach gave an ominous growl.

"The kid's not lost. Assuming she is your grandchild, that is."

"I have proof." Logan pulled a folder from the briefcase he'd carried into the house, and from it he pulled three official-looking pieces of paper. He spread them on the coffee table. "First, Dulcy's birth certificate. You'll note the footprints. Next, here is a complete set of Dulcy's fingerprints attested to and notarized. We had them done during the custody hearing. Premonition, maybe. Third, the order giving me sole custody of Dulcy."

"Impressive."

"There's one more thing," Molly added. She pulled the Dulcy doll from the box beside her. "Is that the child?"

The lieutenant did not ooh and aah. He reached for the doll with interest. "Amazing. Hair's shorter and she's taller, of course, but you've caught the expression. Never smiled. Not once. Not surprising, under the circumstances. Tough little cookie."

"But where is she?" Logan sounded desperate.

"Safe, Mr. MacMillan. Safe. She's with a foster family outside of town."

"Tell me where. We'll go out there at once."

"No, you won't. Look, Mr. MacMillan, if everything you've told me is correct, then this kid really is Dulcy MacMillan and the dead woman really is Tiffany MacMillan and not Terry Rigby. Sooner or later, we'd probably have found that out, anyway."

"How did Tiffany die?"

"Accident. Alcohol-related."

"What sort of accident? Was she driving?" Logan said through clenched teeth. "She's already been convicted of vehicular homicide for driving drunk. One of the people she killed was her husband—my son."

"I'm sorry." Holman seemed to hesitate. "No, she wasn't driving. She was working at one of the bars downtown as a bartender. She left early. Her boss said she was upset and drinking as much as she was selling. I think he wanted to fire her. I also think he was sleeping with her."

"What happened?" Molly asked.

"It's a matter of record. She left to walk home, stumbled, fell against a curb, hit her head." He shrugged. "Apparently, she didn't think she'd been hurt bad, but there was bleeding into the brain. She went home, went to sleep, never woke up."

"Could she have been mugged?"

"No. Couple of people from the bar saw it happen. Doctors found concrete dust in the wound. No, it was an accident, but it probably wouldn't have happened if she'd been sober."

"Poor Dulcy."

"Yeah," the detective said. "She seems pretty tough. Kids forget. She'll be all right." He looked down at the documents on the coffee table in front of him. "Anyway, Mr. MacMillan, we'll try to find a judge willing to execute the order tomorrow morning. Get the social services people to sign off on the paperwork. In the meantime, the kid's doing fine where she is."

"Lieutenant, I'm trying to stay calm, but you've got to know how difficult that is to accept. I want my grandchild."

"I understand that, Mr. MacMillan, I got kids and grandkids too. But you got to understand, we need to be sure that giving her to you is the best thing for the kid."

"Lieutenant . . ."

"Look, you and Mrs. Halliday go find yourselves a nice motel, have a decent dinner, get some sleep. Strictly speaking, it's not my area, but I've been in on it from the first, so I'll meet you down at my office at nine tomorrow morning. I'll get social services and the foster mother there. We'll get it sorted out. You've waited this long. What's another night?''

Logan's shoulders tensed visibly. Then he sighed and relaxed. His eyes were filled with defeat. ''Nine o'clock? That's a promise?''

''Absolutely. Look, Mr. MacMillan, we want to get this squared away as much as you do.'' He ushered them to the door and held it for them. ''One question I got to ask. I don't believe in coincidences, Mr. MacMillan. How come you show up four days after this Tiffany dies? Just in time to pick up the kid.''

''That's an excellent question, Lieutenant. I have only one answer for you, and I doubt you'll like it very much. I don't believe in coincidence, either.'' Logan turned to Molly and stared at the Dulcy doll in her arms. ''I do, however, believe in the intervention of a higher power. Something or Someone is looking out for my grandchild and led us to her now, when she needs us most.''

Molly took the keys to the car from Logan, shoved him in and buckled him up on the passenger's side. ''There's a decent motel out by the interstate,'' she said practically, getting into the driver's seat. ''We'll go there, take two rooms, have hot showers, find someplace decent to have dinner . . .''

''No more steak. These people seem to eat nothing else.''

''Granted,'' Molly said.

''Why do we need two rooms?'' Logan asked.

''Caesar's wife must be above suspicion. You don't want some hanging judge to ask for the motel register and see you've been whooping it up with your doxy, now, do you?''

Logan smiled. Molly was delighted to see that he still could. ''I don't think I'm up to whooping anything, Molly. I don't know whether to blow up city hall or walk into the nearest church and thank God. It is a terrible thing to be grateful that another human being has died. But God help me, Molly, I am glad Tiffany is dead. Now whatever happens, she can't come back into Dulcy's life.''

''Logan, now she'll never be out of it,'' Molly said quietly as she pulled under the arches at the Holiday Inn. ''Sit. I'll take care of this.''

Five minutes later she opened the connecting door into the next room and peered in. Logan lay on his back across the bed behind her, his arm across his eyes. ''Don't go,'' he said without moving.

''I don't intend to,'' Molly said, turning back to sit beside him. ''We may have to avoid the appearance of evil, but nothing says we can't cheat a little behind closed doors.'' She realized what she'd said and blushed. Here she'd promised herself she wouldn't pressure Logan. He'd already said he was tired. She should leave him alone before he made it clear he wanted it that way. In all the years of her marriage, she'd never been able to actually ask Harry for affection. She certainly didn't have the nerve to start with Logan at this late date. She bent to pull off his shoe.

''What're you doing?''

''Getting your outfit off, pard,'' she said dryly, pulling the other shoe. ''First I'm going to get us a couple of club sandwiches from the restaurant, then you can go stand in a hot shower until you're all pruny, and get a decent night's sleep.''

"I can't sleep."

"Want to bet? Even ignoring the exhausting effects of
sex, we've both still had a bitch of a day. When you see
Dulcy tomorrow, you don't want to have little red pig
eyes like an ax murderer, do you? Lie still and practice
looking grandfatherly. I'll be back in twenty minutes."

It was harder and harder to keep the atmosphere light,
Molly thought as she returned ten minutes later carrying
the sandwiches on a tray. She set it down on the ground
and opened the door to their room, then bent to pick it
up and enter. She kicked the door shut behind her.

Logan had not moved. He lay where she had left him,
his arm still across his eyes. He was sound asleep,
breathing softly through his mouth. With his arm covering his gray hair, he looked about twenty-five years old.
She hesitated, wondering whether or not to wake him,
and decided against it. She pulled her mystery novel from
her purse and settled down in the chair by the air conditioner to eat her sandwich.

She tried to read, but she couldn't take her eyes off
Logan. She wanted to wall him around with a bell jar, to
protect him from the assaults of pain that she knew
would come when he found his Dulcy. He'd had so much
pain already.

It was almost as though Tiffany had managed to hang
on to her tortured life until she knew that someone was
coming to rescue her child. For all her self-destructive
instincts, she must truly have loved her little girl. Dulcy
would have that to cling to in the days to come.

"Um." Logan woke and sat up. "You were, I take it,
about to eat my sandwich, as well."

"The thought had crossed my mind."

"Won't work. The smell betrayed you." He swung his long legs to the floor. "God in heaven, I never thought I'd be this tired and still be conscious."

Molly put the tray on the foot of the bed within reach. "Here, get some food in you."

He picked up the tray and set it carefully on the small round table beside Molly. "I don't eat off a tray on my lap unless I'm dying of pneumonia." He bit into the sandwich. "Not half-bad."

"Not poached salmon and watercress, but it will have to do."

He reached across the table to stroke the back of her hand. "I couldn't face this alone, Molly."

She pulled her chair around to sit across from him and watched him wolf down the sandwich. "What precisely do we face? You've told me what it will take for you to get custody of Dulcy, but I don't know anything about the way Tiffany's death will be handled. You're going to have to get her body home for burial, aren't you? There's bound to be paperwork, rules, regulations. Surely in all the construction jobs you've headed up, people have died far away from home. How do you take their bodies back to the people who loved them?"

"Oh, yes, there's always paperwork." He finished the sandwich, drank his tea at a gulp, then carefully laid the napkin beside the plate. "Usually, when there's a death, people are kind, but they're not always helpful. Sometimes they're suspicious and put up roadblocks. Did you get the feeling the Wyoming police think we're kidnappers, after Dulcy for her money?"

"I wasn't imagining things, then. I thought Holman acted very cool toward us. He made me very uncomfortable, as though we were suspected of something awful."

"He was nice enough, but he didn't give us any real information. We still don't know where Dulcy is staying. To give him credit, policemen are by nature suspicious, and our arrival out of the blue less than a week after Tiffany's death must look suspicious. Hell, in his shoes, I'd be suspicious."

"But, Logan, you didn't do anything wrong. You just want your granddaughter back. He can't keep you away from her, can he?" Molly said.

Logan shook his head. "No, but he can probably stall if he wants to. All the paperwork about Dulcy's custody is in order. While you were at the restaurant, I called my lawyer at home. He'll fax information on the case and my good character to Holman's office first thing tomorrow morning. He's also alerting the judge who issued the original order and will have him standing by tomorrow in case the social services people need to talk to someone in authority. That's all we can do at the moment."

"Quite a lot for ten minutes. But Tiffany. What about her?"

Logan looked at his watch. "I have no idea how far in advance of us Madrid is—seven or eight hours, anyway." He sighed deeply. "I'll call her father tomorrow. I'm certain the Laramie police will ask me to identify her body."

"Oh, Logan!"

"Laramie must have some sort of morgue. I'll ask her father what he wants done. My guess is that he will be completely uninterested in what happens to her body."

"His own daughter?"

"You don't know Carlton Edwards," Logan said dryly. He moved back to the bed, taking Molly's hand and pulling her with him. He stretched out and drew her into his arms almost like a security blanket or a favorite teddy bear, as though he drew strength from her mere presence. "Carlton divorced Tiffany's mother when Tiffany was about eight. He didn't even come back to the States to give Tiffany away."

"How awful."

"Tiffany made her own choices, but she certainly had the background to make the wrong ones. Jeremy must have seemed like a kindred spirit—frat parties and fast cars. His record wasn't much better than hers. He simply didn't have access to trust funds."

"Where were you when all this was going on?"

Logan laid his head back against the pillows and ran his hand down his face. "Alaska. The last job before I came home to take care of Sydney. I arrived to stand up with Jeremy a week before the wedding. What could I do at that point except pray?"

"At least you had the excuse of being out of the geographical area." She moved restively in his arms, and pulled away from him. "My ex-husband was physically there when Anne was growing up, but that's all. After the divorce, he simply dropped out of our lives. Anne turned out fine despite us, I think. She sends Harry a Christmas card, but that's the extent of their relationship. He doesn't even care about Elizabeth."

"But he looked after you properly while Anne was growing up, surely?"

"Oh, come on, Logan. Our generation thought that if we gave our kids all the material things we missed growing up, they'd turn out happy and productive. Anne wanted Harry to help with her homework, not send his secretary out at the last minute to spend a fortune on some useless birthday present."

"What should we have done, then, Molly? Let them suffer the way we suffered from not enough of anything? I don't know the answer."

"I don't, either. I'm sure I did terrible things to Anne's psyche out of sheer incompetence. If she were still a baby now, I think I'd tote her around like a monkey baby until she was too big to pick up, and try to teach her that actions have consequences—not always pleasant ones. And I'd still screw up a lot. She might wind up being a serial killer. Nothing's certain."

Logan sighed again and ran his hand down Molly's arm. "Except death."

"What will you do if Carlton Edwards chooses not to be bothered with his daughter's funeral?"

"I will take Tiffany home, have her buried beside Jeremy, then hold a memorial service for her later, after Dulcy is settled. The service will mean a great deal to her daughter when she's older. I don't want her to think we short-changed her mother in any way. She should love the memory of her mother. It's all she'll have."

"I need to call Anne. After all that's happened, I really long to hear her voice. I haven't spoken to her since we left."

"Of course."

"Are you finally going to tell Zoe we've found Dulcy?"

He stiffened. "Not until I've seen her. Not until we have her safely in our hands."

Molly sighed. "I still think you're wrong," she said. "Don't move. I'll go next door to my own room." Molly slid off the bed. Logan captured her hand and pressed it to his lips like a courtier.

"Come back to me afterward, Molly. I want to sleep

in your arms."

She dropped a quick kiss on the top of his head.

TEN MINUTES LATER, she hung up the telephone to see Logan leaning against the door. "Your family all right?" he asked.

"Elizabeth misses me, which is great, and Anne treats me as though I were a brainless baby pigeon she's trying to nurse to adulthood. She's afraid you're Jack the Ripper or Bluebeard."

Logan chuckled and leered.

Molly rubbed her sore neck muscles. "She thinks I'm a delinquent. I didn't buy it."

"Good for you. Come here, Molly."

"You're exhausted, remember, and so am I."

"I was exhausted before the sandwich. Now I've got my second wind. And I remember there were some parts of you I didn't get to explore thoroughly." He reached his hand to her. "Come wrap me in your arms, love, and blow the candles out."

Molly compromised by turning off the light switch instead.

This was the first time that she had undressed in front of Logan. Last night didn't count. That wasn't undressing, it was a comic rout. Tonight, however, she felt as embarrassed as a teenage virgin. She also felt gawky and fat. She managed to slide quickly under the covers while Logan was still in the bathroom. They held each other until they drifted off to sleep.

LOGAN SLID out of bed and left Molly to sleep. Outside he heard strange Laramie birds tuning up to greet the morning. He padded to the bathroom, showered and lathered his face. He hated electric razors and willingly risked the occasional nick to have a shave that would keep his thick beard at bay until nightfall. The shape of Molly in the bed behind him was reflected in the mirror. Just watching her made him smile.

How long had it been since going to bed meant pleasure and not nightmares? How long since he had awakened warm and content in the arms of a woman who truly wanted to lie beside him? Not since the early days of his marriage to Sydney.

He started. His head whipped around to look at Molly. He was in love with her! How could he have let that happen! How could he have locked her so perfectly into the empty places of his life that he only felt whole when she lay beside him? He had a way of disappointing people he loved. And, as a result, they changed into people he barely knew—and eventually he lost them.

He knew he wasn't lovable, as a rule, but Molly showed an alarming aptitude for love. He didn't have Dulcy yet, but there was every reason to believe she would be with him soon. In his experience, granddaughters usually loved their grandfathers. Loving him could put Dulcy in jeopardy—Molly, too. He didn't think he could take it if anything happened to either one of them.

Molly stretched under the covers like a sleepy cat. "Oh, Lord, is that the time?" She rolled out and grabbed her robe from the foot of the bed. She watched him pull a navy suit out of his hanging bag. "Very spiffy."

"I can hardly appear before a judge looking like a sharecropper."

"I see." She did, too. Her voice showed that she'd picked up the coolness in his tone. She didn't touch him as she brushed by on her way to the bathroom. He closed his eyes. *Molly,* he thought, *I love you too much. You scare the hell out of me.*

"YOU SAID you'd have the social service people here at nine," Logan said to Lieutenant Holman as he paced the office like a caged lion.

"I have no control over them," Holman replied. "Ms. Grissom ought to be here any minute. Gives us some time. Some things we need to square away. First off, just when did you leave Memphis?"

"Thursday afternoon. We can furnish airline tickets, hotel receipts, and the word of Tom and Nell Watson with whom we stayed on Friday night, and I have receipts from the motel we stayed in Saturday. If necessary, I can furnish an alibi for my whereabouts all last week. That *is* what we're talking about, isn't it?"

"I'm a cop. We like things neat."

"I'm aware of that. It's why I haven't knocked you down. I take it you've confirmed that Tiffany is dead."

"Memphis faxed me her prints first thing this morning. They match the body we have. Still, we'd like you to identify her. You up to it?" Holman asked.

"If I must." Logan sighed. "And then what?"

"What?"

"Lieutenant, if the woman is Tiffany, I must get the body sent back to Memphis for burial."

"Ah. Yeah. Shouldn't be any problem. The medical examiner issued a certificate. Call your funeral home. They ought to know how to arrange it. Air cargo."

"Not, however, unembalmed. At least in the state of Tennessee. I need the name of a funeral home here in Laramie."

"Sure. Morgue's downstairs. Ms. Halliday, you want to wait up here?"

"Thank you."

Molly stared out the grimy window onto the dusty street. From here, Laramie was not a pretty town.

"Is Lieutenant Holman here?"

Molly turned back. The woman in the doorway looked every inch a professional bureaucrat. She was taller than Molly, slim, and carried a battered black briefcase. Her eyes were tired.

"He's gone down to the morgue for a moment. I'm Molly Halliday." Molly stuck out a hand.

The woman shook it. "Sylvia Grissom, Social Services."

Molly said, "I'm here with Logan MacMillan, the grandfather of the little girl whose mother had the accident last week. He's been trying to find the child. He wants to take her home."

"I see. You a detective?"

"I'm a doll-maker."

"I beg your pardon?" Ms. Grissom said.

"It's a long story."

Logan walked back in the door followed by Lieutenant Holman.

"Oh, Logan," Molly said. "This is Ms. Grissom from Social Services." She felt grateful to be rescued, but one glance at his face made her heart turn over. He looked ten years older. "Is it . . ."

"Tiffany. Yes. Ms. Grissom, I would like to see my granddaughter, please."

"I'm sure you would, Mr. MacMillan, but there are a few legal problems to be gotten out of the way first. We want the best for Dulcy."

"So do I." Logan set his briefcase on the desk, opened it and pulled out the sheaf of papers he had showed Holman.

Ms. Grissom ran her eye over them with quick familiarity. "You seem to have everything in order."

"I am the child's legal guardian and her closest kin now that her mother is dead. Surely she'd come to me even without the papers."

"Probably." Ms. Grissom handed the papers back to Logan.

"I have both my lawyer and the judge who signed the papers standing by if you want to talk to them about my character."

"Fine. Before I do that, I've got a couple of questions. Holman and I have done some talking. Your timing bothers me. You show up on the doorstep just after her mother dies. Does Dulcy have money coming?"

"Her mother's will is with her lawyers in Memphis," Logan said patiently. "I suspect Dulcy will have enough money in trust for her majority to take care of her nicely." The vein at his temple throbbed and his shoulders under the navy jacket were tense with strain.

Ms. Grissom raised her eyebrows.

Logan continued, "I said for her majority, Ms. Grissom. I have plenty of money to take care of her in the meantime. Tiffany's trustees will no doubt handle her estate as they see fit. I'm not one of them."

"I see." She turned to Molly. "You still haven't said how you turned up now."

Molly told her the whole story and watched expressions of surprise and disbelief cross the social worker's face.

"So you see, it really is a blessed coincidence," Molly finished. "Please, call Logan's lawyer. He'll tell you Logan's a fine man. He'll be a good guardian."

Ms. Grissom nodded her head. "Okay. I'll set up an appointment with a judge tomorrow morning to execute your order of custody. Takes about five minutes."

"Tomorrow morning?" Logan asked.

Molly saw his fists clench.

"I'm sorry, but it's too late to get on the docket today." She smiled at him. "Look, I know you're anxious, but I think of every one of these kids as my own. I have to make sure everything is in order before I send them out of the state of Wyoming with strangers."

"I understand," Logan said. "But you must realize that for me it's like getting out of bed on Christmas morning and then being told not to open the presents."

Ms. Grissom nodded. "Good analogy." She turned to Holman. "I called Helen Dalrymple this morning." She turned once more to Logan. "She's the foster parent who has Dulcy at the moment. She can't make it into town until one this afternoon. She'll take you to see Dulcy."

"Can't we just drive out there? Now?"

Ms. Grissom shook her head. "You'd never find the place. Better this way. On the ride out, she can brief you about what to expect." She smiled gently. "I know you're anxious, Mr. MacMillan, but I promise I'm not making this harder than it has to be. Good luck with Dulcy. Let me have your telephone number. I'll call you when the papers are signed."

Logan watched her out the door before he exploded. "Damn!" he said to Holman. "I can't take much more of this waiting."

"Hey," Holman said kindly. "Give you time to make arrangements with the funeral director. And you can bet Sylvia's going to call your lawyer to check out your story. She's careful with her kids."

As they walked down the steps of the courthouse, Molly could see the frustration in every line of Logan's face. He opened her door then got into the driver's side.

"Damn!" He hit the steering wheel with the heels of his hands.

"Holman's right," Molly said. "We have arrangements to make. The funeral home. Find out about air service out of here. Then I think we'd better go back to that apartment of Tiffany's to get Dulcy's things."

"Why? I intend to buy the child decent clothes."

"How about her teddy bear? A blanket she always sleeps with? Her favorite doll? Books? Familiar things? She's got to be terrified, and here we show up out of the blue. I don't know about you, but I'd want something familiar to hang on to."

Logan stared at her for a moment without speaking. He shook his head. "You're right."

Molly took a deep breath. She was about to do something she'd never done in her life. She was going to ask a man for an explanation of his actions. "And another thing while we're about it. What was all that this morning?"

Logan froze. "I don't know what you mean."

She nearly lost her nerve, but kept on doggedly. "You spend the night plastered to me like glue, then roll out of bed and the next thing I know you're treating me as though I were a flesh-eating alien from outer space. If you want to end this thing between us, just tell me straight out!"

Logan dropped his head onto the steering wheel. "I don't want to end it, but I think we should for your sake."

Molly went cold all over. "For my sake? That's the oldest ploy in the book, Logan MacMillan. It's not for me, it's for you. You—"

"Molly, the people I love change. They stop loving me. And then they die. I can't bear to lose you, can't you see that?"

Molly gaped. "Oh." She reached over and turned him to face her. "When my mother and father died within a year of one another I thought some malevolent force was out there feeding off my grief like a candy bar and smacking his lips. I was so terrified of losing Anne that I dragged her to the pediatrician twice a week until she got so fed up she refused to go."

"How did you get over it?"

"I didn't. I still feel that way whenever my life gets screwed up. But you have to keep trying to make things work. What else is there?"

"I've had as much loss as I can handle."

"If you and I go our separate ways the minute we get home, I'll survive. I'm not sure how at the moment, but I will. So will you."

"It won't be *my* decision to go separate ways."

"Don't second-guess what's going to happen later. The point is, my poor old bruised ego already owes you a lot. I'm going to hold on to that as long as I can."

Logan shook his head at her, smiling across the space between the seats. "If I could, I'd take you to bed again right here in front of the courthouse. I suppose I'll have to settle for a chaste kiss."

MOLLY AND LOGAN collected Tiffany's few papers in a manila envelope. They packed Dulcy's pitifully small collection of clothes and toys and put them on the back seat of the rental car. Logan gave Mrs. Washington a check to cover the back rent and another to cover packing and shipping of the rest of Tiffany's and Dulcy's belongings. They returned to the hotel, and Molly waited in her adjoining room while Logan called Tiffany's father, Carlton Edwards, in Spain.

When he opened her door, his face was troubled, but all he said was, "Come on, let's grab some fast-food and get back down to meet the foster parent."

Over lunch Logan stole one of Molly's fries, looked at it in disgust and dropped it onto his tray. "Edwards said Tiffany's been dead to him for years."

"Did he ask about Dulcy?"

Logan shook his head. "He wasn't interested." He slammed his hand down on the table. "Damnation, she's as much his grandchild as mine!"

Molly glanced around at the other patrons. Several looked up curiously. She covered Logan's hand with her own. "Calm down and eat your grease."

Twenty minutes later in Holman's office, the lieutenant introduced them to Helen Dalrymple. She was long and lean. Her slightly horsey face was dark brown and her skin thickened by hours in the sun. Her fair hair was pulled back tight and caught with a scarf. When she shook Molly's hand, Molly felt the calluses on the woman's palms. Working hands.

Without preamble, she said, "I think you should leave Dulcy with us until all the arrangements are made, Mr. MacMillan."

"You can't keep me from seeing her."

"That's not what I meant. How long is it going to take you to get everything finalized here about her mother? Couple of days?"

"I have no idea. Possibly."

"Dulcy's just getting used to the other children. She doesn't need to be snatched away to spend the night in a strange motel with a couple of people she doesn't know exist."

"Perhaps you're right, Mrs. Dalrymple, but we want to tell her we exist. He exists," Molly said, and pointed to Logan.

"Agreed. But we take it slow. And it's Helen. Look, Molly, why don't you ride out with me, Logan can follow. We can talk on the way."

As they drove out of town in a dusty Dodge pickup truck, Molly turned in her seat to watch Helen's hands on the wheel. She drove well. "You wanted to get me alone. Why?"

"Because you're a woman. It's going to be up to you."

"What is?"

"Getting through to Dulcy."

Molly caught her breath. "She's not—I don't know—catatonic or anything, is she?"

Helen shook her head. "No. Outwardly she's functioning pretty well, all things considered. Too well. She does everything she's asked, she's frighteningly polite. But she never smiles, seldom speaks, doesn't interact with the other children at all."

"That's the child I remember—as though she were trapped across a river that we couldn't see and couldn't cross to get to her."

Helen turned to stare at Molly. "That's it exactly."

"Do you have any idea what her life has been? Has she been abused? I assume Ms. Grissom had her checked over by a pediatrician."

Helen braked to avoid a pair of pronghorn antelope that had blundered onto the road and now stood gazing at them from liquid brown eyes. Molly looked over her shoulder and caught a glimpse of Logan braking hard behind them. After a moment, Helen drove on.

"Physically she's fine—no signs of sexual abuse. She's thin and she's lost a couple of baby teeth, but that's normal at her age. No, what worries me is that she's trying not to feel anything. She's taking refuge in routine and trying to create a force field around her emotions.''

Molly put her hand on Helen's arm and withdrew it quickly as the car lurched. ''Sorry. But you see, that's exactly what Logan does. He puts up a kind of psychic force field. I wonder if that kind of thing can be genetic?''

Helen chuckled. ''Stranger things have happened.'' She took her eyes off the road long enough to look at Molly. For a moment Molly read indecision in her glance. Then Helen apparently made up her mind. ''Did Holman or Ms. Grissom tell you what happened?''

''Not in any detail. They found Tiffany dead and took the child to you.''

''Her mother worked the eight to midnight shift and left Dulcy alone in that apartment night after night. No evidence of a baby-sitter.''

''The child is barely five years old!''

''It happens more than you can imagine,'' Helen said. ''Dulcy fed herself, bathed herself, attempted to clean house, watched much too much television, read books and probably held her mother's head over the john when she came home drunk. Unless there was someone with Tiffany. Seems there often was.''

''Amazing Dulcy survived.''

''At least the mother protected her from the boyfriends. A lot of mothers don't.''

''Tiffany was such a mass of contradictions.'' Molly sighed. ''I just wish she could have lived to come home and get her life back together.''

''Luck runs out. Hers did. But I suppose in a sense she saved Dulcy. You know Tiffany died in her sleep Wednesday.''

"Holman told us." Molly shivered, then registered what Helen had told her. "But I thought she died Thursday."

"That's when they broke the door down. When she didn't show up for work or answer the telephone, her boss got mad. Apparently, Dulcy had been taught not to answer the phone."

"My God."

"Dulcy went about her normal routine. We found cereal bowls and glasses in the sink. That's how we know she ate. She told us she'd read *The Velveteen Rabbit* and taken a bath. She assured me she'd brushed her teeth."

Molly sucked in her breath. "The idea of a child that young left unattended in a bathtub—well, it just scares me to death."

"I know. Still, she was used to it. She is a very careful little girl." Helen glanced over at Molly. "That's one of the problems. Anyway, when she couldn't wake her mother up, she just went to bed. I think by then she was getting frightened. The apartment was fairly cool, still, she must have known something was wrong. She just didn't know what to do about it. She took refuge in routine."

Molly fought her rising gorge. "But her mother..."

"Apparently, Dulcy was used to having her mother come home to sleep one off. By the time the police broke in, the body had begun to smell, rigor was passing off. Molly, that child was locked in the apartment with her mother's dead body almost twenty-four hours."

CHAPTER TWELVE

FORTY-FIVE MINUTES later Molly and Helen in Helen's pickup truck bumped over a cattle guard and onto a gravel farm road. Logan followed closely in the rental car. Brown hills stretched away on all sides. The snow that they'd seen earlier had either not made it this far or had melted in the sunlight that dappled the hills. Molly saw no house or outbuildings. Twice they slued sideways on mud the color of old paper sacks. Molly tried to glimpse Logan's face through the windshield, but the glare of the sun turned it into a mirror that reflected only the blue sky and scudding clouds. She could imagine how tense he felt all alone in that car.

They crossed a couple of shallow streams that chuckled over concrete fording pads. Large brown cows raised solemn heads to stare at them as they passed.

They drove for fifteen minutes before they made a sharp right turn down a hill and through a grove of trees. The house, barns, corrals and other farm buildings huddled together as if for warmth and companionship in the bleak open spaces.

Molly saw the children playing before the wind carried their voices to her. She counted seven, from toddler to preteen. They ran and swooped in a fenced paddock that held a sandbox and a large swing set.

As they came to a stop, Molly searched in vain for Dulcy's strawberry hair.

The moment the children saw Helen climb out of her car, they ran to the edge of the fenced enclosure, yelling and shoving at one another. Helen merely smiled and waved. "Scat!" She clapped her hands and they flew apart in mock alarm, then regrouped to stare curiously at the newcomers.

A very tall bronzed man in jeans came out of the barn, pulling off heavy leather gloves. "Hi, pet," he said, and leaned down to kiss Helen Dalrymple's cheek.

"Hi, hon. Molly, this is my husband, Chuck. Chuck, Molly Halliday and that's Logan MacMillan getting out of his car."

"Yeah. We heard." Chuck nodded at Molly and moved to shake Logan's hand briefly.

Logan barely acknowledged the greeting. He couldn't take his eyes off the children. He, too, Molly realized, searched for that strawberry blond head.

"She's not there, Mr. MacMillan. She's inside with Dolores." He laughed and shook his head. "Reading a book, most likely. All she does, seems like. Reads real good, too."

Logan had already started for the house.

"Mr. MacMillan, wait!" Helen called after him. "Take it slow, okay?"

"Mrs. Dalrymple, I've had about as much slow as I am capable of handling."

"I understand. Just remember, she doesn't even know you exist."

Molly trotted along behind Logan. She realized with a start that he was carrying the box with the Dulcy doll under his arm. Helen Dalrymple didn't know the box held a smaller version of Dulcy, but before Molly could say anything, Logan leaped the porch stairs and walked in the front door.

"Hey, Dolores!" Helen called from behind his shoulder. The house was large, cluttered and full of shabby furniture. It wasn't neat, but it was clean and smelled of furniture polish and hot cookies.

A small, cheerful woman leaned around the edge of the door to what was obviously a kitchen.

Helen gestured "where?" with opened arms and raised eyebrows. Dolores pointed toward the room in front of them.

Helen forcefully put her hand on Logan's arm, shook her head and went around him. He followed.

Molly could see that he was breathing hard.

"Dulcy, honey, you in here?" Helen called casually and walked into the large room at the back of the house.

Logan and Molly followed. Molly realized she was shaking. At first she thought the room was empty. Then she saw a glint of sunlight on strawberry hair and moved farther into the room. Dulcy sat curled into a tight still ball in the triangle of floor between the big blue recliner and the fireplace.

She watched them out of Logan's gray eyes. Her small jaw was as square as his, her forehead had that same broad sweep. Molly had never seen a picture of Jeremy MacMillan, but this child was a MacMillan all through. She was painfully thin, and her hair was cropped almost like a boy's. She'd lost all trace of baby fat, but there was no trace of baby in her guarded expression.

Molly thought of cheerful Elizabeth. She longed to fold this child in her arms, to bring laughter to her sad little face.

"Hey, Dulcy, how come you're not out playing in the sunshine?" Helen walked over and reached down a hand toward the child.

Dulcy shrank from her. She didn't cower, she merely moved her body far enough away to avoid Helen's touch.

"What you doing, punkin'?" Helen asked.

"I'm reading." She held up an ancient *Ladies Home Journal* from the dog-eared stack on the hearth in front of her.

"That's nice, honey." Helen sat on the raised hearth a safe distance away but closer to Dulcy's level. "Lookie here, I've brought some folks to see you. I'll bet you can't guess who these folks are, can you?"

Dulcy moved her head from side to side no more than an inch. She kept her eyes on Logan and Molly.

Logan took a deep breath. "How do you do, Dulcy." His voice was strong, carefully polite. He stuck out his hand to her as though she were an adult. "I am Logan MacMillan. I am your grandfather."

Helen made a sound very much like a growl and frowned at him. After a moment she shrugged and said, "Well, go on, honey. Here, I'll keep your place while you meet these nice people. They've come a long way to see you. Didn't you say your momma said always to be polite?"

Dulcy glanced at Helen, then at Logan's outstretched hand. She stood up slowly, but kept the chair between her and her visitors.

She was very tall for her age. For a moment she hesitated and turned to Molly. Molly smiled and nodded to her. Logan should never have stuck that blasted hand out to Dulcy as though he were greeting a chairman of the board. Molly was about ready to throttle him.

Dulcy inched out from behind the chair and came toward them warily.

Suddenly, she stuck out her small hand and brushed Logan's for an instant before she jumped back and smack into Molly. She whirled, stared wildly into Molly's eyes and slid quickly behind her.

In the midst of the chaos their lives must have been, Tiffany had taught her child the manners she had learned as a child. Maybe that was the only remnant of that former life Tiffany could afford. Even as frightened as she must be, Dulcy conquered her fear long enough to do the thing her mother had taught her.

"And this lady is my..." He looked at Molly in sudden bewilderment and opened his hands. "Molly."

Molly blinked back her tears and said to the child at her side, "How do you do?" She stuck her hand in her pocket.

"We have come to take you home," Logan said quietly.

Dulcy looked up at Molly and whispered, "To my mommy?"

Molly caught her breath at the hope in the child's voice and dropped to her knees.

Dulcy flinched at the sudden movement but stood her ground. Her eyes were now on a level with Molly's.

"Honey, don't you remember?" Helen Dalrymple said from the hearth. "I told you, baby, your mommy's dead."

Dulcy ignored her.

Molly closed her eyes. Of course the child had no conception of the finality of death. She glanced at Logan in despair. He seemed to have turned to stone.

"Your mother was my daughter-in-law, Dulcy," he said softly. "Your father was my son. Do you know what a grandfather is?" he asked.

Nothing from Dulcy, not even a shake of her head.

"Dulcy, we've come a very long way to find you," Logan said. "We've looked and looked. Your mother knew you needed someone to look after you."

She glanced at him and then whispered to Molly, "Tell him she looks after me fine."

"But she can't look after you anymore, Dulcy," Logan said. "I've come to take you home to people who will look after you and take care of you and love you the way she did."

"Do you know my mommy?" Dulcy asked Molly. Logan talked to Dulcy, Dulcy talked to Molly and ignored Logan.

Molly heard an edge of desperation in his voice when he answered, "I knew your mother. She was married to my son. You have a whole family that loves you."

Dulcy shook her head. It was obvious she didn't believe that for a minute. Her whole life had been just her mommy. Logan could tell her about another life, but it didn't mean anything to her.

"Do you know how we found you?" Logan asked.

Dulcy moved closer to Molly. Helen moved in protectively on Dulcy's other side.

Logan plunged desperately ahead. "This lady saw you with your mommy and made a doll that looks like you. Would you like to see it?" Logan flipped off the top of the box holding the Dulcy doll, pulled the doll out and held it out to Dulcy.

"My God!" Helen Dalrymple gasped.

Dulcy shrieked and bolted down the hall. They heard a door slam.

Helen threw Logan and the doll a venomous look and ran after her.

"Put that damned thing away!" Molly snapped as she brushed past him to the front door and down the steps to the car. She rummaged in the small store of toys they had brought from Tiffany's apartment until she found an elderly lop-eared rabbit missing an ear and an eye. She raced back to the house.

"But I thought she'd like it!" Logan groaned.

"I know, darling," Molly said.

"Can I come, too?" Logan begged.

"Not yet."

Molly heard the sound of Helen's soft voice through a door at the end of the hall and opened it without knocking. The child on the bed yelped and shrank back.

"Hey, it's okay," Molly said quietly. "I've brought somebody else who wants to see you." She held out the bunny.

Dulcy's eyes lit. "Petey!" She reached for the bunny, and held it tight against her chest, cooing over it like a mother with a beloved child.

Helen gave Molly a silent thumbs-up from her place at the foot of Dulcy's small bed.

"May I sit down, too?" Molly asked.

The child's head nodded. Her bright, butchered hair bobbed on the top of her head.

Molly walked around the other side and sat beside Helen.

After a moment, Dulcy said, her voice muffled by the rabbit, "Thank you, MyMolly."

"You're quite welcome, my Dulcy." She smiled at the child's bent head.

Dulcy peered up at her from under her lashes. There were no traces of tears on her face.

"I'm sorry we frightened you, Dulcy," Molly continued. "Think of how much bigger and more grown-up you are now than the doll. You were just a little girl when I saw you."

The child considered. "Maybe."

"It's just a doll, you know."

"I never had a doll like me. Not a nice doll."

"Your grandfather..." Molly caught the heightened tension in the child's hands. "Your grandfather brought her for you if you'd like to have her."

"Who *is* he, MyMolly?"

"He is your father and mother's daddy. He has been searching for you for a long time."

"Tell him to go away, please. I don't like him."

"I'm not surprised after he stuck that doll out at you like that."

Helen eased off the bed and tiptoed from the room. Molly let her go. She could explain to Logan. Molly had her hands full with Dulcy.

"Why don't you like him, Dulcy?"

Dulcy frowned. "He looks like one of those vampires I saw on television."

Molly gulped. A five-year-old child watching vampire movies? "In what way?"

"He's real big and he's got a real deep voice and he made me shake hands with him and then he showed me that doll." Dulcy shuddered.

"Do I remind you of a vampire, too?"

Dulcy looked her over critically. "Nope. Lady vampires are skinny and got long hair. You're too old to be a lady vampire."

"Thank you, I think."

That settled, Dulcy leaned back against the pillow and stroked Petey. "That Dulcy's a baby." This was said with a great air of superiority.

"Absolutely. But you recognized her, so she's not that different from you."

"No, but she's little. She couldn't take care of herself or anything."

"Children aren't supposed to have to take care of themselves. That's what grown-ups are for."

"I can take care of myself fine. Mommy..." Her bright eyes suddenly went bleak. "Why can't my mommy come back? I want her."

"I know. Sometimes we lose the people who we love most in the world. It's not fair, it just happens. But if we're very lucky, we get to find other people who can sort of fill up the holes in our lives, you know?"

"Like you?"

"Like your grandfather Logan."

"He's scary and he's dumb. He doesn't know what scares little kids even."

"In some ways he's dumb as a doorknob." Molly saw Dulcy's eyes pivot to the doorknob. For a moment she thought she saw the ghost of a smile. She plowed on doggedly, not relishing being thrust into the role of negotiator, but apparently stuck with it. "He used to have little kids, but he's forgotten. Your daddy was his little boy. Did you know that?"

"Don't have a daddy."

"Everybody has a daddy."

"Where is he, then? Is he gonna come and look after me?" Dulcy asked hopefully. Apparently, an unknown daddy was preferable to a known Logan.

Molly shook her head. "I'm afraid he's dead, too, Dulcy. But your grandfather Logan will take care of you."

"Nope." Dulcy shook her head mulishly and Molly was astounded at how much that stubborn little chin looked like Logan's.

"He wants to do better. He's very sorry he frightened you. It's good manners to give him a chance to apologize, you know."

"It is?" Dulcy obviously wasn't certain politeness extended quite that far.

"I'm afraid it is. Besides, if we're going to educate him about little kids, we're going to have to start his lessons sometime, aren't we?"

"Nope. You teach him."

"I've tried, but I need you to help me."

"Do I hafta?"

"Not until you're ready." Molly pulled her legs up onto the bed and leaned against the footboard. "Your grandfather Logan brought Petey, you know. And we've got your other toys and some books in the car. His heart is in the right place."

Dulcy's eyes brightened. "My books?"

"Sure." Molly was not above bribery. "I'll bet he'll get you some new ones, too."

"If I help teach him about kids?" Dulcy frowned as though trying to decide whether the possibility of new books was worth bearding the vampire in his lair. After a moment she shook her head. "Nope. You teach him." Then she made a concession. "I'll watch."

"Sorry, kiddo, doesn't work that way. I'm afraid it's your responsibility. But I promise to help. You know what a responsibility is?"

"Sure. I'm responsible. My mommy told me I had to be responsible."

"You want to go in there and give your grandfather his first lesson?"

Panic flickered across Dulcy's face and she clutched Petey even tighter. "Can I just watch so I can see how you teach him? Then maybe I can help."

Better than nothing. "Deal. We'll go together. I'll hold the hand Petey's not holding."

"That's silly. Petey's just a rabbit. Rabbits have paws, not hands. Does baby Dulcy have hands?"

"Smaller than yours, but yes, she has hands."

"Can I really have her?"

"Do you want her?"

Dulcy considered carefully, then nodded her head. "I think maybe. But you give her to me, not him. My-Molly, do I hafta talk to him?"

Molly considered. "Not right away. Not until you feel comfortable."

Dulcy sneered. Obviously comfort was a long way away.

"Okay. You go."

"We go together, kiddo. I promise I'll hang on to you and you won't have to say one word if you don't want to. Okay?"

Logan sat in the recliner with his head in his hands. Molly could hear Helen's voice but couldn't see her from the hall. The moment Dulcy saw Logan, her hand clenched in Molly's and she moved tight against Molly's side. "Don't let go, MyMolly," she whispered.

"I promise."

Molly hadn't had time to worry about Logan, but the stricken face he raised, the eyes that held both hope and sorrow, made her heart turn over. She wanted to run to him, but she knew her place right now was with Dulcy.

Dulcy stuck to Molly's side like a barnacle. It was like being in the three-legged race. The moment Logan saw them, Dulcy stopped and tugged at Molly's hand. Molly bent her head and Dulcy whispered, "You teach him."

Molly cleared her throat. "Logan, Dulcy and I have decided that when it comes to little kids, you are as dumb as a doorknob." She looked down at Dulcy. "Am I correct?" Dulcy nodded almost imperceptibly.

"We have decided magnanimously that it's not your fault, however, and we are willing graciously to go about teaching you if you promise not to loom over us like a vampire and scare us with dolls."

"Wha...Vampire? Molly, what the—"

Molly held up her hand. "Furthermore, if you promise to give us lots of new books, we might be persuaded to overlook your doorknobness until such time as you manage to correct it." Molly felt Dulcy wriggle against her and knew she'd somehow stumbled on the right tone. Logan was completely bewildered.

For all her fear, Dulcy could recognize the absurd when she heard it. If she had managed to preserve even the tiniest scrap of a sense of humor, there was hope for her. Suddenly Molly's heart lurched. Someday, somehow, no matter what it took, she swore to herself she would hear Dulcy laugh.

Logan cleared his throat. "Uh, yes. Whatever you say, Molly."

Dulcy tugged on Molly's sleeve and whispered, "Ask him, can I have baby Dulcy."

Logan started. "You...I thought she frightened you."

"She's a doll, Dulcy is a real little girl," Molly said.

"Of course you may have the doll. Shall I get her now?" Logan started to stand, but Dulcy caught her breath and stepped behind Molly quickly.

"No!" Molly said. "Later."

"Sure. Would you like to sit down?"

"MyMolly, sit with me, okay?"

Dulcy climbed onto the sofa as far from Logan as possible and pulled Molly down beside her. Her heels beat a steady tattoo against the sofa. Molly saw that her tennis shoes looked nearly new, but her toes were already coming out the ends. She must have been in a growth spurt. Probably Tiffany couldn't afford a new pair.

Logan and Dulcy stared silently at one another until even Molly grew uncomfortable watching them.

"Dulcy, you have an Aunt Zoe and an Uncle Rick, as well, in Memphis," Logan said, finally.

No response.

"That's the town where you were born and where your mother married my son."

Thump went Dulcy's heels.

Logan threw Molly a look of total chagrin.

Dulcy played with Petey and ignored him.

"Your uncle Rick and your aunt Zoe are waiting to see you when we take you to Memphis with us."

Dulcy stared at him in openmouthed horror. "No!" In an instant she was off down the hall again. Petey hit the wall several times on the trip.

Logan threw up his hands in frustration as Molly took after her. "Now what have I said?"

Molly found Dulcy in a ball on the floor on the far side of the bed, busily wriggling under it. Molly lay facedown so that she could see Dulcy peering out of the darkness. "It's okay," she said. "You can come out."

"*No!* I won't go."

"Why not?"

"My mommy won't be able to find me."

Molly dropped her face against her forearms. How could she handle this one? Let Logan drag Dulcy kicking and screaming onto an airplane? Ms. Grissom and Lieutenant Holman would really love that. She raised her head and said quietly, "Dulcy, your mommy won't be coming to find you here, but I think that wherever you go, she'll be there to watch over you. You just won't be able to see her. Do you know about souls?"

Dulcy shook her head, but made no move to leave her sanctuary.

"I believe that everyone has a soul that lives on and watches over the loved ones left behind, no matter where they are."

"So my mommy's here *and* she'll find me in that other place?"

"You got it."

"You sure she'll find me?"

Time enough for deep philosophical discussion when Dulcy was older. Molly swallowed every ounce of doubt she'd ever felt and said as positively as she could, "Yes. I'm sure."

Dulcy considered for a moment, then said, "She won't have to look for me if I stay here. She already knows where I am."

"Do you want to stay here?" Please, Molly prayed, let her say no.

"Nope."

"Don't you like it here?"

"The other kids won't leave me alone. They won't let me read."

"I see. So if your grandfather agrees to give you time to read and not bug you, will you come to Memphis?"

"Not with him. With you?"

"Of course I'll be there until you get settled."

"Promise?"

Molly took a deep breath. God only knew what she was letting herself in for. "Promise."

"Cross your heart and hope to die?"

"Cross my heart and hope to die. Now, will you come out where I can see you? It's like trying to spot a gopher down a hole. Besides, my stomach's all smooshed."

"We going now?" Dulcy asked. She began to work her way backward on the other side of the bed. Petey dragged along the floor.

Molly sat up gratefully as Dulcy climbed on top of the bed and looked down at her expectantly.

"We have to make arrangements," Molly said. "We can't drive all the way to Memphis. It's a very long way. So we'll have to fly." The reality of that struck her at the same moment the words left her mouth. There was no way she and Logan and Dulcy could stay cooped up in that car even as far as Denver without serious damage to all their psyches. Flying would be the only way, no matter how deeply it terrified her. Better to spend the time between planes in an airport, where there would be distractions for Dulcy, than in a car, where Dulcy and Logan would be stuck with one another without respite.

"We don't know about plane schedules and things. It's going to take a couple of days to get the tickets."

"Okay. But I don't want to stay here."

"I'm afraid that's best." Molly looked at Dulcy's face, suddenly set and cold once more. "Dulcy, adults spend their lives telling children what's best for them. When I was a kid, it made me very angry and I'm sure it makes you angry, as well. Unfortunately, we're both stuck with it this time. If you can't understand, can you agree to accept it and tough it out? Won't be more than a couple of days."

Just then, Helen Dalrymple stuck her head around the door. "Hey, you guys doing all right in here?"

Dulcy nodded. Molly shrugged.

"Dulcy, why don't you run out and play with the other kids for a little while so Molly and Logan and I can talk."

Dulcy shook her head. "Nope. Don't like 'em."

"Do you like Sandra?" Helen asked.

"She's okay."

"How about if I take you outside right now and you and Sandra can play in the tree house? There's cookies in about half an hour. Okay?"

"Do I hafta?"

"Just twenty minutes. That's not long. It's a beautiful day."

"If I hafta." Dulcy slid off the bed, thought a moment, then ceremoniously presented Petey to Molly.

"Take care of Petey, MyMolly."

"Of course."

"And come with me when we go past the man, okay?"

Molly nodded and took Dulcy's hand.

When they entered the living room, Logan started to stand, but Molly shook her head at him. Dulcy sidled past as though he were a dragon, and waited while Helen helped her on with her coat and opened the door for her.

Logan sat still until he heard the door close, then he slumped. "My God, Molly, she hates me!"

Molly dropped on her knees beside his chair. "No, my dear, she just doesn't know you. And that was a dumb thing to do with the doll."

"I didn't think. Molly, what am I going to do? She won't even speak to me."

"It'll get easier."

"You were wonderful with her." He stroked Molly's hair. "Dumb as a doorknob indeed."

"Well, you were. I'm not much better. It's like talking to a hundred-year-old woman. She's smart as a whip, Logan, but oh, Lord, she's so *old*."

"And yet part of her is still barely five."

"Logan, we have to fly home. Can you get tickets?"

"But Molly..."

"I know, but cooped up in a car with Dulcy—it doesn't bear thinking about. The thing is to get her home as quickly as possible so she can start a routine. Get to know you."

"She thinks I'm a vampire!"

Molly laughed. "No she doesn't, but what that child has watched on television alone and unsupervised day after day doesn't bear thinking about. We can fly on the same plane that takes Tiffany's body home."

"No! I don't want Dulcy waiting around in an airport while her mother's casket is unloaded."

"She won't have to. She won't even know. The people from the funeral home can meet the plane." He sat with his hand on her shoulder, as if he was drawing emotional sustenance from her very nearness.

"Then if you can endure the flight, Molly, and if the papers are signed, we'll leave tomorrow."

"Good."

He went to the window and stood there, his hands in the pockets of his slacks, following Dulcy's bright hair with his eyes. "Why did Tiffany cut her hair?"

Molly shrugged. "Easier, perhaps. Maybe Dulcy wanted it that way. Kids get cranky about their hair."

"She and Sandy are swinging," Helen said, coming back into the room. "Sandy's her age and quiet, too. I thought you two might like a little time alone."

"It didn't go well, did it?" Logan asked.

"Better than I hoped. She only bailed out twice."

"She won't speak to me or even look at me."

"Mr. MacMillan," Helen said quietly, "think about the men she's known in her short life. To her, every man is big and scary and dangerous. She's learned to be very, very careful. Children of alcoholics do that. Add to that the fact that her mother was taking drugs, and they were on the run. Very isolated, very self-sufficient. But I think she's basically a good kid."

"Polite," he said proudly. "She shook my hand."

"It wasn't easy for her," Molly said.

"Too polite," Helen said. "Most kids would have refused. Some of my juvenile delinquents outside would have told you to stick it in your ear." Helen sank onto the sofa. It sagged under her weight and made a sharp twanging sound. She ran her hand across her eyes. "Dulcy needs to throw one humdinger of a temper tantrum, and then she needs to channel all that anger against her mother into something healthy."

"Anger? All I saw was fear. And she loves her mother," Logan said.

"Sure she does. She also hates her for leaving her, for abandoning her all the time, for being drunk and never able to be counted on. For turning her into a five-year-old parent. She hates herself, too."

"What the hell for?" Logan asked. "She's done nothing wrong."

"She feels that if she were a better girl her mother wouldn't drink, wouldn't yell, wouldn't hit, wouldn't go off and leave her, wouldn't bring strange men home, wouldn't die—the ultimate abandonment. Children are the sum total of their own universes. These things happened to Dulcy because Dulcy caused them to happen."

"Oh, Lord," Logan groaned.

"In my judgment, she's held up remarkably well." She glanced at Logan and smiled reassuringly. "I'm not just a farm wife, Mr. MacMillan, I have a postgraduate degree in clinical psychology with a concentration on children. This is what I do. Dulcy shows no signs of turning into a serial killer or a sociopath."

"Mrs.—Dr. Dalrymple, I read all the magazine articles and newspaper reports about serial killers and sociopaths. They all say the same thing." He ticked off the points on his fingers. "Dulcy's a loner. She's the child of alcoholic parents, isolated, psychologically, if not physically, abused. Her mother has committed the ultimate abandonment by dying. You say she must feel anger and guilt. Of course I'm worried about how she'll grow up."

"You've left out one important point, Mr. Logan," Helen said. "Females don't generally take out their anger on other people. They take out their anger on themselves. I suspect that's why Tiffany drank and did cocaine."

"So what's to prevent Dulcy from repeating her mother's pattern?"

"Your love, your support, the stable environment you will provide her. Professional psychological help if it's indicated. She's a brainy little girl who has stood up to plenty in her short life. I think she's going to be fine."

"But you're not one hundred percent certain, are you?" Logan asked.

Helen laughed ruefully. "I'm not a hundred percent certain about any of those children out there, or about my own, for that matter. Nobody can guarantee that any child will grow up mentally healthy, Mr. MacMillan—not even the top Park Avenue shrinks. There are no guarantees. We do the best we can, and we hope our love will do the rest."

As Ms. Grissom had predicted, the custody hearing took less than five minutes. After the judge signed the paperwork, Logan stopped by to thank Lieutenant Holman for his help. He found him hunched over his desk eating a greasy burrito and drinking a cola out of the can.

Holman waved him to a chair while he finished chewing. "So, you're squared away with the kid?" Something in Logan's face made him narrow his eyes. "Helen did say it's okay to take her with you, right?"

Logan nodded. "Unfortunately, the airline service to Laramie is not quite like service to O'Hare. Tiffany's body is currently at the Johansen Funeral Parlor being prepared. We're picking out a coffin this afternoon. She'll be shipped home tomorrow. Molly and Dulcy and I will take the same plane home."

"So what's your problem?"

Logan sighed. "You are a father, aren't you?"

"Yeah."

"Whatever makes good fathers was apparently not transmuted in my genetic code. I do not understand children. I don't know how to talk to them. And Dulcy is a strange child."

"Hey. You talk to them like grown-ups. What they understand, they understand. What they don't, they ignore or ask about. It's like sex. If they understand it, they're not too young to talk about it. If they don't, who cares?"

"Dulcy doesn't understand death. How do I explain that to her?"

"You don't. She'll have to pick up on it herself. Just do the best you can, MacMillan. That's all I do. So far, it hasn't worked out bad, but then, I got a wife who's a natural. So do you."

"Molly? She's not my wife."

"No, but maybe she ought to be. She could take up the slack where the kid's concerned."

As Logan walked to the car, he considered Holman's words. Molly not only took up the slack with Dulcy, she was the only person who made interaction with Dulcy possible. Dulcy trusted her. She had gotten further than Helen Dalrymple. With Molly's instruction and help, eventually he would learn to communicate with Dulcy, to defuse her anxiety about being with him. Together, he and Molly might well be able to turn Dulcy into a normal little girl. At the moment, however, the prospect of getting Dulcy to Memphis gave him the shakes.

His instinct was simply to let Molly take her home alone then follow by a later plane. No doubt that's what Dulcy wanted, too. Still, that was pure cowardice. She was his child now. If he planned to be her father, he had to start somewhere. The problem was, where?

CHAPTER THIRTEEN

MOLLY AND LOGAN ate dinner in the motel dining room and walked back to their connecting rooms arm in arm. The night had a clear, cold edge that whispered of winter.

"Can we sit outside for a while?" Molly asked. She looked up. "Why do there always seem to be more stars out West than at home? It's as though they snuck in another galaxy on us."

Logan put his arm around her. She snuggled against him.

"You're tense, darling," Molly said.

"I'm worried," Logan answered. "I told myself I could handle anything, but I never dreamed Dulcy would be afraid of me."

"The first time I met you I thought you were pretty formidable."

"Me?" Logan stared down at her.

Molly leaned her head on his shoulder. "Yes, you. From Dulcy's perspective, you loom."

"I want her to feel happy and secure. She can't hide behind the furniture the rest of her life. But how do I help her if she won't even speak to me?"

"Take it slowly. You've only met her once. I changed my mind when I got to know you. She will, too. Let her see that you're not a hobgoblin." She touched his chin and turned his face to her. "Smile."

Logan smiled. Molly laughed. "Now that is scary!"

"She's not afraid of you, thank God." He managed a chuckle. "Nobody could ever accuse you of looming."

"Just remember, darling, this is the easy part."

"It can't get much worse."

"Oh, right." Molly laughed. "Tomorrow we pick Dulcy up and take her shopping. Shopping with Anne and Elizabeth at that age makes the Spanish Inquisition seem like a night at the opera. Jeremy and Zoe probably weren't any better."

Logan shook his head. "Sydney always took them shopping. I never did."

"Not once?" Molly laughed ruefully. "Poor Logan. You have got one rude awakening coming."

"Won't I just be in the way?"

"Not a chance, buster. This is only one of the many glorious perks of raising a five-year-old." Molly stood and pulled him up. He bent to kiss her lightly and walked ahead to unlock the door of his room.

"The child needs clothes, shoes, toys, everything," he said as he held the door for Molly.

"First off, darling, she's not the child," Molly said. "She's Dulcy, and for better or worse, she's already her own person." She sighed. "Even if I were not terrified of flying, I would not relish tomorrow's flight."

Logan caught her, tilted her face and looked into her eyes. "Can you endure it?"

She managed a weak smile. "Just pray the planes aren't crowded so we can spread out." She considered a moment. "Maybe we should put off the shopping spree until we're home."

Logan snorted and turned away. "No way. Did you see those shoes? She can't go home in jeans and a football jersey. She needs dresses, toys, a coat . . . everything!"

"Darling, Dulcy really only needs three things. First, to feel safe. Second, to grieve..."

"Grieve?"

"Her mother is dead, her life has gone up in smoke, she's a refugee among strangers. Darn right she needs to grieve. Wouldn't you?"

Logan ran his hand over his forehead. "I am a complete washout at this. Thank God you're here."

"I'm not doing much better. She turned us down flat when we offered to take her to dinner."

He squeezed her hand. "You said three things. What's the third?"

"To reconnect."

"She's already connected with you. She doesn't want to connect with me." He sat on the end of the bed and began to remove his shoes. "You know all this from your volunteer work?"

Molly shook her head. "Lord, no. I'm no professional. I understand a little about what's happening, but I certainly have no idea how to fix it. Helen Dalrymple sat me down and gave me instructions while you were outside watching Dulcy play this afternoon."

"Maybe time will help her bridge the gap. And being surrounded by people who love her." *As I love you,* he longed to say. Molly would be the bridge between him and Dulcy until he learned to handle her on his own.

Later he lay back on the bed and watched Molly through the open door between their rooms as she pulled her sweater over her head and smoothed her ruffled hair. How lovely she was—not just outwardly, but in her heart. Dulcy had recognized it instantly and turned to Molly the way a flower turns to sunlight.

How different his life would have been with Molly. She'd have come with him on all his jobs and brought their children, as well. She'd have carried home with her like a turtle shell, created a haven for them all wherever he had a job. If she had been Zoe and Jeremy's mother, she'd have taught them herself at home if there was no English school available. With her help, he wouldn't have lost the knack of fathering. His children would have grown up strong and secure.

He longed to take Molly back with him to the places he'd lived, show her the things he had created, introduce her to the people whose lives he had bettered. They would adore her as he adored her. She would put everyone at ease, fit easily into mud huts and marble villas.

He leaned back on the bed with his hands locked behind his head and daydreamed about taking Dulcy with him on his next job. Taking Molly, too.

He'd give Dulcy stability and unflagging love. He'd be there for her soccer games or her ballet recitals, whichever she chose. He did not doubt that she'd make the choices herself. Amazing that deprivation, loneliness, neglect had forged her at five into a much stronger person than either of her parents.

Molly must be there to guide them over the rough spots, he decided.

"Will Zoe and Rick meet the plane?" Molly asked from the other room.

"Well, no." Before she could speak, he continued, "Actually, I've been thinking that if you're willing, Dulcy and I could stay with you our first night. Maybe two." He grinned at her. "I'd sleep very chastely on the sofa, of course." He expected to have to convince her.

She leaned around the doorjamb with her toothbrush in her hand. "I was about to suggest the same thing. I promised Dulcy I wouldn't leave her until she got a little more comfortable with you."

Logan raised his eyebrows. "At the rate we're progressing, that could be sometime in the next century."

"Logan, darling, you'll get there." She disappeared.

He followed her into her bathroom and slid his arms around her waist from behind. She leaned against his shoulder. He grinned at their reflection in the mirror. "I don't want to sleep on the sofa."

She arched her eyebrows at him. "I have a guest room."

He nuzzled her neck. "That's not what I meant."

She laughed. "I know."

"That blasted apartment I live in is not set up for children. She needs whatever little girls want in their rooms. Clothes, lots of clothes. A dollhouse. Maybe some of your other dolls."

Molly laughed. "My dolls aren't for five-year-olds, Logan. She needs you, darling, not things. You tried giving your children things, remember. It bombed."

He turned her face up to his and kissed her gently. "You don't mince words, do you, Molly?" He tucked her head under his chin. "I never thought we'd find her. I've made no preparations, nothing. I don't think there's any food in the house."

"Zoe can shop for you."

Logan let out his breath, released her and walked back into her bedroom. Molly followed, holding a towel. "Yes, well. Let's let Rick and Zoe meet Dulcy at your house. We can buy furniture for her, get things ready."

Molly frowned. "Why not let Zoe choose? She's a professional."

"She can help, certainly, then use her expertise to speed up delivery. She keeps a list of painters and decorators." He began to pace.

Molly watched him in growing unease. He was talking about Dulcy as though she were his latest project. Maybe that was the only way he could express his feelings for her.

"She should start school next fall," he continued. "Definitely an accelerated preschool in January. She can already read. In the meantime, I can help her with beginning math, teach her to write."

Molly's discomfort grew.

"I'll have to interview private schools, select the best one, maybe pull strings to get her in at this stage, locate a pediatrician, a dentist. Do you think she needs braces?"

"No," Molly said, and tried to keep her voice light. "She doesn't need a hairdresser or a full-length mink coat, either. Don't start throwing F. A. O. Schwartz and Harvard Medical School at her."

He subsided. "I doubt even F. A. O. Schwartz could make her like me."

Molly threw the towel at him. "She will, Logan. I do."

"I DON'T WANT a dress," Dulcy whispered to Molly. She glared at the rack of froth and ruffles. Tots and Tykes was a large upscale store in a mall, with boys' and girls' clothing, baby clothes, toys, books, even computer games. Dulcy headed directly for the jeans. Logan and Molly followed.

"Dulcy, you should look pretty when you meet your new family," Logan said, trying to sound reasonable and suspecting he sounded stupid. "You can't travel in jeans."

"You wear jeans, MyMolly," Dulcy said with a side-long glance at her grandfather that was pure "gotcha."

"But why don't you want a pretty new dress?" Logan wheedled. "We'll buy you as many as you like. You need a decent coat and some black patent slippers and some new underclothes ..."

Dulcy continued to shake her head. "Nope. Tell him my mommy says I got to dress like a boy."

"Like a boy?"

Dulcy nodded. "I like it. I hate dresses."

"I think your grandfather just wants to spend some money on you, Dulcy. Men like to spend money on their womenfolk sometimes." Molly leaned down conspiratorially. "Makes them feel important."

Dulcy glanced up at her grandfather and shrugged. "Okay. He can buy me some new jeans." She looked down at the threadbare sneakers that were frayed across her toes. There was a knot in one of the shoelaces. "Could I maybe have some new ones of these, My-Molly?" She stuck her foot up. "And maybe a Cardinals sweatshirt? I like baseball. I watch it sometimes when Mommy's at work."

"Molly, you are turning the child into a tomboy at five," Logan said.

"At least I'm not trying to cram lace and ruffles down her throat," Molly whispered. "I don't think she's any more the lace and ruffles type than I am."

"Nope." Dulcy smiled cheerfully. "I liked it when my mommy cut my hair all off so I look like a boy." She curled her lip in a remarkably grown-up sneer. "She put some stuff on it that turned it brown." She rolled her eyes. "It smelled when she put it on. It grew out though. I thought it looked silly but Mommy said I had to when we moved."

Molly froze and gaped at the child's innocent upturned face. "She dyed your hair?"

"I guess." Dulcy could not have been less interested. She wandered off to stare at a stuffed lop-eared bunny wearing a pink satin romper.

She didn't touch the toy, merely gazed at it, her head cocking from side to side in silent appreciation. She sighed and wandered off to look at a line of children's books on shelves beside the stuffed toys. Molly saw her small hands reach out for a book on a shelf above her head, then drop to her sides.

Logan's gaze swiveled from Dulcy to Molly and back again. "Tiffany dyed her hair?" he asked incredulously. He walked over to Dulcy who jumped when his shadow fell across the shelves. She looked up at him and moved sideways out of his reach. "I wasn't going to hurt them," she said to Molly.

Logan wanted desperately to pick her up and crush her against him, but he'd begun to learn that he must move slowly, softly. "Would you like some books?"

"They cost a lot," Dulcy said. She sighed. "Mommy and me got books from the library. You got to give 'em back and if you don't they make you pay money."

His hand hovered over her head like a benediction. At least Tiffany had given her books to read, if not to keep. The woman was an incredible contradiction—allowing Dulcy to fend for herself most of the time, yet taking her to the library.

A child who read the *Lady's Home Journal* wouldn't be interested in the books that were supposed to be for five-year-olds. Without thinking, he reached down, scooped her into his arms and held her up so that she could see the top shelf. He felt her gasp and stiffen. Instantly, he regretted his gesture. He'd backed her into a corner. She couldn't escape.

"I'll buy you as many books as you like," he said quickly. He expected her to struggle. Instead, she froze and every muscle strained away from him. Then over Dulcy's head he saw Molly shake her head. "That is, I'll buy you—" Molly held up her left hand, fingers extended "—five books—any five you like."

Dulcy gasped. "Five whole books? Not my birthday or Christmas or anything?"

"Right." For the first time since that awful meeting, she'd spoken directly to him, not to Molly. Glowing with relief, he turned his body sideways to the shelf so that she could reach it from his arms. Her body felt weightless, her bones fragile as bamboo reeds. She bent forward, and in the sheer delight of selecting the books, no longer seemed concerned that he held her. Molly came over and took them from her as she chose. Several times she changed her mind, but finally Molly held five.

"Please tell him to put me down, MyMolly." Her voice shook.

Obviously it had been only a momentary break in her defenses. Still, it was better than nothing. Logan set her down gently.

She flew to Molly's side. Logan could see her chest heaving.

She held her hands up to take the books from Molly and began to caress them. "Can he afford five whole books?"

"Yes, Dulcy," he said as though she'd spoken to him. "I think I can manage it."

"Can we wait outside, MyMolly?" She grabbed Molly's hand and dragged her toward the door.

"But the jeans?" Logan called.

"I'll come back and load up while you and Dulcy start lunch," Molly answered. Dulcy shook her head. "You don't have to talk to him, Dulcy. It'll be all right.'' Then she said to Logan, "We'll have barely enough time to get everything packed, check out and get to the plane.''

"Come *on*, MyMolly.'' Dulcy pulled on her.

"We'll be at the shoe store,'' Molly said over her shoulder.

Logan watched them. Dulcy wouldn't get off the plane looking like a princess. More like a prince. He shook his head and smiled.

THEY BOARDED the plane with little time to spare. Dulcy's new jeans whished when she walked, and her feet in their shining white Nikes looked twice as big as they were. She carried only two of the five books. Molly had convinced her to pack the others in the new backpack that Logan had bought to hold her new clothes and her few toys. Molly carried the Dulcy doll. Dulcy had refused to check her.

"What if they lose baby Dulcy?'' she had asked.

"How about we ask them to put baby Dulcy up front in the hanging rack?'' Molly asked.

"She'll get smooshed.''

The flight attendant smiled down at Dulcy. "No, she won't. Promise. You can have her in Denver as good as new.'' She picked up the doll, looked carefully at Dulcy and laughed. "Why, she's you!''

"Is not,'' Dulcy said angrily. "I'm bigger. She's a baby.''

"Sorry.'' The attendant raised her eyebrows at Molly. Molly shrugged. So Dulcy did have a temper. Molly hoped she wouldn't pick this fully booked flight to let rip with Helen Dalrymple's "humdinger of a temper tantrum.''

There were two single lines of seats along each side set on top of a small ledge. Molly bumped her head fitting Dulcy into her seat. For a moment she balked at the seat belt, but let Molly close it when she saw the other passengers buckling theirs. Logan sat behind her. Molly slid into her seat across the aisle and fastened her own belt.

As soon as the other passengers settled, Dulcy reached across the aisle for Molly's hand and gripped it tightly. The engines began to rev. Dulcy drummed her feet on the front of her seat. Molly felt her gorge rise and began to pray silently.

Dulcy stared straight ahead. She was breathing hard.

The flight attendant, a slim blond woman with a warm smile, knelt in the narrow aisle by Dulcy's seat. "I'll bet this is your first flight," she said.

Dulcy nodded. Her eyes were wide.

"You're going to love it. Just look out the window and you'll see all the people and cars like toys down below."

Dulcy gulped and held Molly's hand even harder.

The flight attendant took her seat facing them, strapped herself in and the plane began to taxi. Dulcy stared at Molly, who tried to smile reassuringly.

Molly began to lose the circulation in her fingers. Dulcy had the grip of a stevedore.

The plane lifted safely into the air and banked sharply. Dulcy keened. Her heels drummed faster. "I don't like this, MyMolly," she shouted above the engine noise. "I want to go home right now."

"We're way off the ground, Dulcy. Look out your window."

Dulcy glanced to her left. "Nope. I want to go back."

"Baby, we can't," Molly said. The plane lurched. Molly's stomach lurched, too. She tried to smile. "Read one of your new books. We'll be there in no time."

"Nope. You read." Dulcy handed her a paperback with dragons flying across the cover. "Read loud."

Molly leaned her head as close to Dulcy's as she could and began to read at the top of her voice.

Logan watched them, the bright burnished head and the soft silver one. He could see Molly's lips move, but couldn't distinguish the words over the noise of the airplane engines.

He felt a wave of heart-stopping love wash over him. Molly was right. She wasn't "the child." She was Dulcy—a grave, tough little creature with a mind of her own. She was the formidable one. He wasn't even in her league. She'd survived everything her young life had thrown at her without breaking. He had to nurture that strength, even if it meant she fought him too.

But not without Molly. He'd known Molly for less than two weeks yet she'd taught him to feel again when he thought he didn't dare. She'd brought him joy and laughter and ecstasy.

She'd brought him Dulcy.

She must remain a part of his life and Dulcy's. She had to marry him. Together they could build a life. If she wouldn't do it for him, surely she'd do it for Dulcy.

"WHERE'S DULCY?" Molly asked as she sat down.

Logan looked from his newspaper to the seat beside him in the airport waiting area. "Isn't she with you?"

Molly felt a chill run up her backbone. She stared at the crowd of people around the waiting area. "Of course she's not with me."

Logan caught the fear in her voice. "She said she had to go to the bathroom while you were in there. I naturally assumed..."

"God, Logan, she could be anywhere!"

"Don't panic, Molly." Logan fought his own sense of panic. "Check the bathroom. I'll ask at the desk. Maybe she's wandering around and can't find us."

Molly ran into the ladies' room and began calling for Dulcy. She duck-walked down the line of stalls and tried to identify Dulcy's shoes under the doors. "Dulcy! Come on, honey, Molly's waiting for you."

A broad woman wearing a cerise polyester shirt and slacks that had been made for a much smaller woman slammed the door of the stall back against the wall and stepped around Molly, her eyes hard. "Move it, lady."

Molly looked up. "Have you seen a little girl wearing jeans and a red sweater? Short reddish hair, about this tall?"

"Why, ya lost one?" the woman asked.

"Yes!" Molly called after her.

A young girl looked up from the table on which she was changing a fat cheerful baby.

"There was a kid in here a few minutes ago. Bobby Lee, you settle down now, honey." She dropped a diaper hastily over the baby's private parts as a stream of urine began to arc upward.

"Did you see which way she went?" Even as Molly said the words, she knew how stupid she sounded. Dulcy was either here or gone—there was no "seeing which way" to it.

The girl shrugged and shook her head. "No'm."

"Well, if you see her, grab her, please, and get someone from airport security to find me. My name is Molly Halliday. Thanks." Molly ran out the door.

She stood in front of the ladies'-room door and sought a glimpse of Dulcy's head among the throngs who moved down the corridor. To her left, a crowded moving walkway glided to the even more crowded main portion of the airport. On impulse she ran alongside it. She easily out-paced it, but reached the end without spotting Dulcy.

She heard a loudspeaker demanding that Miss Dulcy MacMillan please come to any check-in counter, her family was looking for her. In all the noise, Molly had difficulty deciphering the words. Dulcy wouldn't con-nect Dulcy MacMillan with Dulcy Rigby. She'd been Dulcy Rigby much longer than she'd been MacMillan. Surely Logan must know that.

How could he have let Dulcy go wandering off by her-self? Didn't he remember what five-year-olds were like?

She tamped down her anger. Logan must be terrified and calling himself much worse names than she could think up.

A five-year-old child loose in this airport could be anywhere, with anyone. Dulcy was unused to crowds. She'd be terrified. Anyone might pick her up, take her away. Horrible things happened to unattended children.

"Just let her be all right," she prayed under her breath. "Just let us find her. Please, God, just let her be all right." She began to check the snack shops and souvenir stalls that ran along the right side of the concourse.

LOGAN OFFERED himself as a sacrifice even as he prayed for Dulcy's safety. If anything happened to her because of his stupidity he'd die anyway, so let the powers that be take him instead of putting her into danger.

He should have been more careful, but Dulcy seemed so grown-up, and he'd been so delighted that Dulcy stayed with him while Molly went to the bathroom. He didn't blame her when five minutes later she demanded to follow Molly.

He couldn't very well take her into the ladies' room. When they didn't show up after a couple of minutes, he'd assumed Molly was trying to clean Dulcy up. Airports made everyone feel dirty.

He'd lost track of time because he'd been so certain Dulcy was safe with Molly. Now he realized he should have been more alert. Dulcy wasn't used to either of them, wasn't used to airports. She must be worn-out by the long day and the strange things that had happened to her.

He gave the nearest security guard a description and stood by while the guard talked to the head of security. He heard the loudspeaker.

He was torn between staying in the waiting room so that if she found her way back she'd see him, and needing to do something—anything—to find her.

He turned to the motherly lady who had been sitting beside them on the plane from Laramie. "Madam, are you by any chance taking Flight 630 to Memphis?"

The woman nodded. She dropped her knitting needles in her lap. "You lost your little girl?" she asked.

"She's not used to airports. I thought . . ."

She reached up and touched his arm. "You go on. I know what she looks like. If she shows up, I'll hang on to her for you. I got grandbabies of my own." She laughed. "Sometimes they can be a caution. Squirt out from under you like toothpaste."

"You do remember her?"

"Lord, yes. Couldn't forget that hair."

"Her name is Dulcy. Thank you, Mrs. . . ."

"Mitchell. Irene Mitchell."

He tore off down the concourse before he remembered he had not given Mrs. Mitchell either his name or Molly's.

He could hear the request for Dulcy to communicate with security repeated over and over as he raced down the concourse where Molly had run only moments before. His head swiveled as he searched for Dulcy's head at thigh level among the adult travelers.

Business travelers rushed to catch evening flights that would send them home to sleep in their own beds. Too many people, too many colors. He raced after a child in a red sweater only to find, the moment the crowd cleared, that the child had blond hair and was a boy, not a girl. Under his breath he continued a silent litany for Dulcy's safety.

She'd done this on purpose. When she couldn't find Molly, she'd run away rather than come back to him. He was used to running, but not through crowds that closed in front of him like a football huddle, and not with the adrenaline of his fear pummeling his heart like a sledgehammer. He slowed down for a moment to catch his breath.

Anger welled up in him. How could she do this? When he found her, he'd kill her for frightening them so! He caught his breath.

He knew that when he found her—he refused to allow himself to consider anything else—he'd hug her until her bones cracked and thank God she was safe. If she was.

He skidded to a stop. There were snack bars and shops all along the concourse. Where would she go? He considered going back to have someone check all the ladies' rooms along the concourse. Time enough to do that later, he decided as he scanned the crowd. He couldn't see either Molly or Dulcy.

He began to scout the shops on the left. Dulcy had no money, no identification. There hadn't been time to get her any. Where would she go? he asked himself again.

The ordinary child would go for food or toys. But Dulcy was no ordinary child. He thought back to that first meeting at Helen Dalrymple's. Dulcy had been frightened then. What had she done? She'd bolted to familiar territory.

But there wasn't any familiar territory here. No one who knew her.

What was familiar? What could give her solace?

Books.

He scanned the shops. Halfway down the concourse on the other side he saw a rack of paperback books sitting on the edge of the walkway. He sprinted toward it, barely avoiding falling over a woman in a wheelchair. He sidestepped a baby stroller and kept running.

The shop was deeper than the snack bars. There were rows of magazines and newspapers at the front. In back were racks of hardcover thrillers and romances, paperback mysteries, and finally, in one corner, a rack of books for children.

He spotted her hair before he saw her. She sat in the farthest corner at the back of the store with her feet tight against her rear end and her knees in the air. Her feet in their big white athletic shoes shone like a beacon. She held a large bright book open across her bent knees.

He gulped and tried to slow his breathing. He realized he was sweating and wiped his palms down the sides of his slacks. He didn't want her to see his fear.

Slowly, casually, he sidled into the store until he stood just outside her line of sight. Then he hunkered down. "We lost you," he said softly.

She raised her head. Her face was streaked with tears. There were dark wet patches on her sweater. Her eyes were anguished.

She threw the book aside with a wail and launched herself at him. He felt her thin arms go around his neck.

Her heart beat against his chest like the wings of a mockingbird caught in a snare.

He wrapped his arms around her and stood up with her hanging from his neck like a chain.

The moment they cleared the ground, she wrapped her legs around his waist.

"Where's MyMolly?" she said, sobbing. "I went into that bathroom and she wasn't there and I came out and I couldn't find her and . . ."

"It's all right, Dulcy. I've got you."

"I want MyMolly."

"She's looking for you, too. We'll find her." With the child still attached to his chest, he stooped for the book, picked it up and carried it with him to the counter. He handed it to the bored woman reading *People* magazine. "How much?" he asked. She told him. He tossed a bill on the counter and picked up the book in his one free hand. "Keep the change," he said, and carried Dulcy out of the store.

"Logan! Dulcy!" Molly shouted.

Dulcy turned her face away from Logan and began to wriggle. "MyMolly! Where were you?" she called.

"Not where you thought I was, obviously." Molly ran up to them and threw her arms around Logan, enclosing Dulcy between them in a sandwich. "What possessed you to go running off like that? You scared us pea-green!"

"I get down now, okay?" Dulcy said. Logan slid her down his body until her feet touched the ground. She reached at once for Molly's hand. "MyMolly, I saw you go in and you didn't come out and I thought you were still there and I went in and I couldn't find you and I came out and I couldn't find you and I went looking for you and . . ."

"Hey, kid, it's okay," Molly said, and stroked her hair. "Take a breath. Your grandfather Logan found you." She smiled brilliantly up at Logan.

Dulcy looked at him shyly from beneath her dark red lashes. "I guess so," she said grudgingly. Logan realized she was deeply embarrassed that he'd seen her cry, that she'd lost control so badly that she'd clung to him. He nodded. In a crazy way, he was beginning to understand his grandchild. He decided to respect her privacy.

"Dulcy was fine," he said to Molly. He walked along the concourse beside the two of them. Dulcy held Molly's hand but made no move to take his. "She handled getting lost extremely well, I must say." He glanced down at Dulcy and winked.

She looked at him with suspicion, glanced up at Molly and back at Logan. He thought he caught the tiny flicker of a smile.

Finally. He shared a secret with Dulcy. Maybe, just maybe, she might actually start talking to him instead of through him.

Ten minutes before scheduled departure, a bored voice announced that the plane had been delayed and would leave in an hour. The weather had deteriorated. Through the large windows of the waiting area they watched wind whip tatters of gray fog like dirty cotton batting. Molly shivered.

The day had worn them all out. She had persuaded Dulcy to snuggle down on the two seats at Molly's left, and to pillow her head on Molly's thigh. She brushed the hair back from Dulcy's damp forehead as the child's eyes closed. On the other side of Dulcy, Logan sat with his head dropped to his chest, his eyes closed. He looked exhausted. Molly suspected he'd had no idea how much effort a child Dulcy's age required. No wonder God gave children to the young.

Molly ached from the top of her head to the soles of her feet. The back of her neck felt as though someone had taken every muscle and ligament and tied them into a series of complicated seaman's knots. Even her hair hurt. She longed to doze, but couldn't get comfortable with the weight of Dulcy's head on her thigh. She couldn't disturb the child, so she sat quietly as her leg lost all feeling. From time to time, Logan jumped and shifted in his sleep.

Unfortunately, no matter how long and uncomfortable the wait was for the airplane, Molly knew that at the end of the wait she faced two hours in the air.

When at last they called the plane, she woke Dulcy, who whimpered and tried to go back to sleep.

Logan shook himself and offered to carry her. That snapped her awake.

"Nope," she said, and reached for Molly's hand. He followed them onto the plane.

"This is big," Dulcy whispered as they funneled to their seats. Molly saw that the plane would be full, with no extra room to bed Dulcy down. They sat three abreast, Molly by the window and Dulcy between. Logan slid baby Dulcy into the overhead bin while Dulcy watched him suspiciously. Her eyes were still heavy, but she wasn't sleepy enough to trust Logan. She flinched away from him when he sat down and whined grumpily to Molly, "I want to go home."

"We are going home, Dulcy," Logan said. Dulcy buried her face against Molly's shoulder.

The moment they were airborne, Molly raised her armrest and cradled Dulcy against her. Dulcy fretted, then seemed to settle.

Which was more than Molly managed.

They flew into nothingness. No stars, no city below them, only the thick cotton wool of cloud outside the window. No matter how high they rose, there seemed to be no top to the clouds. The seat-belt sign stayed on, the engines throttled back.

The plane bucked and tilted like a roller-coaster ride. The captain's loud apology for the bumpy ride woke Dulcy, who rubbed her eyes fretfully and sat up whimpering. Only the arrival of the flight attendant with milk and soft drinks kept her in her seat.

She perked up when the cardboard chicken sandwich and tiny cup of ice cream were served. She ate every mouthful as though she were a baby wolf. Molly ate, too. Fear increased her appetite.

Logan picked at his food and finally thrust it away. Dulcy whispered to Molly, who reached over and offered his unopened ice cream to Dulcy, who ate it quickly and without comment.

The pilot continued to apologize for the weather. Molly wished he'd just shut up and fly the dad-gummed plane.

"Shall I read to you?" Molly asked after the snack had been cleared.

"Nunh-unh," Dulcy said. "Are we nearly there?"

"An hour or so," Logan said. "Can you tell time?"

She glanced up at him with pity. "Sure."

"Good, then we'll have to get you a watch so you'll know what time it is."

If Logan expected the offer of a watch to go over big, he was disappointed. Dulcy cut her eyes at him with something approaching a sneer.

Then she threw up.

DULCY SLEPT so deeply in the car that she didn't wake up when Logan carried her into Molly's house.

Molly went ahead of him to Elizabeth's room and turned down the twin bed nearest the hall. The furniture was all white French provincial. The beds were covered by matching log-cabin quilts in pink and turquoise. Horse models and books sat on the shelves. Logan looked around approvingly, then deposited Dulcy carefully onto the bed. She grumbled but did not wake.

"Both of you need a bath," Molly whispered. "I couldn't do much in the plane, even with the attendant's help."

"You're not going to wake her up for that, surely?" Logan asked. "Let the child sleep."

Molly touched his face. "Of course I'm not. Come on before she wakes up." She removed Dulcy's shoes and jeans, but left her sweater on.

Logan thought her legs looked as fine-boned and thin as a stork's. Hadn't Tiffany fed her properly? Had she been living on cereal and milk? Molly took his hand and led him out.

"Except for that one yelp, you handled being thrown up on better than I would have dreamed," Molly said. "Poor Dulcy. She was so embarrassed."

Logan shook his head. "Not her fault. I've done my share of throwing up." Molly trailed him as he went to the car to bring in their bags. He handed her the Dulcy doll. "I'd forgotten children never warn you before they vomit."

"I don't think they know they're going to." Molly picked up Dulcy's duffel in her other hand. "We'll leave these on the other bed."

After Molly left the room, Logan opened the duffel, found Petey and slid the toy rabbit carefully between the covers, by Dulcy's face. Her hair lay damp against her cheek. He brushed it away. She whimpered and wriggled deeper under the covers. She'd seemed so tall and grown-up, but lying in Elizabeth's bed she looked as tiny and fragile as a baby bird.

The smell of childhood vomit clung to her hair. He stood at the door watching her in the glow from Elizabeth's horse-head night-light. Her breathing barely raised the covers.

"What if she wakes during the night?" he asked Molly.

"I'll look in on her." Molly wrinkled her nose. "You hit the shower, buster. You smell like a goat."

"Aren't you going to join me?" he asked hopefully.

"Get real. That's one of the problems with having children. Remember what a crimp Jeremy and Zoe put in your love life? The problem with having babies is that thereafter you have them."

Twenty minutes later, Logan padded barefoot into Molly's living room. She had lit a single lamp in front of the windows and had curled into the wing chair. Her eyes were closed, her breathing soft and regular. From beneath her long lashes, he could see dark circles below her eyes. The face that he thought so full of luscious curves seemed broken into triangles by the shadows.

He'd had no right to push her this way, but he couldn't see any alternative. At least now they were home. He looked around the room. The couch needed re-covering, there were piles of doll and decorating magazines haphazardly spilled on the scarred coffee table. He'd been in this house only twice, yet it already felt more like home than his apartment.

He felt something soft against his ankles. Elvis brushed past him and leaped onto Molly's lap.

She jumped and opened her eyes. In the shadow of the lamp they were not blue but dark as midnight. He dropped beside her chair and put his arms around her. She leaned her head on his shoulder and sighed.

"We found her, Molly. Dear God, I can't believe it even now. Thanks to you, I have my granddaughter back."

CHAPTER FOURTEEN

ANY SATISFACTION from the sandwich they'd eaten on the airplane wore off about nine o'clock that evening and left Molly and Logan famished. Molly checked on Dulcy to see whether she had grown restless from hunger, saw that the child had barely moved in her sleep and let her sleep on.

Molly fixed a Denver omelette and English muffins for herself and Logan. They ate at the kitchen table in a silence not so much companionable as exhausted. Molly saw that Logan's eyes were empty and very far away.

After he was done, she picked up his plate and took it with hers to the sink. "You've got to call Zoe," she said. She turned on the water and rinsed the plates, then arranged them in the dishwasher along with the skillet.

"I don't know what to say to her." Logan handed her the silverware as casually as though he were in his own home. "Besides, it's after ten. I'll call tomorrow morning. If I call tonight, she'll rush over here."

"You've got to tell her you're home safely. That's just good manners. Tell her Dulcy's asleep and ask both her and Rick to come for breakfast tomorrow morning," Molly said reasonably. "Dulcy will probably get up very early. It's a strange bed in a strange house. She'll be ravenous. She threw up everything she ate. I'll give her some cereal to take the edge off her hunger, get her bathed and dressed, then you can take her down to feed Maxie and Eeyore and the geese while I fix breakfast for all of us."

"Do you think she'll go with me?"

"You don't have to talk, just walk. Besides, she actually spoke to you in the car. You didn't yell when she threw up. Could be she's decided you're not Dracula, after all. Check it out. Ask Rick and Zoe for about nine. Then if Dulcy should sleep late, which I doubt, we'll wing it."

He put his arms around her waist from behind and pulled her to him. "You are a remarkable woman."

"No, merely a practical one." She leaned against him gratefully. "And at the moment, both a very tired and a very dirty one." She turned her head so that she could kiss his chin. Stubble pricked her lips. "I'm sorry you have to sleep in the guest room."

"Not nearly as sorry as I am." He turned her so that he could kiss her lips. Her head dropped back and she came against him, fitting into the curves of his body as though she'd been formed to match him. He kissed her gently, softly, and then more urgently. She felt his passion growing to match her own.

Gasping, she shoved him away. "At this rate, we're going to wind up in the middle of the kitchen floor."

He laughed and waggled his eyebrows at her. "Sounds good to me." He ran his hand up her back beneath her sweater and began to fumble with the hook of her bra. "Dulcy's sound asleep. We'll have time..."

Molly twisted away. "No we don't. The last thing she needs is to walk in on a wrestling match between Tugboat Annie and The Incredible Hulk."

Logan chuckled. "You win. Go take your shower while I phone Zoe." As she turned to go down the hall, he patted her rear and she swatted at his hand.

Five minutes later, she stood in the shower and let the remains of the hot water sluice over her clean body and hair. She wondered if anyone had ever fallen asleep in a shower and drowned.

Suddenly, the door to the bathroom opened. "Molly! She's gone again!" Logan pulled the shower curtain back.

Molly grabbed a towel and stepped out of the shower. "Gone? She can't be!"

"God, Molly! I was sitting in the living room talking to Zoe on the telephone. I could see both the front and back doors. The chains are still on."

Molly grabbed her terry-cloth robe from its hanger behind the door and slipped it onto her still-damp body. "She went out a window?"

Logan ran ahead of her. "The window in her room's still shut and latched."

"Did you check under the bed?"

"Of course I did. First thing."

"Then she must be in the house." The door to the hall stood open. Molly looked into Elizabeth's darkened room across the hall. In the light from the bathroom and the night-light, she could see the covers on the single bed pulled back, the pillow missing.

She turned to Logan and whispered, "Is she in the bathroom?"

"No, I looked," Logan said.

Molly shoved him back down the hall toward the kitchen. He was right. Chained from the inside. "She's got to be here."

He leaned on the counter with both hands. "I hung up the phone. I could hear your shower. I walked down the hall to check on her, opened the door to her bedroom, and nothing! She can't have vanished."

"Of course she didn't vanish." Molly turned around in a circle as though she expected to find the child hiding beside the refrigerator. "Okay. I'll start in the guest room. Maybe she sneaked by my room while I was in the shower. You start in Elizabeth's bedroom. A child can hide in very small spaces."

Elvis wound around Molly's ankles as she followed Logan down the hall. It was as close as the cat ever came to welcoming her home after one of her trips, but tonight he was also jealous of all the interlopers and demanding her undivided attention. Molly picked him up and slung him across her shoulders like a feather boa. "You can sleep with me tonight. Nobody else is going to." She tossed him onto her bed. He jumped off and raced back into the hall after her.

She opened the door to the guest room, flicked on the lights, saw the undisturbed candlewick spread. A week's worth of dust lay on the nightstand.

"I found her," Logan whispered.

Molly jumped. "Don't sneak up on me like that." Then she registered his words. "Where is she?"

"On the floor in the very back of Elizabeth's closet. She's made a bed with the quilt and her pillow. She's got Petey in her arms and baby Dulcy sitting up beside her."

"Thank God."

"I suppose she woke up in a strange room and went back into hiding. I'd hoped we were past that."

"Pretty good way to handle her fears, if you ask me."

"But what are her fears?" he asked. "How can we help her if we don't know how she got to this point?"

Molly leaned against his shoulder and hooked her arm under his. "Maybe Tiffany taught her to hide to keep her safe."

"Maybe she had to hide from Tiffany," Logan said. "She's like a fawn, Molly."

"More like a coyote pup." Molly chuckled. "No hiding in the long grass while the wolf pack circles. She dives for the den and hunkers down. There are neither sheets nor blankets on this bed, Logan. If you're going to sleep in the guest room, you can help me make it up."

Wearily, she pulled herself erect and went to bring blankets and sheets from the linen closet in the hall.

Logan caught the other side of the fitted sheet when she flipped it at him and tucked it under the sides of his mattress. "I can move her back to bed without waking her. We can't leave her where she is."

"Why not?" Molly tucked in her side of the sheet and flipped the top sheet toward him.

Absently, Logan smoothed the sheet and made a neat hospital corner at the foot.

Molly tilted her head. "I never tuck in sheets. You're much too neat for me."

"Are you sure we shouldn't move Dulcy back to her bed?"

"And have her wake up thinking she'd been teleported? Now, wouldn't that disorient the dickens out of anybody?" Molly flicked the blanket into place. "There. You're all set."

Logan looked at the bed. He wanted a bed with Molly in it, sleeping beside him, curled against his back or snuggled against his shoulder. That wasn't possible.

But damnation, neither was this. He gathered up the blanket and added a pillow. "If that child can sleep on the floor, so can I. If she wakes up in the middle of the night, I'm going to be there. She may not want to see me, but I'll be damned if she'll wake up alone."

Molly started to protest, then stopped. She came around the bed and leaned across the bedding to kiss him softly. "I think that's a very good idea, my dear."

MOLLY WOKE to the sound of mockingbirds and the pressure of small bony feet against her backside. She groaned and just managed to turn over without falling off the edge of the bed. Dulcy lay curled on her side in the center of the bed with Petey clutched to her chest. She must have wandered in during the night and wriggled in beside Molly, then spent the next several hours staking out most of the bed as her own. Molly raised herself onto one elbow. Elvis slept in the angle behind Dulcy's knees, snoring.

In Elizabeth's room, Logan woke from his pallet on the floor beside the bed and remembered why he hated camping. Every place his bones had come in contact with the carpeted floor, he hurt. He groaned, stretched and struggled to his feet. Then he looked in the closet.

This time he didn't react. Dulcy's disappearing-child routine was becoming just that—a routine. He decided to look over the house before alarming Molly. If Dulcy had wakened during the night to find him guarding her like a German shepherd, she was perfectly capable of going to sleep in one of the kitchen cabinets.

He glanced into Molly's room, saw the bright head curled on the pillow beside the silver one and smiled. He went to see if he could find the makings for coffee.

He looked through the overhead kitchen cabinets with no success. Where would Molly keep coffee? A coffee grinder sat on the kitchen counter beside an electric coffeemaker. So, she ground her own beans. He thought a moment and opened the refrigerator. No beans. Then he opened the freezer. Bingo. He began to search for measuring spoons.

Molly was the key to living with Dulcy. That much was obvious. The child trusted her, sought her out, connected with her in a way that even Helen Dalrymple hadn't managed.

He found a scoop, measured the beans into the grinder and turned it on. The buzz sounded like a fire alarm in the silent house. As soon as he judged it prudent, he shut the thing off.

Dulcy hadn't mentioned her mother since they got on the plane at Laramie. He knew she hadn't forgotten, but she'd been too busy dealing with new problems. Should he talk about Tiffany or leave it to Dulcy to bring up her mother?

He found a box of coffee filters tucked in behind the coffeemaker and began to make the coffee strong. This morning he needed extra caffeine. The next few hours were not likely to be pleasant.

Elvis padded into the kitchen and growled expectantly at his food dish.

"I have no idea what to feed you, cat. Or how much. You'll have to wait for Molly."

The cat sat and began to wash itself. Its tail lashed impatiently.

"He wants his cheese," Molly said. She still wore her morning face, devoid of makeup, shiningly clean. Her eyes were too bright, too young, too aware for a woman who had spent the day from hell yesterday. She came to him and snuggled against him with her arms around his waist. "A while back, I started giving him a bit of cheese in the morning. Now he expects it and grumbles if he doesn't get it."

"I am too old to sleep on floors," he whispered against Molly's hair. "And Dulcy still managed to climb over me without waking me. Fine watchdog I am." He kissed her.

"She kicks," Molly said, and rubbed her backside. "I'd rather sleep with you."

"MyMolly?" Dulcy trotted into the kitchen. "Where are you, MyMolly?"

Molly swung so that she could smile at the child, but she didn't release her hold on Logan's waist. "Right here. You scared us half to death last night."

"How come?"

"Your grandfather went to check on you and you'd disappeared."

"That's a really big bed."

"And a strange one, I know. Your grandfather Logan found you, so he slept on the floor in your room all night so you wouldn't wake up and be scared."

"I wasn't scared." Dulcy's head went up and her jaw stuck out. "I don't ever get scared." Her eyes dared her grandfather to snitch about her bout of tears in the airport. Logan winked at her.

"How about some cereal?" Molly asked, and moved away from Logan. "We'll have breakfast in a little while but you're probably hungry."

Dulcy shrugged. "I guess."

"Then we'll get you bathed and dressed. Did you know my granddaughter Elizabeth keeps a pony here?"

Dulcy's eyes glowed. "A real pony? Can I see it?"

"After you're dressed, your grandfather will take you down and you can help feed the pony. And the donkey and the geese."

Dulcy looked sideways at her grandfather who stood mute, one arm around Molly's waist. "I guess." She shrugged and trailed away down the hall, dragging Petey behind her.

"Yes!" Logan whispered. It took a pony to do it, but Dulcy had agreed to go walking with him without Molly along. That was real progress.

Elvis lashed his tail and prepared to attack Petey, then heard Molly open the refrigerator door and came instead to yowl at her feet.

"See, I told you so," Molly said. "And please give me some coffee. Then you can use my bathroom while I help Dulcy take a bath. Hop to it, man! Zoe and Rick will be here before you know it!"

"WHAT DID Zoe say when you told her about Dulcy?"

Logan poured another cup of coffee. "I didn't tell her."

"What?"

"Now, listen, Molly, before you lose your temper. She and Rick should be here any minute now. All I told her was that I had an incredible surprise for her."

Dulcy sat between them at the kitchen table working assiduously on one of Elizabeth's old coloring books. A large box of well-used crayons sat open in front of her.

Logan looked at her bent head fondly. He reached out a hand as though to caress her hair, let it linger in the air a few inches above her head, then withdrew it without touching her.

"Who's Rick and Zoe, MyMolly?" asked Dulcy without looking up from her book. She spread the boxed crayons with her fingers so that she could insert the dark green crayon carefully with the other greens. She appraised the emerald cow with a frown, nodded in satisfaction, selected a purple crayon and began to color the pig a vibrant fuchsia.

"They are your aunt and uncle, Dulcy, my daughter and her husband," Logan said. Dulcy glanced up at him, nodded once and bent her head to the emerging purple pig. "How many more?"

"Excuse me?" Logan asked.

Molly laughed. "These are about the last. Certainly the last you'll have to meet today. I have a daughter named Anne. She's married to my son-in-law, Phil, and they have a granddaughter named Elizabeth. She's a few years older than you. You won't have to meet them right now. We'll wait until you're used to these before we spring any more on you."

"Good." Dulcy sighed deeply and replaced the purple crayon with a salmon-pink one. She started on the sky.

Logan had been staring over her shoulder. "Do you think she's color-blind?" he whispered.

Dulcy raised her head. "Tell him I know cows aren't green." Then she did an extraordinary thing. She patted his hand. "But the sky gets pink sometimes."

Logan froze at her touch. She went immediately back to her coloring. Logan looked at Molly over Dulcy's head and saw that she was on the verge of tears. So, he realized, was he.

Then Molly laughed. "I think purple pigs might be a distinct improvement."

The alarm sounded. Dulcy jumped and stared at Molly in terror. "It's okay, Dulcy," she said. "I have a bell down by the road. It bongs when people drive in the driveway."

"I got to meet 'em?"

"Won't hurt a bit, I promise."

"Nunh-unh."

"Then how about you stay here and keep coloring. After a little while, you can come on in. It's just your uncle Rick and your aunt Zoe. They don't bite. I'll be right with you."

Dulcy considered. "Okay, I guess."

Logan grabbed Molly's arm on her way to the front door. "God, Molly, what if they don't see the resemblance? What if they don't believe me?"

"They won't have a choice. Come on, pardner, you got yourself into this. Let's see you get yourself out."

Dulcy called, "MyMolly, don't go away, okay?"

"Wouldn't think of it." She opened the door.

"Hello, Mrs. Halliday," Zoe said. She looked at her father, her eyes full of suspicion. "What's the surprise? Did you and Mrs. Halliday get married?"

Molly gulped. Logan glanced over at her and smiled. "No, although that's a suggestion worth pursuing. Maybe you two had better sit down. This may come as a shock."

"Oh, Lord, what now?" Zoe asked.

"Molly and I went on a quest. I'm glad to say we have been successful. We have found Dulcy alive and well and brought her home to stay."

Dulcy picked that moment to peep around the edge of the kitchen door. Zoe took one look at her, locked her hands across her mouth and shrieked.

Dulcy bolted. She raced down the hall and into the guest room. The door slammed. Molly went after her.

Behind her she could hear Zoe's hysterical sobs mixed with Rick's comforting murmurs and Logan's explanations.

Molly knocked on the door. "It's just me. I'm all by myself. Can I come in?"

No sound.

Molly tried the door. It was unlocked. She opened it just far enough to stick her head in. Dulcy was nowhere to be seen. The door of the closet was suspiciously ajar. Molly went in softly. A moment later she heard footsteps behind her and turned to see Rick, his hands in his pockets, standing in the doorway.

"Where is she?" he whispered.

Molly pointed to the closet.

Rick walked over to the nearest twin bed and sat down Indian-fashion on the floor. Molly gave him a thumbs-up sign and sat in the rocking chair at the corner of the room. The two sat without speaking. The only noise in the room was the creak of Molly's rocker.

Finally Rick said to the closet door, "Sorry about that. Zoe wasn't expecting to see you, Dulcy. Sometimes she gets a little uptight."

Silence. Molly continued to rock to let Dulcy know that she was there. She smiled encouragingly at Rick.

"You see," he said to the closet, "you've been gone a very long time. Zoe didn't think she'd ever see you again."

The door moved an inch.

Rick propped his hands on his knees, closed his eyes and leaned his head back against the mattress. "You want to come out, I promise I won't yelp at you."

"Men don't yelp," Dulcy said from the closet. Her voice was surprisingly strong and deep. Apparently she had no trouble speaking directly to Rick, but then maybe he didn't remind her of a vampire.

"Some do." He leaned over and picked Petey up from the floor beside the bed. "Nice rabbit. He yours?"

The child's bright head appeared around the door of the closet, her gray eyes focused on the worn rabbit as though she was prepared to do battle over him.

Rick reached out to the closet as far as he could, and when Dulcy made no move to come toward him, he laid the rabbit on the carpet between them and dropped his hands to the floor.

Dulcy knelt in the doorway on all fours. She looked over at Molly, then reached a tentative hand toward the rabbit. She drew back when she realized she couldn't touch Petey without coming all the way out of the closet. She looked Rick over appraisingly.

"I won't grab at you," he said.

"Cross your heart and hope to die?"

He crossed himself and locked his hands behind his head.

Molly stood. Dulcy looked up at her from the floor and scooted back into the closet doorway.

"He's okay, Dulcy," Molly said. "I need to go back up the hall to talk to Zoe. I trust him."

Dulcy dropped her head and peered at Rick from beneath pale red eyelashes. "You sure, MyMolly?"

"Promise." Molly walked softly to the door and into the hall, but left the bedroom door open behind her so that Dulcy had an escape route if she chose to take it.

Dulcy sat back on her haunches and raked Rick with her eyes. She sighed.

Rick waited.

Slowly she slid out of the closet on her hands and knees and crawled close enough to pick up Petey. She sat flat on the floor between her heels, as only supple children can do. She listened to the drone of words from the living room, her head cocked on one side.

Rick followed her glance and smiled. "Your aunt Zoe's a nice lady. She didn't mean to scare you."

"What's your name?"

"I'm your uncle Rick. Rick Jackson."

"I gotta call you Unca Rick?"

"Rick's fine. May I call you Dulcy?"

She relaxed. "Sure, that's my name."

After a moment he asked, "Where did your grandfather and Molly find you?"

"On a big ranch with cows and lots of big kids." She wrinkled her nose as though the memory was not a particularly pleasant one. "My mommy's dead," she said.

He caught his breath.

"It's okay. MyMolly says that means she's here looking after me but you can't see her." She glanced at the ceiling. "MyMolly and my grandfather Logan came and got me out of that place with all the kids and we got on a little airplane and then a big bumpy airplane and I threw up all over Grandfather Logan." She laughed, a deep laugh for a child.

Rick laughed with her. "That must have been some picture."

"He didn't yell at me or anything." She considered. "I thought he would but he didn't."

"Wasn't your fault."

"MyMolly says we got to teach him about little kids. I'm trying, but it's hard." She inched closer until she leaned her back against the bed. She sat Petey in her lap and locked her hands behind her head in perfect imitation of Rick. "I colored a green cow and a purple pig and he thought I didn't know better." She shook her head and sighed.

Rick heard Zoe's footsteps coming tentatively down the hall.

Dulcy stiffened, dropped her hands and prepared to bolt again.

Rick leaned over toward her, but did not touch her.

"It's okay," he whispered. "Zoe won't yell again."

Dulcy cut her eyes at him and held her ground. She inched over so that her shoulder touched his arm.

"Hang tough," he told her. "Women get emotional about little kids."

Dulcy whimpered and leaned harder against Rick.

Zoe opened the door slowly and carefully. Her cheeks were wet with tears, her eyes and nose fiery. She breathed in hiccups. Her pulse jumped at the base of her throat. She stared at Dulcy with a kind of awe.

Rick bobbed his head at her, dropping his eyes to the floor and back to her face again.

Zoe caught the signal and sank to all fours, then sat down on the floor with her legs crossed. He winked and smiled at her.

Zoe cleared her throat. "Hi, Dulcy. I'm your aunt Zoe."

"Hi," Dulcy whispered. She glanced up at the man beside her for support and went on in a stronger voice, "Rick says I don't have to call him Unca Rick."

"You don't have to call me Aunt Zoe, either. Just call me Zoe."

"That's a funny name."

Zoe laughed shakily. "I agree. It's my father's mother's name, so I got stuck with it."

"Who's that?"

"My father—your grandfather."

Dulcy sighed and recited, "Grandfather Logan is your daddy. He's my daddy's daddy. My daddy's dead. So's my mommy." She looked up at Rick. "If my mommy's up there looking after me, is my daddy, too?"

"Absolutely."

"And now you've got me and Rick and your grandfather to look after you, as well," Zoe said.

"And MyMolly. She looks after me best. I love MyMolly."

"Yes, but..." Zoe began.

Rick shook his head at her. "Of course you do," he said.

"I'm going to stay here with MyMolly forever and ever."

CHAPTER FIFTEEN

"I CANNOT BELIEVE my father is letting Dulcy think she's going to live with Molly Halliday," Zoe said. She stared out the window of Rick's truck. He could hear the quaver in her voice. She dragged a hand across her cheek under her eyelashes. He saw the flash of moisture on her fingers in the morning sunlight that streamed in through the windshield.

"Logan's just staying there long enough to get things ready at the apartment. Isn't that what he said?"

"That's not what Dulcy thinks. God, what a mess!"

"Aren't you happy he found Dulcy?"

"Of course I am, but Rick, my father has no more business raising that child than he . . . than he had taking care of me and Jeremy. He hasn't a clue about children."

"And you do?"

"Yes I do! At least I know she doesn't belong in that damned mausoleum over the store without even a backyard to play in."

"Look, you've got to open the store and I've got a job in Germantown." Rick pulled over to the curb, switched off the engine then turned to her. "But this is more important."

He took her hand. "Zoe, you told me how your mother always treated him like an outsider, made him feel incompetent. Isn't that what you're doing? Making him feel guilty for all those years he wasn't there and at the same time not giving him a chance to atone?''

She whirled to look at him, her face tight with rage. ''He's the one who's shutting me out! My God, the most important thing to happen to this family since my mother died and he goes off with that woman and doesn't even give me a hint!'' She jerked her hand away. ''How dare he! Atone? By giving Dulcy all the care he should have given me and Jeremy? It doesn't work that way.'' She burst into tears and beat her fists against her knees. ''Oh, Lord, listen to me!''

Rick pulled her over against him and wrapped his arms around her. ''I know, baby, I know.''

She wrenched away. ''You can't know.'' She banged her head back against the headrest. The pulse at the base of her throat thrummed like a jungle drum. ''One part of me is so glad we found Dulcy—I can't begin to get a grip on how I feel.'' She reached into the purse at her feet, dug around and came up with a tissue. She blew her nose. ''The other part is so jealous that every time my father looks at her with that sappy smile on his face, I want to slug him.''

''She sure doesn't smile back.''

Zoe turned to look at him. Her eyes grew contemplative. ''No she doesn't, does she? She doesn't smile at all, even at you.''

He grinned and reached across to knead her shoulder. ''And women find me irresistible.''

She smiled back mistily. ''He's wrong for her. I feel it, Rick. You're the father she should have.''

''Baby, I'm not the father on the custody papers. And you're not her mother. All we can do is be there for her, give Logan as much help as he'll allow. That means we stay on his good side and don't rock the boat.''

"For the moment."

He took in the set of her jaw, the faraway look in her eyes and groaned inside. He knew the signs. Zoe had a plan. And Zoe with a plan could be dangerous.

"THAT WENT better than I hoped," Logan said. He stood on the front steps with his arm around Molly's waist long after Rick's truck disappeared from view.

"Better than you deserved."

"You're right. Strange, I've considered myself the unluckiest man alive for a long time. Since I met you, Molly, my luck has changed. You're my guardian angel."

"I am nobody's angel. Ask my friends. Oh, Lord, I haven't even called Sherry to tell her about Dulcy, and she's the oldest friend I've got."

"Where is Dulcy?"

"In her room playing with baby Dulcy."

"I need to take her home, Molly, to my apartment."

"Not yet. Her room's not ready. You're welcome to stay until it is."

He nibbled her ear. "I was hoping you'd say that. Just for a couple of days. It's a problem moving the child again so soon."

"But I absolutely have to get to work. Quentin Dillahunt's grandmother will be after my hide. You'll have to baby-sit."

"Of course." He ran his lips across the nape of her neck, smiled at her involuntary shiver and replaced lips with the tip of his tongue.

She caught her breath. "Whoa, there. At this rate, I'll never get any work done."

"My dear Molly, I haven't held you in my arms for a century. You are a difficult habit to break."

She leaned her head against his shoulder. "Logan, have you thought that maybe there's another solution?"

He tightened his grip. "Of course." So Molly had realized the same thing—the three of them, Dulcy, Molly and he, should be a family.

"Maybe she belongs with Rick and Zoe."

He stiffened. "Absolutely not. Don't be ridiculous."

"But—"

He dropped his arms and turned away. "I won't discuss it."

"But Logan, can't you see—"

"MyMolly, MyMolly, where are you?" Dulcy called.

"Right here, my Dulcy. On the front steps," Molly called.

Dulcy ran onto the porch, spared Logan a quick glance and launched herself at Molly. "You won't go away, will you?"

Molly picked her up with a grunt.

Dulcy wrapped her legs around Molly's waist and her arms around Molly's neck. "Can I see the pony again? And the donkey? And the geese and stuff?"

"Of course you can, Dulcy." Work would have to wait. "Come on, Logan, we'll all pay a social call on the animals."

Logan watched Molly teach Dulcy how to throw the corn for the geese as far as she could, and how to hold sweet feed for Maxie and Eeyore flat in the palm of her hand so that they didn't nibble her fingers by mistake. Dulcy didn't smile, but her small face glowed as she concentrated on flattening her hand. She threw the feed too close, then hid behind Molly when the geese toddled up. Molly shooed them and laughed as they waddled away snicking grumpily.

"Now, Dulcy, let me show you where I made baby Dulcy."

Molly walked down the path, unlocked the front door to her workshop and flipped on the lights.

"You made baby Dulcy here?" Dulcy looked around at the couches and tables.

"No, darling. Through my showroom to the little room in back. I generally go in through the back door directly into the workroom, but I thought you might like to see my other dolls."

Dulcy grew quiet and took Molly's hand.

"Now, these aren't dolls like little girls play with. These are big-girl dolls—very expensive. Zoe is going to sell them for a great deal of money in her store. I know it'll be hard for you not to touch, but these dolls are made of bisque—that's like glass. It breaks very easily. Think you can manage not to touch?"

Dulcy nodded gravely. Molly unlocked the door to the showroom and turned on the lights.

Logan followed them inside. Suddenly he felt as though he'd been thrown back to the moment when he discovered the Dulcy doll. He could barely believe so much had happened in such a short time. That Logan MacMillan had been lonely, angry, frustrated and driven to despair by too much grief. He didn't recognize that man any longer. Before Molly came into his life, he had fought any kind of feelings. Now he drowned in love as then he had almost drowned in despair, but this time he didn't fight. He surrendered.

Dulcy walked the room silently as he had walked, her hands clasped behind her back as his had been clasped. She reminded him so much of Jeremy as a child that he felt tears start in his eyes.

He would bring Dulcy up strong and straight. He couldn't fail so long as Molly was with him. How could she even consider giving Dulcy to Rick and Zoe? Dulcy was his just as Molly was his.

"The dolls are very beautiful, MyMolly," Dulcy whispered reverently.

"Thank you, Dulcy."

"But I like baby Dulcy best. She don't break."

"Doesn't break."

"Uh-huh. That's what I said."

Molly smiled at her. "So would you like to see my workroom where all these dolls start? That's the room I really care about." She went back to the front door. Logan moved aside.

"Sorry, Logan. Security system. This room is locked off from the others front and back. I unlocked it before you came the other day."

Logan followed her as she unlocked the door at the back of the room, stepped through, turned on the lights, then stood aside to let him and Dulcy go through before she locked the inside door to the showroom behind her.

"Oh, MyMolly, look at all the little feet and hands!"

Logan had never seen this room. In contrast to the others, this room was as antiseptic and utilitarian as a hospital. Floor-to-ceiling white shelves held body parts segregated by size and type. The floor was bare red quarry tile. A kiln squatted in the corner like a square brown toad. A high worktable ran across the back wall. Under the left side of the table ran a bank of shallow drawers next to a small refrigerator. Then came a clear space with a single bar stool shoved against it, then another deeper bank of drawers.

There were no pictures on the walls, no distractions from the work except a portable CD player that sat on brackets above the worktable.

The upper bookshelves held square Styrofoam boxes, small wig blocks, some with wigs on them, and dozens of small oblong boxes. The lower shelves held painted and unpainted arms, legs and bodies, and even some unpainted heads.

Logan looked at the small boxes and frowned. "What goes in those?" he asked.

"Eyeballs," Molly said.

She laughed at his horrified expression. "The best ones come from Germany. They're made of glass and of course they come in pairs. The boxes are molds." She took one down from a high shelf and opened it. "See, Dulcy, there's room for a doll's head inside this box. The others have places for hands and feet and bodies and arms and legs and all the parts that make you a doll—and a person."

"This is where you made baby Dulcy?"

"Right here. And I'm going to be working here most of the time the next few days. I've got some catching up to do."

"Can I help?"

"You can keep me company some if you'd like." She looked up at Logan. "But your grandfather is going to have lots for you to do."

Dulcy looked over at Logan sulkily. "Like what?"

"We have to buy you some more clothes and some furniture," he told her. "We have to go see my apartment. Zoe's asked us to come have lunch with her tomorrow."

"I got furniture."

"That's Elizabeth's furniture. You need some of your own."

"I guess."

"And Friday afternoon after school my granddaughter Elizabeth is coming to spend the night," Molly told her. "She's eleven."

"A big girl?" Dulcy asked hopefully.

"Maxie is her pony."

"Will she maybe let me ride him?"

"That's up to Elizabeth. But I'll talk to her."

"Okay, MyMolly." She sighed and yawned.

"It's been quite a day already, hasn't it, darling? How about a glass of milk and an apple?"

"Can I have a cookie instead?"

Molly glanced up at Logan. He raised his eyebrows and shrugged.

Molly smiled. "Apple now, cookie later."

Now it was Dulcy's turn to shrug.

Logan followed the two up the hill with a short detour by Maxie and Eeyore's paddock to rub both equine noses.

He didn't know the right answer to the simplest questions Dulcy asked. He didn't even know for certain if she should have an apple or a cookie. He couldn't manage without Molly.

Dulcy complicated everything and speeded everything up, as well. He no longer had the luxury of allowing his relationship with Molly to develop slowly. He'd ask Rick and Zoe to let Dulcy spend the night with them Saturday. He was certain Zoe would jump at the chance to have the child to herself. He and Molly definitely needed some time alone. He didn't just want her company, he wanted to make love to her. Sleeping in the same house and not in the same bed as Molly had been hell.

He would make love to her, and then as they drowsed in each other's arms, sated with love, he'd ask her to marry him.

He'd remind her of her promise to stay close to Dulcy. He wasn't above making Molly feel guilty if she hesitated. He knew he was right. The three of them belonged together. Molly would see that. Besides, he needed Molly to be his wife and Dulcy's mother, and he needed her now.

Sunday morning when he picked Dulcy up from Zoe and Rick's he could announce to them that he and Molly were to be married as soon as possible.

AFTER LUNCH, Logan moved Molly's rocking chair from the reception room of the workshop to Molly's workroom so that Dulcy would have a place to read. She refused to nap—that was for "little girls." His instinct was to force her to lie down in her bed, but when Molly told her she could come read in the workroom instead, Logan accepted her decision.

While he was alone in Molly's house, he called Adam Carswell, the owner of the mortuary that had picked up Tiffany's casket at the airport.

"We've taken care of everything just as we discussed over the telephone," Carswell said. "We've made all the arrangements for a private graveside ceremony next Wednesday morning at ten."

"And the headstone?"

"Should be finished in plenty of time."

"Thank you." Logan sighed as he hung up the telephone. His instinct was not even to mention the graveside service to Zoe, but he knew he must. She would certainly not want to attend. Molly would go with him. He could always count on her. No doubt Zoe would be happy to keep Dulcy with her at the store while he and Molly were at the cemetery.

Someday he would take Dulcy to see the graves of her parents, someday he would have a memorial service for Tiffany, but not now, not while he was trying to integrate Dulcy into her new life.

He had to admit that Dulcy's constant need for attention wore him out. He leaned back in Molly's wing chair and closed his eyes. When the telephone rang, he jumped. He cleared his throat and answered the phone, expecting to take a message for Molly.

"Lieutenant Holman, Mr. MacMillan."

Logan froze. He and Dulcy were no longer under the jurisdiction of the state of Wyoming. How had they tracked him to Molly's? What could they possibly want now? "Yes, Lieutenant," he said as calmly as he could. "How did you find me here?"

"Mrs. Halliday left her name with me, too. When all I got at your place was an answering machine, I decided to try her place."

"You're a good detective. What can I do for you?" Logan cleared his throat. His mouth was suddenly so dry he couldn't swallow.

"Something's come up here, Mr. MacMillan. I thought you might want to know."

"Something about Dulcy?"

"Not directly, no." Logan heard the hesitation in Holman's voice almost as though the lieutenant had changed his mind.

"Whatever it is, tell me."

"Yeah. Okay. We found where Terry Rigby did her banking here in Laramie."

Logan relaxed. "Good. Her trust officers will need that information for her estate. It's probably going to be a month or so before we even start considering probate. I'm perfectly capable of supporting Dulcy without her mother's money."

"No, you don't understand. You got a fax machine?"

"In my daughter's store."

"Let me have the number. Got some real interesting checks you might like to see copies of."

Logan gave him the number. "What's this all about?"

"First you got to promise me you won't go off half-cocked."

"I don't make promises I don't understand."

"Look, MacMillan, I probably shouldn't be giving you any of this, but, oh, what the hell." Logan heard the deep breath over the phone. Holman plunged ahead. "Seems like every month since Terry Rigby moved to Laramie, there's been a three-hundred-dollar check sent to somebody in your town. A Mr. Youngman."

Logan sat down hard. "Damn it to hell! I knew it!"

"That's not all. I had a hunch. I got onto your local police, and they pulled his phone records for the last couple of months. Guess what?"

"I have no idea."

"Somebody at that number called the place where Terry Rigby worked at seven the evening she died."

"That bastard! He was trying to warn her so she could vanish again."

"Thing is, the bar manager now admits Tiffany really freaked after the call. That's when she started drinking shooters like there was no tomorrow. He sent her home. Said she was too drunk to stand up, much less tend bar. Took her car keys away from her. Told her to take a cab. She walked, fell, and the rest you know."

"So that bastard Youngman was responsible for Tiffany's death."

"You can't say that—not exactly."

"The hell I can't."

"Anyway, I asked your locals to talk to him. Seems this Youngman has taken a powder. Not surprising."

"Why haven't the police called me?"

"No reason to until they find Youngman—maybe not even then."

"So why'd you call me?"

"I knew you were upset about what happened to Tiffany, and I didn't want you to find out about Youngman some other way and go after him."

"Wise of you." Logan wiped his free hand down his face, and looked down at the moisture in surprise. He hadn't realized he was sweating. "Molly and I suspected he knew Dulcy was alive, but until now there was no way to prove it."

"Hey, this is still no proof he knew the kid was alive. Maybe he was just blackmailing Tiffany."

Logan leaned back in the wing chair. Finally he could be the one explaining to Holman. "Lieutenant, unless Youngman knew that Dulcy was alive, there was no basis for blackmail. Tiffany had disappeared before, she could do it again, particularly if she no longer had a small child with her. But so long as Youngman knew that Dulcy was still with her mother, all he had to do was threaten to tell me my granddaughter was still alive. Tiffany would have paid him any amount of money to keep that particular secret."

"Yeah, well. It's weird, you know. According to the locals, this Youngman's got a clean reputation."

"That's why my lawyer recommended him, but I can't believe this is his first try at blackmail. He must be smarter than he looks."

"Maybe he didn't start out to blackmail Tiffany. Maybe he does her a favor by telling you Dulcy's dead, then he sees a great way to get himself a steady income out of the deal. Not so much that she can't pay him every month, but enough to tide him over when things get tight in the detective business."

"If I had the little bastard in front of me at this moment, I'd beat the living hell out of him."

Holman sighed. "Yeah, I thought that's what you'd say. Look, Mr. MacMillan, the kid doesn't need her grandfather in jail for attempted murder." There was a chuckle at the other end of the telephone. "Although I might come down and testify in your defense. Get you off with a suspended sentence."

"I hope that won't be necessary," Logan said. "So what happens now?"

"Not much. Too many other crimes out there to investigate. Anything violent always goes to the head of the line. This was vicious, but he didn't shoot anybody. Youngman can always say he didn't know the checks were from Tiffany. They were signed by Terry Rigby."

"But how could he explain why Terry Rigby of Laramie, Wyoming, would pay him three hundred dollars a month?"

"So he makes up something. We know he's lying, but Tiffany's not around to contradict him. It's not enough to indict him for blackmail, but maybe you can get his license pulled, sue him for malfeasance, force the cops to follow up on that little item about aiding and abetting a fleeing felon. Worth a try."

"Indeed it is. I'll get the lawyer who recommended him to pursue it. He owes me that."

"One last thing. When Terry started drinking the night she died, the manager said she started crying and talking about having to move again fast. Said she didn't think she could stand it. Kept saying she wanted to go home."

Logan kneaded the back of his neck and sighed. "If Youngman hadn't called her, if she hadn't fallen, maybe I could have found her and persuaded her to come home with me. Youngman ought to hang over this."

"He didn't kill the woman, MacMillan, any more than you did. Still, it's ironic."

"It's more than ironic. It's damned tragic." Logan drew a deep breath. The hand not holding the telephone was clenched into a fist. He flexed his fingers.

"I want your promise, MacMillan. Don't get yourself into trouble over this."

Logan laughed mirthlessly. "As you said, the last thing Dulcy needs is her grandfather facing jail for murder."

"Thing is, you're not supposed to know about this, so when the local police get around to you, make sure it's a big surprise."

"I will. Thanks for calling, Holman."

"Don't make me sorry I did."

"I won't." Logan hung up the phone and went to tell Molly about the conversation.

She was sitting at her workshop counter with her bare feet hooked around the rungs of her stool. There was a streak of dried clay, like a scar, along her jaw and her hands were caked with it. She looked up, put a finger to her lips and nodded toward the rocking chair.

Dulcy's book lay on the tiles. She was in the rocker under an afghan. Her hair lay damp against her forehead and her chest rose and fell with her soft breathing.

Logan motioned to Molly. She slipped out onto the landing outside the back door. He eased the door shut behind her.

"What's the matter now, darling?"

"Is it that obvious?"

"You've got that granite-faced look you had when you broke the Dulcy doll. As though you're hanging on to your temper with your fingernails."

He told her about Holman's call.

Molly leaned against the wall and drew a deep shuddering break before she spoke. "I knew it."

"I can sure pick 'em, can't I?"

"Stop blaming yourself. You're an ethical man, Logan. Honest people expect other people to be honest. Holman said even the police thought Youngman was honest. If he fooled them, it's no wonder he fooled you."

"In any case, he's their problem now."

Later that evening after Dulcy was asleep, Molly joined Logan on the couch. She snuggled back against him, and he wrapped his arms around her.

"Are you still mad about Youngman?" she asked.

"Hell, yes." He slid his hand down her arm, but absently, as though he was finding it difficult to concentrate. "I think he warned Tiffany to get out of Moundhill," Logan said. "After he convinced me Dulcy was dead, I mean."

Molly turned to him and shook her head. "That may not be what happened." She slipped off the couch, found her handbag in the kitchen and brought it back with her. She dug around in it for a moment and handed Logan the folio of photos in which he'd first seen Dulcy.

He glanced at them and at her, a question in his eyes. "So? These are the pictures you took when you were in Moundhill. I saw them before, remember?"

"When I showed them to you, I told you to ignore the people in the foreground—my tour group. Now I want you to look at them."

He looked and shrugged. "I don't understand."

"Look at the sweatshirts. We're all wearing University of Memphis sweatshirts. We bought them before we left. We decided to wear them that day as kind of a joke." She leaned forward and put a hand on his arm. "Put yourself in Tiffany's place. Her picture was on the front page of our newspaper half a dozen times during her trial and after she ran away with Dulcy. Now she's settled down in Moundhill, found a job, bought off Youngman, convinced everyone Dulcy is dead. She's starting to make a life for herself. Then one day when she and Dulcy are in the park she sees a lady wearing a Memphis sweatshirt taking a picture of her child—her child with the strawberry blond hair. And then she sees a battalion of middle-aged people all wearing the same sweatshirt. I think she took Dulcy straight home, cut her hair, dyed it brown, moved out of her apartment and ran again. All because of me and my little Nikon."

Logan looked at the picture again and nodded silently. "You could be right."

Molly stuffed the pictures back into her handbag and dropped her purse onto the desk. "Youngman didn't even have to trace her again. She had to pay him no matter how far she ran so that he wouldn't tell you Dulcy was alive. Three hundred dollars a month! No wonder they lived in a fleabag. I could kill Youngman. That money should have been spent on Dulcy."

Logan put his arm around her waist and sat her down beside him once more. "In spite of the man, Molly, we got her back. I wish we could have gotten Tiffany back, as well." He realized with a start that he meant what he said. When had he stopped hating Tiffany? Was it when he began to understand her? He brushed his lips across Molly's hair. She tasted a little like chalk, but he didn't mind. He smiled and drew her closer. He had stopped hating Tiffany the moment he began to love Molly. She lifted the darkness from his soul. If they had found Tiffany, he had no doubt Molly could have helped her, too. "Poor Tiffany," Logan said. "She tried to come home too late."

CHAPTER SIXTEEN

MOLLY SPENT the next two days with Dulcy and Logan. She fired Quentin's head one final time and left it on a top shelf to cool. She selected a mold to start her next portrait, a girl the same age as Dulcy, but much different. She was a laughing, chubby little princess who'd never been denied a single thing in her sunny young life.

After being interrupted for the fifth time, Molly decided to put off starting on Kimberly until she got Dulcy and Logan settled.

Dulcy took root in the rocking chair when she wasn't chasing the geese or petting Maxie and Eeyore. Molly shopped for groceries, picked up, scrubbed bathrooms, cooked three meals a day. She remembered how much she hated housework. Logan and Dulcy tried to be helpful. Dulcy made up her bed with lumps. Logan offered to help but never seemed to see what needed doing until Molly had done it. Molly gave thanks that the only thing she was a perfectionist about was her tools and her studio. The mess in the house really didn't matter.

Logan wanted so badly to win Dulcy over that he insisted they take her to the zoo, to the museum, to the movies. He shopped for more clothes, more toys, more books. Molly felt guilty when she tried to stay home alone. Dulcy demanded, even begged, Molly to go with them.

They had fun. Molly had to admit that Dulcy and Logan brought life and energy into her life. They saw the latest Disney movie, and ate pizza served by creatures dressed in fake fur. Dulcy saw dinosaurs at the museum and Rembrandts at the art gallery. She asked questions, demanded answers and seemed intrigued by every bit of information. She never seemed to run out of steam. Molly and Logan were too worn-out for more than a quiet kiss and drowsy cuddle on the sofa every night.

Anne dropped Elizabeth off after school on Friday for her sleep-over. Molly had warned her granddaughter about Dulcy and Logan, but Elizabeth still acted annoyed when she discovered that "someone was sleeping in her bed," and that someone would probably eat her porridge, too, given half a chance.

"Are you going to marry that Mr. MacMillan?" Elizabeth asked as she helped Molly set the table for Friday-evening dinner. Logan had driven Dulcy to the store for a gallon of ice cream for dessert. It was the first moment Molly and Elizabeth had managed to be alone.

Molly started. "No!" She tried to keep her voice casual. "He hasn't asked me, Elizabeth, and I'm not at all certain I'd accept if he did."

"You like him, though, don't you?"

"Yes, I like him. But I've known him a very short time, and frankly, we come from two very different worlds."

"If you married him would you move?"

"No. Definitely not." Molly handed Elizabeth napkins and reached for the salt and pepper shakers. "I know this is hard on you, Elizabeth, but hang in there for tonight. And don't sulk. By next weekend, Dulcy and Logan will be living in Logan's apartment."

Elizabeth flounced away. "I'm not sulking. But you go away for a week and all of a sudden there's this strange man and his very peculiar child staying in your house. Besides, she follows me around. Yuk."

"You fascinate her. Deal with it."

Elizabeth spoke little during dinner. Logan tried to draw her out about school, the upcoming horse show and her friends. Elizabeth replied in monosyllables and kept a watchful eye on Dulcy.

Dulcy went to bed first. Elizabeth went to her room and came back out. "Gram, that child is sleeping on the floor!"

Molly sighed. "Don't worry about it, Elizabeth. She's fine down there."

"I mean, really. The floor! Can't you do anything about her?" She flounced off again.

Later, as she crawled into bed, she heard Dulcy whisper, "G'night, 'Lizabeth. I'm glad you're here."

Elizabeth hid her head under her pillow.

After she finished cleaning the kitchen counter, Molly sat beside Logan on the couch. "Elizabeth's nose is severely out of joint," she said.

He dropped his arm around her shoulders, cuddled her against him and began to nibble her earlobe gently. She wriggled with pleasure, but when his hand came up to encircle her breast, she held it away. "We can't. Dulcy may not wander around at night, but Elizabeth does."

"So? What's wrong with necking on the couch?"

"Logan, stop that!" She turned to him. "Elizabeth does not think of me as a sexual being—come to that, until I met you, I didn't think of myself as a sexual being, either."

"Molly, you are the most sexual being I have ever met." Logan pressed his cheek against hers and bent her head to the side, then began to tease the fine hairs at the nape of her neck with his tongue. She gasped.

"Oh, God, I am when you do that." She turned in his arms and raised her face to be kissed.

He broke the kiss first. "Thank God Dulcy's spending the night with Rick and Zoe tomorrow. I don't think I can stand another night without you in my arms. I had forgotten how I hated being a teenage boy. There is a certain rhythm to these things, Molly, at least for a man."

"For a woman too, you ass."

"Necking with you is delightful, but if I don't get the bells and whistles before long I'll go nuts." *Now,* he thought. *Ask her to marry you. Now while you can feel her nipples hard against your shirt, her soft breasts engorged, her face flushed in the lamplight.*

No, better stick to the plan. Tomorrow night, without anyone else in the house, as they lay in each other's arms, after a beautiful dinner and a bottle of champagne, he'd ask her. He knew she loved Dulcy. She'd have to marry him. It should be obvious that he couldn't manage Dulcy without her.

MOLLY POURED the dregs of Elizabeth's morning orange juice down the sink, rinsed the glass, dropped it into the dishwasher and started it.

Elizabeth stalked into the kitchen. "Gram, Dulcy's messing with my stuff."

"Just a couple of the Breyer horses, Elizabeth. She hasn't touched the Barbies. She's got her own toys."

"She's reading my books."

"So? That's what books are for. Why don't you try reading her one?"

"Why does she have to be here, anyway? She's not kin to us."

"No, Elizabeth, but she's my houseguest. Look, I know this isn't easy for you, but Dulcy is only staying until Mr. MacMillan gets things ready for her at his apartment."

"So how soon are they leaving?"

"Soon." She took Elizabeth's hand and pulled her over against her side. "She's a little girl and you're a big girl. You've always talked about being a teacher. Think of this as a chance to get a little experience of what it's like."

"I want to teach high school or college. I can't relate to anybody under four feet tall." She sniffed, then suddenly she grinned. "It's not for long, right?"

Molly laughed. Elizabeth's sulks never lasted long. She was essentially a sunny child and despite her current attack of jealousy, generally a compassionate one, as well. She often brought home wounded animals. One summer, she carried in a four-foot king snake she'd found caught on barbed wire at the bottom of the pasture. Molly had nearly drawn the line that time. Elizabeth had begged until Molly made a bed for it in the barn. Molly still saw it there occasionally.

It was because of Elizabeth that Eeyore lived with Maxie. Elizabeth had seen him in a pasture next door to a friend's stable, with sores on his back, his hooves so long they turned up like Turkish slippers. Elizabeth had begged and cajoled her grandmother into giving him a proper home. Molly, Anne and Phil had nursed baby birds, abandoned squirrels, a Canada goose with an injured wing, even a family of possums discovered alive in their mother's pouch after a hunter had shot her.

If only Molly could convince Elizabeth that Dulcy was no different from any other wounded and abandoned animal, she knew she'd have it made.

Molly tried again. "Look, Elizabeth, Dulcy's had a really rough time. She needs all the help and stability she can get at the moment. So just hang in there for me, please."

"So where've they gone now?" Elizabeth leaned her head on Molly's shoulder. She held Molly's hand and patted her shoulder. The gesture was touching and a little sad.

"They're out buying furniture for Dulcy with Mr. MacMillan's daughter, Zoe."

"Great. That means they'll be out of here quick, right?"

"Elizabeth, this isn't like you." Actually, Molly understood her granddaughter's mood. Elizabeth was used to being able to show off her "with-it" gram to her friends, give them rides on her pony, show them the dolls in the showroom. Now Dulcy slept in "her" room, read Elizabeth's books, put her clothes in Elizabeth's closet, stacked her toys on the floor. It must be truly unnerving for an only child. Most children who had to deal with new arrivals in their families started out with baby brothers and sisters, not five-year-olds who appeared out of the blue.

Even Maxie was getting used to Dulcy now. So far, Molly hadn't put her up on the pony, but the little girl wasn't afraid and begged for a ride. Molly wanted to make sure Dulcy understood that the pony belonged to Elizabeth although she was tempted to lead the child around when Elizabeth wasn't there. She made a decision. "Elizabeth, why don't you put Maxie on a lead line and walk around the pasture with Dulcy in the saddle sometime. I know she'd be thrilled."

"Maxie's mine!"

"Of course he is. But it would give you a chance to show off a little and give Dulcy a treat at the same time."

"Do I have to?"

"Of course not." Molly sighed. "But it would be a nice gesture. Wouldn't cost you anything."

"Give you and that Mr. MacMillan some time alone, you mean."

"That's not it at all." Although, Molly admitted, it would be nice to see Logan alone during the day, if only for a few minutes.

"Well, all right. But if she falls off and breaks her neck, don't blame me."

LOGAN DREADED buying Dulcy's furniture. After lunch Molly had persuaded him to take Zoe along on the trip because his daughter was an expert. He came close to sending off Dulcy and Zoe without him, but decided that he couldn't fob off Dulcy on Zoe the first time the child needed something important. He would pay for the furniture, so he should help select it. Period.

He remembered that unpleasant shopping expedition with Dulcy in Laramie. He still longed to see the child dressed up in satin and lace, but he probably wouldn't until she put on her wedding dress, if then.

"Why didn't MyMolly come with us?" Dulcy asked from the back seat of the BMW.

Zoe glanced at her father. "She had to work on her dolls."

"I wish she'd come with us," Dulcy grumbled under her breath.

"Dulcy, we are going to pick out furniture for your room," Logan said. "Zoe is a professional interior designer. She can advise us."

"I got furniture."

"That's Elizabeth's furniture," Zoe said reasonably. She swiveled so that she could see Dulcy. "Do you want furniture like that?"

"I get to pick?" Dulcy asked suspiciously.

Zoe took a deep breath. "Within reason. I don't know what the budget is. You like Elizabeth's furniture?"

"No way," Dulcy said, and wrinkled her nose. "It's all white and fancy and ruffly. Yuck. I want red. Like the Cardinals."

Three hours and four showrooms later they hadn't found anything that suited Dulcy. After the second showroom, Logan gave up and sat on the first piece of solidly upholstered furniture he found, leaving Zoe to deal with Dulcy and the salespeople.

He had to give Zoe credit. Dulcy was tired and getting whiny, but Zoe never lost her temper or her cool. She plowed doggedly down aisle after aisle, looked at suite after suite, charmed every salesperson. He'd never watched her work with a client before. If she treated every customer at MacMillan's with this tireless courtesy, no wonder the store made money.

He was ready to give up in disgust, when he heard Zoe's shout from the back of the store. "Yes!"

He stood up wearily and wound his way to where they stood in the back corner looking at a suite of simple Shaker-style furniture painted dark barn-red.

"It's even got bookshelves!" Zoe said excitedly. Dulcy was bouncing on one of the twin beds. "And it's not that expensive." She glanced at her father. "Relatively speaking, that is."

"Doesn't look much like a little-girl's room," he said.

Dulcy stopped bouncing and rolled her eyes at Zoe. "You said I could have what I wanted. I want this. Yeah!"

"Look, it's got great lines, it's solid wood so it'll hold up, the finish is excellent, the drawers are even dove-tailed. She won't outgrow it even when she's a teenager. It's a reputable manufacturer...and it's what Dulcy wants." Her lip curled. "Or didn't you mean what you said?"

He heard the sarcasm dripping in her voice. She might cut Dulcy unlimited slack, but not him. "How much and when can you deliver?" he asked the hovering salesman.

Dulcy whooped and plunged off the bed. Logan saw an incredible thing. Zoe and Dulcy exchanged a very creditable high five. He'd never have believed it if he hadn't seen it with his own eyes.

Then an even more amazing thing happened. Dulcy threw her arms around Zoe and hugged her.

LOGAN DROPPED Zoe back at MacMillan's and drove Dulcy home to Molly's, where she immediately attached herself to Elizabeth like a limpet.

Molly gave the children apples and milk, then sent them out to groom Maxie and Eeyore. Elizabeth grumbled that she wanted to be alone, but Dulcy trailed after her just the same.

"Stop following me," Elizabeth said as she reached the door of the stable. Dulcy stopped six paces away, but when Elizabeth reached for Maxie's halter, she slipped in behind her and stood against the wall, watching her from wide gray eyes. Elizabeth ignored her, cross-tied the pony, picked up a currycomb and began to curry the pony's muddy shoulder. Dulcy ducked around Elizabeth, picked up a brush and began to brush the other side.

"Stop it. That's wrong. You have to curry first, then the dandy brush and then the soft brush. Don't you know anything?" Elizabeth asked.

"Okay, 'Lizbeth." Dulcy stood aside watching for a moment, then picked up the dandy brush and began to brush the mud from the pony's front legs.

Elizabeth shoved her out of the way. "Wait till I'm finished."

"You gonna ride him?" Dulcy asked. "Can I ride, too?"

"You're too little." Elizabeth moved down the pony's flank. "Besides, he's my pony, not yours."

"I know, 'Lizbeth." Dulcy stroked the pony's nose. "I bet you ride good. Maybe when I'm bigger My-Molly'll get me a pony."

"She won't buy you a pony because she's not your grandmother, she's mine," Elizabeth snarled. "She's not your Molly, she's my Molly, she's always been my Molly and she'll never ever be kin to you. You're going to go live with your grandfather in an apartment and never ever see my grandmother again!"

Dulcy stared at her in horror, then flew out of the stable.

Elizabeth started after her, then stopped. She picked up the currycomb in her trembling hand and began to curry the pony again, but she couldn't see the dirt for the tears that ran down her cheeks.

CHAPTER SEVENTEEN

"THIS DAY has been hell," Logan said. He reached into the refrigerator for a soda, closed the door and leaned against it as he popped the top and drank deeply. "Dulcy had her mind set on red furniture for her bedroom. Red! Do you have any idea how tough that is to find? Then she read a book all the way home in the car and ignored Zoe and me both."

"Logan, she's five years old. She was tired and hungry."

"I guess. Actually, we all were." He drank the rest of the soda, then dropped the empty can into the recycle bin beside the stove. "When Zoe miraculously found what she was looking for, they couldn't deliver until Wednesday afternoon." He sat on one of the bar stools at the counter and reached for Molly, encircling her waist with his arm and pulling her against him.

At the store he had hesitated momentarily before giving the salesman the address of his apartment. If everything went well with Molly tonight, he could always call on Monday and change the address to Molly's house. She wouldn't really need a guest room once they were married. Elizabeth would have her room for when she came to stay, and Dulcy would have her red bedroom. They could store the guest-room furniture or sell it. Everything would be perfect.

Suddenly he decided not to put off asking her to marry him one moment longer. Once she said yes, they could tell Dulcy this afternoon before she left with Rick.

Still, he wasn't quite certain how to start. Molly seemed distracted and a little on edge. Had Elizabeth been difficult? He could tell the girl resented him. Once he married Molly, he'd have to work to win over her granddaughter as hard as he was working to win over his own. Why was nothing ever simple?

"I didn't plan to move in on you like this," he continued. "One or two nights has stretched out, hasn't it?" He nuzzled Molly's neck. She shivered and leaned against him quietly.

"I don't mind the company."

For a moment he wondered about her syntax. Not "I like" but "I don't mind." He was creating roadblocks where none existed, he admonished himself silently. He nibbled her ear. "Rick and Zoe will be here any minute, then your daughter's picking up Elizabeth. Tonight will be just you and me for a change."

She laughed softly. "I warned you about the differences between fatherhood and grandfatherhood, didn't I? Grandfathers can send the kids home."

"True, you warned me. Unfortunately, at the time I hadn't yet discovered how much I hate sleeping in your guest room and how much I want to sleep with you." He turned her in the circle of his arms. "Molly, Dulcy is so happy here it seems a mistake to move her."

"She'll get used to living with you."

"I don't have geese and ponies and donkeys."

Something in his tone made her suddenly uncomfortable. She slipped away from him, dug into her junk drawer for the kitchen scissors and began to snip the brown edges off the basil leaves that grew in a pot on the windowsill. "You could move," she said. "Get a house."

"I could. As a matter of fact, I know the perfect place."

"Wonderful. Where?"

He didn't answer her.

She felt him behind her, his breath warm against the curls at the nape of her neck. She felt the same intense ripple of desire she always felt with him, but she felt something new—a wariness. She didn't know why, exactly, something about his tone, perhaps, a new depth, an earnestness. Why didn't he answer her question? Was he planning to move to the other side of the world and take Dulcy with him before she'd even had a chance to get used to Memphis.

He took her shoulders and turned her to look at him. "Put down the scissors a moment. We have to talk seriously about Dulcy's future. Molly, you have to marry me."

Molly gulped. Whatever she'd been expecting, this wasn't it. At least not in those words. "I beg your pardon?" She wanted to be certain she'd understood precisely what he had said. She looked at his gray eyes, eyes she had once thought glacial, now warm and caring. So why did she shiver suddenly, as though he'd left the refrigerator door open? The man had just asked her to marry him. She loved him, didn't she? She loved Dulcy, too. Why didn't she throw herself at him and say yes?

She knew why in the next moment, with his next sentence.

"It's the perfect solution to the problem." So reasonable, so well thought out. So logical. So horrifyingly, appallingly insulting.

He warmed to his subject now that he had her full attention. He had no idea how full that attention was. "Dulcy already thinks of you as her mother, and she loves living here."

Molly cleared her throat. She wanted to sound equally reasonable. Maybe she could still salvage the situation—or at least some semblance of dignity. But instead, she felt all her old insecurities bubble to the surface of her brain, felt the old sense of inadequacy twine icy fingers around her body even as she felt Logan's warm ones on her shoulder. He couldn't possibly realize what he'd just said. "She doesn't think of me as her mother. She had a mother."

"But you're taking Tiffany's place damned well. Why, in a year Dulcy won't even remember the horrors she's been through. You've already more than half replaced her mother."

"No, Logan, I haven't, any more than you're taking the place of the father she's never known."

"But I will." He sounded so sure of himself. "Don't you see? Together, we'll be her family. All the family she needs. It's obvious I can't manage her without you. With you as my wife, we'll be mother, father, child. It's perfect."

"I was a mother, Logan, I don't want to start over at this point. I have a role to play in Dulcy's life—or at least I hope I do, but not as her mother." She twisted away from him. She had to get away before this got out of hand. She'd seen this side of him when he'd peremptorily forbade her to trudge out into the snowstorm to call Anne. He made decisions and expected people to follow them without question.

She felt her pulse quicken, her breath surge in her lungs. She fought to get herself under control before she hyperventilated. Surely he didn't mean to insult her. He'd just picked the wrong words to express his feelings. Surely he didn't even realize how deeply those words wounded her. All she had to do was explain things to him simply, so that he'd understand and apologize.

She heard the rough edge of exasperation in his tone when he said, "Come now, Molly, what would you do if, God forbid, Elizabeth's parents died? Wouldn't you take custody of Elizabeth and raise her?"

"Of course I would, and we'd manage somehow. But Logan, I wouldn't have any alternative. Her grandfather probably wouldn't recognize her, assuming he pulled his head out of the bourbon bottle long enough to notice." She wanted to hit him over the head with the closest blunt object—maybe a two-by-four would work. Something to get through to him before he destroyed everything. "You do have an alternative."

Logan drew himself up. "I don't know what you mean."

"Rick and Zoe."

"Rick and Zoe? Don't be ridiculous."

"What's ridiculous about it?" Molly asked. "Rick and Zoe are the right age, they adore Dulcy, they've got the stamina to deal with a small girl. Rick is wonderful with her..."

"Whereas I'm not, is that what you're saying?"

"Not at all. She needs everyone in her family, Logan. She needs her aunt and her uncle and she needs her grandfather. You're her grandfather, Logan. You are not, and never can be, her father."

"No, she needs a father and a mother. That's me, Molly, and that's you. My God, I would have thought you'd jump at the chance. I had no idea you were so selfish. Think of that poor child, for God's sake. It's your duty to marry me, dammit!''

"Jump at the chance? My duty? To marry you to provide Dulcy a home?" Molly stared at him, open-mouthed.

"Yes!" He expelled his breath as he fought to get himself and the situation under control. "Listen, Molly. Be reasonable. You and I, we're good together. We get along, we have great sex. I want to show you and Dulcy the world—my world. Dammit! You promised Dulcy you wouldn't walk away from her."

Molly went dead calm. She felt empty, as though he'd sliced her open and drained her of every drop of blood in her body. His words had destroyed them and he didn't even know he'd done it. "I have no intention of walking away from Dulcy, Logan, not unless you force me to."

Suddenly her face flamed, not with love this time, but with anger. "You once said Tiffany had used Dulcy. She'd taken Dulcy with her because the child was the only person who loved her. Now *you're* planning to use Dulcy—to get a second chance at being a father."

He recoiled as though she'd slapped him, but before he could answer, she continued, "How dare you talk to me about my duty! Is that all this has been from the beginning? You choose a nice, eccentric earth mother to bake cookies and run carpool so you won't have to? Manage your household and warm your bed? Take up the slack so you can have someone handy to blame for your mistakes as a parent? So you can become the absentee father again? Is that why you seduced me? Because I'm cheaper than hiring a nanny?''

This time, before he could answer, Elizabeth ran in. "Gram!" Her white face was streaked with tears and her chest heaved. "Gram, come quick! Dulcy's in the workshop. I think she's making a mess!" She grabbed her grandmother's hand and began to pull her out the door. Molly hesitated only a second, then ran out and down the path with Elizabeth. Behind her, she could hear Logan shouting for her to come back. Then she heard his footsteps pelting behind her.

"What's this all about, Elizabeth?"

"Oh, Gram!"

Molly heard the crash and tinkle of broken glass. The back door to the workroom stood open, light spilled out. Molly rounded the corner and dashed into the room.

A twelve-inch arm sailed past her right ear to explode into shards of bisque on the concrete landing. A softball-size skull flew past her shoulder and into the darkness. Molly heard it pop against the bole of a pine tree.

Dulcy flailed at the shelves of legs, arms, feet, heads. Her thin arms swept back and forth like scythes. Body parts flew from the shelves as though they'd been ripped apart in an explosion. They rained down onto the tiles and snapped and cracked like dry branches breaking.

With every sweep of her arms, Dulcy screamed, "No no no no no."

Molly reached her in two strides, wrapped her arms around the child, lifted her off her feet and spun her away from the shelves. Dulcy twisted and fought like a trapped animal. She snapped like a rabid dog, rolled her eyes and clawed at Molly's encircling arms.

Dulcy's heel caught Molly hard on the shin. The pain took Molly's breath away. She stumbled, but held on to Dulcy doggedly.

They staggered around the room until they faced the open door. Elizabeth and Logan stood silhouetted in the doorway, too stunned to move or speak. An unbroken arm rolled under Molly's foot. She slid back against the corner of her workbench. It caught her across her right kidney. She saw stars and gasped with sudden agony. But she held on.

Little by little Dulcy quieted. Her screams died away to gulps and gurgles. She hung stiff in Molly's arms like a marble statue. "I hate you, I hate you!" she said again and again.

"Why, Dulcy?" Molly gasped. Her lungs burned. She didn't dare let go of Dulcy, but wasn't certain how much longer she could hold on to her. "Why do you hate me?"

"You don't love me! You're not MyMolly. You're going to send me away and I'll have to live with *him!*" She kicked backward, and her heel caught Molly across the kneecap.

"Ow!" she yelped. Her knee buckled momentarily, then held. Dulcy slipped. Molly tightened her grip.

Molly looked over Dulcy's head. "Elizabeth," she said ominously. "What's this all about?"

"How should I know? She's crazy. She just ran out. I thought she went to find you, and then I heard all the noise and—"

"Elizabeth."

"Well, she said she was going to live here and you were going to buy her a pony and I told her you weren't her grandmother, you were mine and then she went crazy." Elizabeth stopped for breath, her frightened eyes staring into her grandmother's with every bit of innocence she could muster. "And I saw her run in here and I thought I'd better get you and look what she did."

"My God, Molly," Logan said from the doorway. He took a step inside and pointed at Dulcy. "And you, young lady..."

Dulcy began to squirm again. She and Molly were both slippery with sweat. Dulcy was like a bony eel. Molly could feel her hold slipping.

"Logan, get out," Molly said. "Rick and Zoe are due any minute. Go wait for them at the house. You and I can talk later. At the moment, just get the heck out of here and let me deal with this."

"Molly, I intend to discuss this monstrous attack right now. Dulcy—"

Molly's voice rose dangerously. "Not now, Logan. I've got all I can handle. Please just go."

He glared at Molly, then without another word turned on his heel and disappeared.

"Elizabeth, come in and shut the door, please," Molly said. "And Dulcy, if I let you go, will you sit down and discuss this intelligently?"

Dulcy braced herself against Molly as though gearing up for another fit.

"No more yelling and no more kicking. My shins can't take it."

"I hate you," Dulcy said softly.

"That's your prerogative. Hate me all you like. What you can't do is kick me or bite me or scratch me. And what you also can't do is destroy any more of my property. You got that?"

"But..."

"No buts. We are going to get to the bottom of this now, you two, and then the three of us are going to clean up this mess. Do I make myself clear?"

"Yes, ma'am," Elizabeth whispered. She had never called her grandmother "ma'am" before.

"All right." She set Dulcy down on the floor but kept her pinioned. Molly knew she wanted to run.

"I mean it. Nobody's going anywhere until we find out what all this is about." She felt Dulcy stiffen. "You do owe me an explanation."

Dulcy began to relax.

"That's better. Now, the three of us are going to sit down right here in the middle of the floor and talk this out." She released Dulcy warily, walked around in front of her and sank onto the tiles. She pulled Elizabeth down beside her.

Dulcy stared at the floor mulishly. No one said a word.

After a moment, Dulcy sank onto her heels, but with her back to the others. She stared at the ceiling.

Molly felt a stab of pain under her left hip, reached under her and brought out part of a foot. She held it a moment, sighed and tossed it into the corner where it broke. Both Dulcy and Elizabeth jumped as though she'd fired a rifle at them.

"Settle down, both of you." She reached out a hand toward Dulcy, who flinched away without taking her eyes from the ceiling. Molly sighed and let her hand drop. "All right, we'll take Dulcy first."

Dulcy stiffened, but gave no other sign that she'd even heard. Elizabeth watched her as though expecting her to explode like a hand grenade.

"Dulcy, let's take care of this business of my not being your grandmother first. I'm going to talk to you as though you were a lot older than you are. If you don't understand anything, it's up to you to ask me to explain. Okay?"

Dulcy ignored her.

"Elizabeth is right. I am her grandmother. I am not your grandmother."

Dulcy's lip began to quiver. Her chest heaved once, then she set that jaw of hers that was so like her grandfather's and blinked back her tears.

Molly kept talking. "The first time I saw Elizabeth, she was a tiny baby. I've watched her grow up. I have loved her for eleven years. I remember how cute she was, and that helps a great deal when she pulls a stunt like this one." She turned toward Elizabeth. "You get me?"

Elizabeth nodded.

"I have known you, Dulcy, less than a week. I saw you once before, but I have only known you since I saw you sitting reading that magazine in Mrs. Dalrymple's den. I have no memories of you as a cute little baby to draw on. I don't have your yesterdays in my heart. I can only love you as you are today, right this minute. Not as my grandchild, not as my kin, but as Dulcy—a person. And I do."

"Do what?"

"Love you, you silly goose. I plan to love you long after you have children of your own. Do I make myself clear?"

"But 'Lizabeth says I'm not kin to you."

"So? Since when do you get to love only your kin? I can pick anybody I like to be kin to me and I pick you."

Dulcy gulped and cut her eyes at Molly. "I broke stuff."

"You sure did." Molly shook her head at the devastation. "I'm glad you're not taller."

She saw the corner of Dulcy's mouth twitch.

"I understand why you did it, just as I understand why Elizabeth said those awful things to you. But that doesn't mean I approve. You both screwed up." She and Logan had screwed up, as well, but that wasn't either Elizabeth's or Dulcy's business—not at the moment, at any rate. Logan was no doubt storming through the house right this minute, fuming because she'd kicked him out. Hadn't she done exactly what Sydney used to do to him? Kicked him out of the problem?

She had enough on her plate with this mess and the feud between Elizabeth and Dulcy. She didn't have time to listen to Logan's commanding-general routine. He'd have to wait his turn. She dreaded talking to him. Compared to the problems his cheerful little marriage-demand—she refused to call it a proposal—created for the two of them, this war between Dulcy and Elizabeth was a minor skirmish on the day before World War III started.

She took a deep breath. "Now it's your turn, Elizabeth."

Elizabeth sat up straight. Molly saw the trails of tears down her flushed cheeks and the glint of more tears brimming in her eyes.

"Kiddo," Molly said, "you've never had to share me with a living soul since you hit this earth. Most kids have to share their grandmothers with brothers and sisters and cousins, but you've had my undivided attention, plus ponies and toys and fancy shoes and clothes whenever you wanted them. Pretty cushy."

"But Gram..."

"I'm not condemning you. Just stating facts. Then here comes Dulcy tagging along. All of a sudden, I'm asking you to share your things, look after her and teach her. Maybe I asked too much."

"No, you didn't, Gram, please."

"I'm not dumping guilt on you, either. All I'm saying is that Dulcy is a part of my life now. You think because I love her I've got less love for you?"

"No," Elizabeth whispered. She dropped her eyes, then her chin set hard, as well. She glared at her grandmother. "Not less love. Less time."

Molly caught her breath. "I see. I really do see. Okay, let's look at this time thing from the other direction. What if I called Anne and told her not to pick you up this afternoon? Told her not to let you go to the movies with your friends because I wanted you to spend more time with me?''

"Oh, Gram.''

"Hey, it's a valid question. We've both got other lives, Elizabeth. Your other lives are going to take more and more time from now on. I'll always have time for you, but believe me, you won't have five minutes for me three years from now. That's just the way it is. But I promise you, I'll always have as much time for you as you want. Cross my heart and hope to die.''

Elizabeth was crying in earnest now.

"Now let me give you a tip.'' She winked at Dulcy. "Big girls can really show off to little girls if they play their cards right. Think how much you could teach Dulcy. And I'll bet she'd enjoy learning, wouldn't you, Dulcy? Like how to groom Maxie?''

"Dulcy said you were going to buy her a pony,'' Elizabeth said.

"No, I'm not, but you and I both know you've nearly outgrown Maxie. Next year you'll be moving up to a horse if we can find one we can afford to buy. Wouldn't you like to have Maxie stay here for Dulcy to ride rather than be sold to some stranger?''

Elizabeth's eyes widened. "I don't want Maxie to go away.''

"So teach Dulcy to ride him. Then he can stay to keep your next year's horse company.''

Elizabeth looked at Dulcy with her eyes narrowed. She thought for a moment. "Okay, Gram. But she's got to leave my stuff alone.''

"I promise, 'Lizabeth,'' Dulcy said softly. She gazed at Elizabeth with something close to adoration.

"Good,'' Molly said. She slapped her hands on her knees. "Then let's get this mess cleaned up. Later on we'll figure out just how the two of you are going to make amends."

"But Gram, I didn't break anything."

"No, but you sure had a hand in it, Elizabeth. Now you scoot back to the house, bring the broom, the mop, the bucket, the dustpan and the big black garbage bags under the sink. Can you carry all that?"

"Sure." Elizabeth unfolded easily from the floor, ran out the door and up the hill toward the house.

Molly turned to Dulcy. "Well, kiddo?"

Dulcy sucked in her breath, then dived at Molly and hit her full in the chest so hard she dumped over backward with the child on top of her.

"Oh, MyMolly, I'm so sorry."

Molly held her, caressed her thin back and crooned to her while the child sobbed her heart out with her arms around Molly's neck like a noose.

"Sweet patience, when'd the tornado hit?"

Molly looked over the top of Dulcy's head. Rick stood in the open doorway. Molly sat up and let Dulcy go.

"Long story." It wasn't surprising under the circumstances that she hadn't noticed the gate alarm sounding.

"You have a raccoon get in or something? Boy, I've seen hurricanes that did less damage than this."

Dulcy wailed.

"What's the problem, short stuff?" Rick hunkered down. Then he glanced at Molly with sudden comprehension. "Uh-oh."

Molly nodded. "Uh-huh. You guessed it."

"Gram, here's the stuff." Elizabeth ducked around Rick and brought her armload of equipment into the room. She stood the broom and mop against the wall, then set the bucket and the dustpan on the floor.

"Okay, here's the drill," Molly said. "You and Dulcy see if anything survived in one piece. Put the whole stuff, if any, on top of my worktable. Elizabeth, you start in that corner, Dulcy, you start over there. After you've rescued what can be rescued, Dulcy, you hold the dustpan, and Elizabeth, you sweep. Dump everything into the trash bag."

"Why do I have to do the sweeping?"

"Because you're eleven and Dulcy's five. Now get started. I need to talk to Rick a minute." She pulled him up and walked him into the autumn afternoon. She closed the door to the workroom behind her softly, leaned against it and rubbed her knee. "Helen Dalrymple said she'd be glad when Dulcy pitched a temper tantrum. I think she'd be real pleased about this. I'm not sure I am." She walked past Rick and up the path toward the house, her feet dragging with every step. She didn't think she could face Logan's fury right now. She felt totally drained. At least Rick was here to keep things civilized. "Didn't Logan tell you what happened?"

"What Logan? His car's gone. He's not here."

Molly ran to the house and into the guest room. He'd taken everything, from his shaving equipment to his bathrobe. She looked in Dulcy's room. Dulcy's suitcase sat open on the bed, all packed for her sleep-over with Rick and Zoe. Baby Dulcy and Petey lay on the bed beside the open suitcase. Molly leaned against the doorjamb.

"What's going on, Molly?" Rick asked.

"Logan asked me to marry him."

"Hey, great."

"I turned him down. We got into a fight about it, and right in the middle, Elizabeth ran in to tell us Dulcy was destroying the workroom. Apparently, Elizabeth convinced her that because I'm not officially kin to her I was going to abandon her. Just the way everybody else in her life has. She decided to hit me where it would hurt the most—in my dolls."

"Boy, kids sure know how to get to you, don't they?"

"Absolutely. Anyway, Logan started yelling at Dulcy so I kicked him out. He must have come back here, packed his things and walked out."

"Why'd you get into a fight?"

"It's complicated. Look, Rick, we've got to help the girls clean up the mess. Then you take Dulcy with you."

"Logan'll be back. You can work it out."

"There's nothing to work out."

"I'm sorry." He kneaded her shoulder. "I'd like to have you for a mother-in-law."

Molly blinked back her tears. "He wanted a mother for Dulcy. I don't think he considered any other relationship."

Rick looked at her carefully. "I see. Or I think I do. So what do I do about Dulcy?"

"You'll have to tell Zoe what happened. Whatever happens with Logan, I do love that child, Rick. I don't want to lose her. But I can't be her mother. I just can't."

"No, you can't. Come on, let's go pick up some dolls."

AN HOUR LATER, Dulcy still clung to Molly. She kept whispering "I'm sorry" as she had said "I hate you."

Finally, she said, "Do I got to go with Rick?" She gulped convulsively and hid her face against Molly's shoulder. "I want to stay with you. I got to help."

"You've done your part, kiddo," Molly said, and smoothed her damp hair away from her forehead. "Rick and Zoe are really looking forward to having you sleep over just like a big girl. Just the way Elizabeth sleeps over with me."

Dulcy raised her face, her eyes wide. "Like Elizabeth?" She considered a moment. "Okay, I'll go. I can come home tomorrow right?"

Molly caught her breath. When would she see Dulcy again? Logan might simply walk out of her life and take Dulcy with him. She didn't think she could bear that.

Dulcy definitely did not need to hear that was even a possibility, so Molly simply smiled and kissed the child before she put her down.

Rick drove out with Dulcy as Anne drove in to pick up Elizabeth.

"Gram, can we maybe not tell my mom about what happened?" Elizabeth whispered as Anne opened her car door.

"I plan to hold it over you for the rest of your life, kiddo. Blackmail."

"Oh, Gram."

Five minutes later, Molly stood alone in her workroom. Five arms of varying sizes, a dozen sets of eyeballs and three mismatched legs sat undamaged on the counter. Elizabeth had taken the shards to the trash. Molly was too exhausted and dispirited to try to salvage anything else.

"At least the eyeballs survived," Molly said aloud. She looked at the top shelf. "And Quentin, you little troll, you lead a charmed life. God, what a mess." She sank into her work chair and dropped her head in her hands. "What a mess it all is." She began to cry.

"SHE TURNED HIM down? My father?" Zoe laughed shortly. "Nobody turns my father down."

"Come on, Zoe."

"You know what I mean. It's a ploy—a lovers' quarrel. Mark my words, I've got a new stepmomma right over the horizon."

"Would that be so bad?"

"Bad? The earth mother of the universe? Of course it would be bad. You and I should have Dulcy. If Molly wasn't around to take up the slack, sooner or later even my father would understand that."

"Don't count on it."

"He could take Dulcy out of the country Monday morning. It's just the sort of thing he would do now that Molly's said no."

"So what do we do?"

"I don't know. Make Dulcy so happy with us that she'll want to stay. Talk to my father, Rick. I can't do it."

Rick shook his head. "If we talk, we do it together. But I'm not standing between the two of you. It's time you worked out your problems."

"Work anything out? With my father? Ha!"

"So maybe we could have Dulcy stay with us unofficially. Give her to him on weekends. That's how most grandparents work it."

"Rick, you know my father. He has to control everything, make all the decisions. He'd never agree, and even if he did, he'd be calling here a dozen times a day. No, I want Dulcy for good. We need to make the decisions about which pediatrician to use, which school she goes to. She needs friends, a backyard, a bicycle."

"You fight him on this, you could destroy your relationship forever."

Zoe shrugged. "What relationship?" She turned her head, listening. "I think Dulcy's waking up from her nap. Is the swing set finished?"

"And the sand's in the sandbox."

She smiled and kissed him. "Good. You know, we should really think about getting a puppy. Maybe a Labrador retriever." She trotted up the back stairs toward the guest bedroom.

Rick watched her. He shook his head. He wanted Dulcy as much as she did, but Logan had to make the decision himself. He didn't think that would happen.

"SHERRY, I've got to talk to you."

Sherry Carpenter stood in her front doorway and rubbed a bright blue towel over her damp hair.

She peered at Logan curiously, but stood aside without asking questions, then passed him and led him out to the heated pool house. "Fix yourself a drink. You look as though you could use one. I'll be back as soon as I get some clothes on."

Logan watched her trot into the house and up the front steps. He'd always thought her a remarkably beautiful woman, but today she seemed too thin, too taut, too chic. Like Sydney.

He pulled a diet soda from the small refrigerator nestled under the counter of the bar, opened it and drained half.

Sherry came back wearing a flowered broomstick skirt and a yellow T-shirt. Her feet were bare. She raised her eyebrows at the diet soda in Logan's hand but stretched out on the chaise without speaking.

"Have you talked to Molly?" Logan asked.

"When?"

"Today, this afternoon."

"No. Logan, what's happened?"

"I asked Molly to marry me. She turned me down."

"Good Lord, Logan, why? She's nuts about you."

He threw the can at the garbage can so hard he knocked it over. "That's it, Sherry. I don't know."

He sat on the end of the other chaise and dropped his head into his hands.

"What exactly did you say, Logan? Maybe she didn't understand what you were talking about. Give me the entire conversation from the start."

Before he'd uttered two sentences, Sherry began to groan. He looked up at her to find her shaking her head at him pitiably. "Logan, you are a first-class jerk."

"What?"

"Molly was married to a horse's patoot of a corporate executive who convinced her she was little more than an upper-class servant. Then he walked out on her for a twenty-five-year-old baby corporate lawyer with legs to her shoulders and enough streaky blond hair to stuff a sofa pillow."

"What's that got to do with me? With us?"

"Did you ever in the midst of your generous job offer to Molly mention that you love her? You do, don't you?"

"Of course I do."

"Instead of saying something like, 'Molly Halliday, you are the most beautiful woman I've ever met in my life, I want to make love to you a dozen times a day for the rest of our lives because I love you passionately,' what do you say? 'It's your duty to marry me to provide a mother for Dulcy.' Good grief, Logan, you sound as though you were hiring a nanny."

"That's what Molly said. But, Sherry, she didn't give me a chance to explain."

Sherry threw up her hands in a gesture of frustration. "Logan, you have spent too much time bossing a bunch of roughnecks. You know about women as much as I know about astrophysics."

"So, how do I fix it?"

"Get your tail over there, bang on her door, break it down if you have to and tell her you're an idiot who loves her."

"But Dulcy."

"What about Dulcy? You and Molly need to make a life for yourselves."

"She told me I ought to give custody of Dulcy to Zoe and Rick."

"Of course you should. Anybody can see that."

"Listen, I love Molly, but my first consideration has to be for Dulcy." He stood abruptly.

"Where are you going?"

"Back to Molly, of course. Somehow we've got to work this out, but for the life of me I can't think how."

HE CALLED MOLLY repeatedly from his car phone. Her answering machine was on. The first three times he hung up. The last three he left messages. He moved from demanding she call him back to begging she call him back. He reached her driveway at dusk.

The front gate was closed. He hadn't even realized there was a gate, yet there it was, wrought-iron, five feet tall, and wrapped with a chain, locked with a formidable padlock. He pulled the BMW in front of the gate, stopped it and rattled the chain in impotent frustration.

He had to see her. He vaulted the wooden fence, pushed through the shrubs and loped up the driveway to the house. He rang the bell, beat on the door and shouted for Molly.

Maybe she was in the workroom. He walked down the path, sidestepping the geese. There were no lights in the workroom and the door was locked.

He walked back to the house and peered in the window of the closed garage. No car.

Back in his own car he called Sherry, then Anne Crown. Neither had heard from Molly. He asked both women to have Molly call him at his apartment if they heard from her.

He'd barely seen the inside of his apartment since he and Molly returned with Dulcy. He'd taken the child there this morning to show her the room that would be hers. Zoe's old room, but long since fitted up by Sydney as a sitting room for herself. Nothing remained of the child, Zoe, at all.

He drove home to wander through the silent apartment. Jeremy's old room had become a guest room after he married Tiffany and moved to his own apartment. The only things left in this house from his children's early lives were the pieces of exercise equipment in the attic where Logan exhausted himself every night so that he could sleep.

He sank onto the nearest sofa.

He'd had no trouble sleeping and no nightmares since he'd first slept pillowed on Molly's breast, his body spent from loving her. He'd even slept well in her guest room because he knew that she was only a few feet away. Now he didn't think he'd ever asleep again.

How had he allowed things to get so badly out of kilter with Molly? Surely she knew he loved her, that he didn't want her just as a mother for Dulcy.

He stood up and prowled the apartment like a tiger. He'd used Molly's promise to Dulcy against her. He'd blasted her with a cannon. According to Sherry, he should have tried a dozen roses.

He called Zoe twice. She said Dulcy was getting along beautifully. Both times, Dulcy was too busy to come to the phone.

He prowled some more. Maybe Molly was right. Rick and Zoe were young enough to stand up to Dulcy's constant need for attention. But could he trust them to bring up the child properly? He shook his head. He didn't dare. Dulcy's future was too important. He had to make the decisions.

He called Molly every five minutes and hung up in disgust when her answering machine picked up. At ten o'clock, he began to move from annoyance to fear. Where was she? Had she checked into a hotel?

At midnight he called Sherry and woke her up. She said that she had not heard from Molly and threatened to sic Leo on him if he called again before nine in the morning.

He fell into bed at 1:00 a.m. and counted the pleats under the canopy of his bed until they blurred. As dawn broke, he fell into an uneasy sleep.

The moment he woke, he dressed and drove back to Molly's. Her gate was still locked. He considered reporting her to the police as a missing person. But he had no standing. He wasn't her husband, he was only a fool who loved her. She'd probably been so upset she'd left on one of her trips. How could he have acted so stupidly?

As he sat in his car, Anne's Jeep Cherokee rolled up to the gate. Elizabeth got out of the passenger side, unlocked the padlock, removed the chain and pushed the gate open. Anne drove through and Logan drove through right behind her. He followed the car to the house.

"Mr. MacMillan, good morning. Didn't expect to see you here," Anne said.

"Where's Molly?"

Anne blinked. "Why, I assumed she was with you. She called last night to ask me to feed the animals this morning. I figured you two had driven to the lake or someplace since Dulcy wasn't here." She turned to Elizabeth who stood watching Logan narrowly. "Elizabeth, go feed everybody." Then, as Elizabeth started toward the stable, she said, "And don't let those darned geese break your leg." She watched her daughter for a moment, then turned to Logan. "Should I be worried?"

"When did Molly call you?"

"Nine, ten o'clock last night."

"Did she say where she was?"

"No, she just said to feed the animals. You didn't answer my question. Should I be worried?"

"About Molly? Apparently not. Look, Anne, the next time you talk to her, tell her I've got to see her, speak to her. Will you do that for me?"

"Lovers' quarrel?"

"You could say that." He turned on his heel, climbed into his car, swept around in the turnaround and drove away. How could Molly be so irresponsible? How could she go off without telling him on their first night without Dulcy? She didn't even give him a chance to explain. It was their first fight. Surely she could have waited around long enough to talk to him.

If he intended to convince Molly that he loved her for herself alone, he had to be sure he could look after Dulcy by himself.

He'd pick her up at Zoe's and take her home with him. There'd be just the two of them. He'd prove to Molly, to Zoe, to Rick, to everyone that he could be a responsible father. He'd win Dulcy over to his side. Once Dulcy accepted him, he could woo Molly to be his wife and the other woman in Dulcy's life.

One night might not be enough to accomplish all that. It might take months. A prospective client had been bugging him for weeks to take over a project in the Yucatán that was way behind schedule. Six months max, they said. A lifetime to be without Molly, but it might take her that long to cool down. He'd write her to explain everything. Maybe she didn't want to talk to him, but he knew she'd read his letters. He could rent a villa in Mexico and hire a nanny for Dulcy. Dulcy would love Mexico. In six months, he and Dulcy would be a family. Then Molly would realize that he wanted her for his wife, and not just as a mother for Dulcy.

The more he thought about the idea, the better it sounded.

He picked up fast-food on his way back to the apartment. Molly had certainly messed up his eating habits. He had to admit that a bacon cheeseburger and fries was more fun than steamed broccoli and poached whitefish, but at the rate he was going, he might actually have to start watching his cholesterol. He spread the food on his desk in the apartment and looked up the telephone number of Bob Harriman, the man who'd been speaking to him about the job in Mexico.

Fifteen minutes later he had a solid job offer to head up the construction of a plant in the Yucatán.

"Beautiful country, plenty of nice houses complete with servants," Harriman said. "Shouldn't be any problem to take your granddaughter with you. You can show her all those ruins. Start educating them young, right?"

Logan agreed and hung up.

He drove around aimlessly in Zoe and Rick's neighborhood until five minutes to five. He didn't want them to feel as though he was checking up on them. The houses were comfortably large neat colonials and mock Tudors. He stopped in front of the Jackson house. He'd never noticed the pleasant front yard, the late chrysanthemums in the well-tended flower beds, the euonymus and lucidum banking the front door. A pleasant house. He'd only been inside it on Christmas and Thanksgiving.

He rang the doorbell. No one answered. They knew he was coming. They must be home. He fought a moment of panic. Zoe wouldn't take Dulcy and run. That was ridiculous. He stared up at the windows, then walked down the driveway toward the backyard.

As he reached the garage, he heard Dulcy laugh. He knew it must be Dulcy. She had a deep, husky chuckle that chattered along his nerve endings like champagne. He heard Rick's baritone laughter and Zoe's alto, as well. At least, he thought it must be Zoe's laughter. He hadn't heard her laugh in years. The sound stopped him cold.

He walked down the side yard by the garage until he could glimpse the backyard.

An enormous swing set dominated the yard. It had swings, a treehouse, a slide, a jungle gym.

"Higher, Rick, higher!"

His heart stopped. Dulcy swung so high the chains loosened for a moment at the top of the arc. Rick pushed her. And beside her, Zoe, his staid Zoe, swung just as high and laughed just as hard. For a moment, she looked so like the happy child he remembered that he couldn't catch his breath.

He stepped into the yard.

CHAPTER EIGHTEEN

MOLLY SAT on the bank of Pickwick Lake and watched the sailboats ghost in. Running away was cowardly, but she couldn't face Logan yet.

She'd done more crying than thinking. She'd thought her self-esteem had hit bottom after the divorce, but Logan's marriage proposal had brought her to a new low.

He had made her feel alive, sexy, even beautiful. She loved the feel of his face in her hands, the feel of other parts of his body, as well. She still carried the woodsy scent of him in her nostrils and felt his fingertips caressing her breasts. Of course she'd dreamed what it might be like to marry him. But not this way.

Was she only a convenient mother for Dulcy?

Apparently.

And dammit, as much as she loved Dulcy, she had no intention of becoming the parent of a five-year-old girl.

She had never planned to love Dulcy, but now she could no more cut the child from her heart than she could Anne or Elizabeth. She'd promised herself that one day she'd hear Dulcy laugh. That hadn't happened yet. She wanted to be around when it did.

She'd done what she promised, had gone on Logan's quest, found his Holy Grail and brought her home. She had the right to retire to her cloister again. This was not the time to become a mother. She was a grandmother. That was different.

Dulcy could visit on weekends as Elizabeth did, but no more endless carpools, no more sitting through ballet and riding and piano lessons. She'd done that with Anne. It was somebody else's turn now.

The somebody elses were right under Logan's nose. He was just too stubborn to see them.

Zoe and Rick could search the town for the only kind of science folder some teacher would allow, attend parent-teacher conferences, make trips to the mall for the "only" shoes without which Dulcy's life would be over. Zoe could bake cookies at midnight because Dulcy forgot to mention she needed them until she was ready for bed.

Zoe and Rick would thrive on that kind of craziness, and Dulcy would thrive with them.

But what if Logan took Dulcy off to live in a mud hut on the Upper Volta where you could find a cobra in the bathtub?

Didn't he realize Dulcy needed roots more than any child she'd ever known? She needed the same school every year, the same friends, the same house. She needed two loving parents to convince her that her world couldn't be torn apart at a moment's notice.

Molly had decided Rick was a natural-born father the first day she met him, when he gave her an estimate for plumbing her workshop. As he did the work over the next few weeks, she'd grown more certain she was right about him. He was kind, patient and competent. He listened to people. He was a good teacher.

The strange thing was that in the last few days she'd decided Zoe would make a good mother. Zoe was certainly nervous, too hard on her father and probably on herself. Yet her love for Dulcy was obvious. Dulcy certainly sensed it. Zoe warmed up and loosened up whenever the child was around. Together, Zoe and Dulcy might wind up healing one another.

If Logan would just give them all a chance.

Molly had tried to tell him that Dulcy belonged with Rick and Zoe. He didn't want to hear. Cuddled in his arms two nights before, he had said, "Molly, how different my life would have been if I had married you."

When she asked him how, he'd gone on and on about how she would have made a home for him and their children no matter where he'd been stationed.

She'd been stunned.

"Logan, I am an army brat. I grew up moving from post to post every year, leaving schools and friends at a moment's notice and having to be the new kid over and over again. Then I spent the next twenty years doing the same thing to my daughter, except that it was the blasted company that moved us, not the army. It's a god-awful way to raise children."

"But you did it, and damned well, too."

She tried to explain to him that her log house in the woods, her overgrown land, her animals and the responsibilities that kept her anchored in one place were the only good things to come out of her divorce. He'd listened patiently, but he hadn't heard one word.

She should have known better than to fall in love with him. He'd always said Dulcy was his only consideration and that he alone knew what was best for her.

She couldn't believe he'd made love to her to tie her to him more closely so that she'd stay with him for Dulcy's sake. They gave each other more than pleasure—they came together with joy. Still, they hadn't made love once they found Dulcy. So, all right, it was tough with Dulcy sleeping in Elizabeth's room. So maybe he had planned to make love to her tonight while Dulcy was at Rick and Zoe's. Heck, anything to keep the old girl happy!

She'd hated all the moving and so had Anne. Anne picked a husband who never expected to live more than five miles away from the house in which he was born. How dare Logan expect her to turn her world upside down because he crooked his little finger? What was he changing about his life? Nothing!

No way. Not if she spent the remaining years of her life celibate. She intended to spend the rest of her life meeting her own expectations and nobody else's.

So why did she feel so damned miserable about it?

IN THE DARKNESS of her kitchen, the red light of her answering machine blinked wildly. She clicked the button and played Logan's calls. They began in frustration, progressed to worry and ended in anger.

She picked up the phone to call him, held it a moment, then put it down again. What they had to say to one another should be said face-to-face, not over a telephone, and she'd pick the time to do it.

She fixed herself a salami sandwich, then fed most of the salami to Elvis. Food tasted like cardboard. Without Dulcy and Logan, the house was as still as a cave. Elvis jumped up on the arm of her chair and purred for more salami.

Everybody had an angle! Even the blasted cat!

The phone rang again. The answering machine picked it up. This time, however, it was Zoe Jackson.

Her heart skipped. God! Not something wrong with Logan or Dulcy!

She grabbed the phone in time to hear Zoe say, "My father has taken Dulcy home to his place. She didn't want to go. Molly, it's none of my business what happened between you and my father, but—''

"Forgive me, Zoe, but you're absolutely right. It isn't."

"Molly, you're back. Could Rick and I come over and talk to you? It's important or I wouldn't ask."

Molly looked down at her muddy jeans and sighed. "Of course. I'll put the coffee on."

THEY WALKED IN hand in hand twenty minutes later. Zoe's eyes were red, her skin mottled. Rick guided her to the sofa, sat beside her and draped his arm behind her, not quite holding her, but available if she needed him.

"My father's very upset," Zoe said without preamble. She shook her head at Molly's offer of coffee.

"I know." She handed the mug to Rick who took a single sip and set it on the coaster beside him.

"Do you think he's right?" Zoe said. "About keeping Dulcy himself, I mean?"

Molly took a deep breath. She propped her feet on the ottoman in front of her and took a long sip of her own coffee to gain time. "No, Zoe. I don't. I think Dulcy should live with you and Rick."

"Thank God."

"But maybe there's room for compromise. Logan could retain legal custody, but leave her with you."

Zoe leaned forward. "That's not a good idea. You don't know my father. It would be like what he does with my store, only worse. He'd want to approve everything—from which pediatrician we use to what she eats for breakfast. He never trusts anybody else's judgment. My mother always said that was the engineer in him. I— Rick and I—couldn't raise Dulcy like that. Always looking over our shoulders, always being second-guessed, being blamed if anything didn't go the way he expected it to go."

"Do you hate him that much?" Molly asked softly.

Zoe's mouth dropped open. "Hate him? I don't hate him. I just know him." She began to sniffle. "I love him—not that he's ever noticed. He tried to be a good father when he was around. He's too old and too set in his ways to raise Dulcy. She needs *us.*" She reached across Rick and grabbed his other hand.

"Did you ever tell him you loved him?" Molly asked.

Zoe blinked. "Maybe not in so many words, but..."

"Oh, Zoe," Molly said wearily. She set her mug on the coffee table. "Look. I agree you and Rick should have Dulcy. I also think you need to tell your father you love him and stop blaming him for decisions he made when you were six. He did the best he could, and if he screwed up, well, we all do. If you do get Dulcy, you'll find that out. You're going to put that child in a psychological minefield that may not explode under her until she's forty. Every parent does it. We're human. We mess up. And frankly, Zoe, it's about time you started defusing your own mines." She stood to signal the meeting was over.

"Then you won't talk to my father for us?"

"To quote Dulcy, nope. I'll back you up every step of the way, but if you want Dulcy, you're going to have to convince Logan on your own." She smiled to take the sting out of her words. "Do it right and you may wind up with a father again."

"But why aren't we going home to MyMolly's?" Dulcy asked.

"Because it's time we went home, Dulcy, to our real home, the home that we'll be living in together from now on," Logan said.

"Not with MyMolly?"

"No."

"Oh."

Logan would have felt better if she'd argued, screamed, cried or hit him. This calm acceptance, as though she realized how powerless she was over her own destiny, tore at his heart. His fault. All his fault. He should never have assumed Molly would marry him. Hadn't she said all along she liked living alone? That she liked having the freedom to travel? That she was happy being a grandmother? She'd gone along with him because he'd promised her a new kiln.

Some portion of his brain told him that she'd stayed with him, come into his arms and his bed, taken him and Dulcy into her home and her heart because she wanted to, but he refused to listen.

He parked the car in his space behind MacMillan's, leaned over and unbuckled Dulcy's seat belt. Generally she beat him to it, but tonight she didn't seem to care.

She sat in the car while he pulled her duffel bag from the trunk, and didn't even look at him when he opened the car door for her. She slid out with Petey clutched under her arm, and walked beside him.

He unlocked the back door of the silent shop and ushered her into the dim twilight that spilled over from the night-lights left on in the store. He pushed in the code that disarmed the alarm, shut the door, bolted it and reset the alarm.

Dulcy waited patiently beside him.

She might have been going into the hospital for major surgery. He wanted to hug her, pat her shoulder, reassure her in some way, but he had no idea how to start or what to do if she rebuffed him.

They rode silently in the elevator. He showed her to the guest room and put her suitcase on the carrier under the window.

Dulcy looked at the high four-poster bed. "It's big."

"Do you think you might fall off?"

She rolled her eyes. "I don't fall off beds."

"I see. Speaking of little people, where's baby Dulcy?"

"I left her at Rick and Zoe's for when I come back. She's too big to take all over. Besides, I sleep with Petey."

"I see. Are you hungry? Thirsty?"

She shook her head.

"Do you need help getting into your pajamas?"

She snorted. "'Course not. Don't I got to take a bath?"

"Do you need one?"

Dulcy wriggled her nose. "I'm pretty dirty."

He took a deep breath. "Fine. I'll run your bath. Do you need help getting undressed?"

She raised her eyes in disgust. "Nope. I take my own baths all the time." She went over to her suitcase, hunkered down, opened it and began to rummage.

"Uh, can I help you?"

"I got to find my pj's." She dipped into the case and came up with a pair of flannel pajamas with yellow ducks on them. Logan didn't recognize them. Zoe must have bought them for her. "Okay. You got a toothbrush?"

"There's a new toothbrush on the sink."

She stood with her left hand on her hip. "You got to turn on the water."

He ran her bath, tried to remember how to test it for babies, decided Dulcy could test it herself and went to find her. She stood in the middle of the room in her underwear. She walked past him into the bathroom, gave him a stare over her shoulder and pointedly closed the door.

"Call me if you need anything," he said through the door. "Dulcy?"

"Okay."

"Do you need me to wash your hair or anything?"

"Nope."

He paced and listened to water splashing. "Be careful getting out."

"Sure."

He waited anxiously with his ear pressed against the door, ready to barge in if he heard her cry out or flounder in the water. After five minutes of discreet splashes, he heard her climb out of the tub, heard teeth being brushed, heard the toilet flush. The door opened. Dulcy stood there in her pajamas and bare feet, her short hair damp around the nape of her neck, her face shining in the lamplight. Logan exhaled gratefully. At least she hadn't drowned.

"Do you need me to tuck you in?" he asked.

"Nope."

"Would you like me to read to you?"

"I can read to myself."

Logan walked to the door and turned to watch her watching him. "Well, good night."

"Uh-huh." She didn't move.

He paused with one hand on the doorknob. "Dulcy, are you sure you'll be all right in that bed? Maybe you'd prefer I make you a bed on the chaise in my bedroom."

"Uh-uh."

"Do you plan to sleep in the closet? Is that it?"

"Maybe." Her eyes scanned the room.

He came back in and sat on the slipper chair beside the door. "Dulcy, I know you don't like me much, but we've got to learn to get along somehow."

"You're okay."

"I know I'm not as good at this stuff as Molly is..."

"Rick's good, too."

"I shouldn't have stayed at Molly's this long or let you think we'd be staying there permanently." *Except that I thought we were.*

"Why won't MyMolly marry us?" Dulcy asked. "Is it because of me?"

He reached out to her and she stepped back quickly. "No, Dulcy. No. It's not because of you. She loves you very much. It's because of me."

"Maybe you asked her wrong?"

He smiled grimly. "Maybe I did."

"So ask her right and maybe she'll marry us."

"I would be delighted to, but I don't know where she is."

Dulcy caught her breath. For the first time, she seemed frightened. "MyMolly's gone?"

He hastened to reassure her. "No, not gone, Dulcy, or at least not for long. She's just taken a little time off. She'll be back."

"Then you'll ask her right to marry us?" Dulcy nodded her head as though encouraging him to agree with her. She was like a teacher coaching a really slow student.

"I promise I'll try. But I can't guarantee she'll say yes."

"If she won't, do we got to stay here by ourselves for-ever and ever?"

"You don't want to?"

"You don't got a pony and a donkey and a swing set and geese and Elvis and a backyard."

Logan sighed. "No, but I can get them."

"You don't got Rick and Zoe and Elizabeth and MyMolly, either."

That was the real problem. He didn't have anyone except this grave child, and he was more and more certain he shouldn't have her either.

"We'll work it out some way so we can be happy. I promise you, Dulcy. Just give me a chance. I'm not so bad."

She cocked her head, assessing him, then she sighed like a grown-up and walked slowly over to lean against his knees. "My mommy used to say she was bad, too, but she wasn't, Grandfather Logan." She patted his arm gently. "I had to talk to her about being bad lots so she wouldn't feel sad. Don't you feel sad either, okay?" She nodded several times as though adding up a column of figures in her head.

"You found me, that's good. You gave me baby Dulcy, that's good after I got used to it. You found me again when I got lost in the bathroom. And you didn't tell MyMolly. That's good. And you slept on the floor at MyMolly's so I wouldn't be scared when I woke up. That's good." She nodded once more and smiled up at him. "Okay?"

He didn't think he could take much more without breaking down completely. "Okay."

"And you're going to ask MyMolly to marry us right. That'll be good. And you're going to let me stay with Rick and Zoe sometimes. That'll be good." The last was said with a sly sideways glance.

"Of course I am."

"Okay." She dismissed him as though the audience was over and went to burrow in her suitcase. After a moment, she found the book she wanted. "I'm going to bed now, Grandfather Logan. G'night."

He wanted to hug her, to give her a good-night kiss, but he didn't offer and neither did she. Apparently, patting his arm was as close to physical contact as she intended to get.

He walked to the door again. "Good night, Dulcy. And thank you for the pep talk."

She waved a hand at him without looking at him, and climbed up onto the big bed. He watched while she turned down the covers and crawled between them. Only then did he realize he should have turned the bed down for her, removed the spread. She propped herself up on the lace pillows and opened the book. She looked over at him dismissively. "I'll go to sleep in a minute, okay? I like to read first."

"Not too long. Should I leave your door open or closed?"

"Open, okay?"

"I'm right next door." He pointed. "Call me if you need anything." He didn't add "or get frightened." He knew that would offend her. He clicked off the overhead light. She lay in bed holding her book in the small circle of light from the bedside table lamp. The light turned her curls into an aureole of soft pink feathers around her head.

He half closed his own bedroom door, then leaned against the jamb. Dulcy was clean and safe, and if not content, at least comfortably settled. He hadn't drowned her or sent her scurrying to the closet in terror. At least not yet.

"I can do this," he told himself. "If I have to, I can raise this child alone, but God in heaven, I don't want to, and I'm starting to think I shouldn't. Oh, Molly, where are you now that I need you?"

CAROLYN McSPARREN 277

"Exactly this," he told Bianca. "If I lose so I can't make the child-support payments, and so everybody, and TV, can see I've struck out, they'll—" He broke off. "I'm sorry, I can't do this."

CHAPTER NINETEEN

LOGAN STOOD in the kitchen doorway and watched Dulcy. She hadn't noticed him or heard him over the rap music playing low on the radio on the counter. The clock read six-thirty in the morning. She must have wanted to avoid waking him, but she'd figured out not only how to turn on the unfamiliar radio, but how to tune it to the station she wanted. The insistent bass beat was identifiable even if the words weren't.

She'd probably used the radio for company on the lonely mornings when her mother was too tired or too hung over to fix her breakfast. Her very self-sufficiency wrenched his heart.

Dulcy hummed along, her head bobbing and her shoulders moving rhythmically. She found the kitchen stool, climbed from it to the counter and began to hunt through the cupboards. On her second try she found a box of raisin bran—the only cereal Logan ate, and only occasionally. She pulled down the box, set it on the counter beside her and slid along to the next cabinet on her knees. Her new jeans made small scraping sounds on the marble countertop.

He watched her with his heart in his mouth. She was such a little person, and suddenly the counter seemed miles above the quarry-tile floor. He made a quick movement toward her, then stopped. He wasn't really spying on her. She had only to turn her head to see him in the doorway. He knew he stood close enough to catch her if she slipped.

She found a cereal bowl, set it on the counter, slid back to the place she'd left the kitchen stool and climbed down carefully, humming and bobbing all the while. When she turned to set the bowl on the table, she saw him. She jumped, but didn't drop the bowl.

"Good morning," he said.

"G'morning." She reached for the cereal box. The bobbing motion stopped. She became all business again. "I got hungry. You want me to maybe fix you some, too?"

He shook his head. "No, thank you. Is that what you usually have for breakfast?"

"Uh-huh. My mommy didn't let me use the stove."

She spoke of her mother in the past tense, but he was certain that indicated awareness of his point of view, not her own. He cleared his throat and asked, "May I help you?"

"Nope. You got milk?"

He nodded. He wasn't certain whether there was anything else in the refrigerator except a six-pack of beer and a jar of olives. There should be orange juice, and the milk should be relatively fresh. Zoe usually picked up extra cartons for him when she did her own shopping. He'd taken her small kindness for granted. He made a mental note to thank her when he saw her.

He watched Dulcy pour her milk neatly, found her a spoon in the drawer that held the everyday silver and reached down two glasses. "I have orange juice. Would you like some?"

Dulcy nodded. "You gonna make coffee? My mommy drinks lots of coffee. She lets me pour the water. I know how to make it real good, but that's not the same kind we have.'' She pointed to the coffeemaker.

Logan glanced at the stainless-steel apparatus in the corner. ''Yes. I think I will.'' Dulcy watched him warily over her cereal spoon, but when he set down her orange juice, she drank it greedily, holding it with both hands and making gulping sounds. ''We don't have big glasses like this,'' she said as she set it down half-empty beside her cereal.

While he waited for his coffee to hiss into the pot, he sat down opposite Dulcy. She ate neatly, but even so, she dripped. He reached over and pulled a paper towel off the roll and handed it to her. She took it without comment, wiped her mouth daintily and slid it into her lap.

Maybe he could do this, he thought. He and Dulcy could live together amicably. In Mexico, it would be easier. There would be servants to look after them both, a swimming pool... No, maybe not a swimming pool. He'd be working long hours. He couldn't risk having servants watch over Dulcy in a house with a pool. He'd hire an English-speaking nanny, and in the spring he'd hire a tutor.

In Mexico, he wouldn't have to see Molly. He already missed her the way he'd miss a leg or an eye. He didn't know how he'd react if he ran into her accidentally at Sherry's or saw her at MacMillan's. No, Mexico was better.

''You got a newspaper?'' Dulcy asked. ''I like to read the comics at breakfast.''

He nodded, then realized it would be downstairs at the back door. He went to get it. When he came back, he saw that Dulcy had rinsed out the dishes and his orange-juice glass and was loading them into the dishwasher as though she did it every day. Hell, she probably did do it every day, at least when Tiffany had been able to afford an apartment with a dishwasher.

Dulcy turned unsmiling eyes toward him. She'd turned off the radio. She watched him expectantly while he unfolded the newspaper and handed her the comics section. She opened it, climbed back onto the kitchen chair, set the paper on the table, cupped her chin in her hand and began to read. She blocked him out entirely.

Maybe books, newspapers and magazines were Dulcy's way of locking out the world she didn't understand and couldn't handle. He was part of that world.

He poured himself a cup of coffee. "Would you like a glass of milk?" he asked.

She shook her head.

He sat opposite her and opened the paper, but even the report of the latest commuter-plane crash emblazoned across the front page didn't interest him. He watched her bright head surreptitiously, hoping for any sign that she was even aware of his presence. Once, she glanced up at him gravely and immediately dropped her eyes back to the paper.

In that instant, he made his decision. He could take her off to Mexico, to a world of nannies and servants, where she would be as isolated as she had been with Tiffany. He could live with her, perhaps with time reach a kind of ease with her, but would she ever let him past that wall she'd built up around herself? Even worse, could he drop his own walls?

He wanted to hear her laugh again. He remembered the joyful whoops and giggles he'd heard from Rick and Zoe and Dulcy just before he'd stepped into their backyard the night before. That was a different Dulcy from the one he'd seen even with Molly, and certainly different from this little girl reading her newspaper.

He was a selfish idiot. He couldn't use Dulcy to expi-
ate his guilt over being a lousy father. The past was gone.
He must not screw up the future—Dulcy's future—even
if it meant he spent the rest of his life alone. He kept
talking about knowing what was best for her. Now that
he did know, he'd better put his money where his mouth
was, no matter how much it hurt.

"Grandfather Logan?"

He realized she'd climbed down and stood beside his
chair. He looked into her upturned face. Her eyes held
concern. Obviously, she'd picked up on his distress.

"You gonna ask MyMolly to marry us right today?"

Without thinking, he bent down and swept her into his
arms the way he had in Laramie and at the airport, and
sat her on his lap. For a moment, she froze as she had
then, every muscle straining against him. Then she slid
one arm around his neck. He heard her heart beating
against his, smelled the sweet mingled scent of child and
milk and orange juice, and feared it was the last time he'd
ever hold her this way.

"Today may not be the right time."

"But I miss MyMolly." She lowered her head and her
voice was so soft he had to strain to catch the words. "I
did a real bad thing, didn't I? That's why MyMolly won't
marry us, isn't it?"

He hugged her fiercely. "No, child, no. It doesn't have
anything to do with you. She loves you, I promise you
that." He released her and looked into her face. God,
how could he reassure her? He had to make her see that
she wasn't responsible for any of it. And he didn't know
how.

"I promise you, Dulcy, Molly will always be a part of
your life." It was a safe promise. He knew Molly well

enough to know that whatever he did, Dulcy would be safely under her wing forever.

He slid Dulcy off his lap and smiled at her. Maybe he'd finally gained a little wisdom. He knew his choice was right. Knew with a certainty so powerful that for a moment he was afraid the weight of it would crush him, and then a moment later the pain lifted, leaving him feeling lighter than he had in a long time.

He stood and took Dulcy's hand. "Come on, kiddo," he said in obvious imitation of Molly. "I've got some telephone calls to make."

"WHERE'S DULCY?" Zoe asked as she walked into Sherry's front hall. Rick sauntered behind her. At first glance he seemed relaxed, but his eyes followed Zoe. He nodded at Logan and smiled, but did not take his hands out of the pockets of his jeans.

"Out by the pool with Sherry," Logan said. When Zoe moved past him, he stopped her. "Not yet, please, Zoe. She doesn't know you're here. I would prefer we keep it that way until after we've talked."

The look Zoe gave him was cool. "It's your party." Logan held the library door for her and pointed her toward the couch. Rick followed.

"Well?" Zoe turned without sitting down.

Logan shook his head. "I only want to say what I have to say once. If you don't mind, we'll wait for Molly."

Zoe started to protest but caught Rick's small headshake and subsided. "Oh, all right."

The doorbell rang. Logan answered it.

Molly stood on the doorstep clutching her satchel in front of her like a barrier between her body and Logan's. His heart turned over at the sight of her. She'd put on a dress—the first time he'd ever seen her wear one—

and makeup, even a pair of high-heeled pumps. He read the signals. She was using the unaccustomed clothes as another barrier so he would know that nothing remained between them but a strained formality. The smile died on his lips.

He greeted her and led her to the library. When she was seated in the wing chair, he went to stand by the fireplace.

"I've taken a job in Mexico," he said without preamble. "I leave next Friday."

Zoe jumped up. "No! You can't take that child to Mexico." She turned to Rick. "Rick, do something, say something. We've only just got her back."

Logan opened his mouth to speak, but she rounded on him. "We won't let you. I don't know how we'll stop you, but we will. Come on, Rick." She headed for the door. Rick followed her, but whether to join her or to stop her Logan couldn't tell. Molly sat quietly, her feet neatly crossed at the ankles, her hands clutching her satchel. He glanced at her and the look of concern that he read in her eyes heartened him. He'd get through this somehow. Then it would be all over, and these people could get on with their lives.

"Zoe, come back, please, I'm not finished."

"When are you ever? You go off without telling me, find Dulcy, bring her home, plop her into the middle of our lives and then just like that you snatch her away again before we, she, any of us have had a chance to become a family again."

"You'll have a chance to become a family," he said quietly. "This morning I instructed my lawyer to sign over custody of Dulcy to you and Rick."

Zoe gaped. "What?"

Logan turned away. He couldn't bear to look at Molly or Zoe until this was over. He took a deep breath, glanced at Molly and addressed Zoe. "You don't know how hard it is for me to apologize, to admit I was wrong, but I've been wrong from the beginning. I should have told you we were going to find Dulcy. I treated you like a child, not like the very fine woman you have become." He turned to Rick. "This is my day for apologies. You're the one who made my decision for me." He shook his head. "Dulcy doesn't laugh with me. With you she does—she will. I can't deny her joy. Molly was right when she said you were a natural-born father. Unfortunately, I am not."

He walked to the window to stare out into the front yard. Instead of the chrysanthemums, he saw twenty-hour days spent driving himself until he could fall asleep in an unfamiliar house alone among unfamiliar voices. He'd survive, somehow. He always had, but then he hadn't carried in his heart the memory of Dulcy's laughter or the touch of Molly's sweet lips. Those memories would get him through the coming months and years. If anything could. They wouldn't come close to the joy of holding Molly in his arms, waking up with her beside him, of hearing Dulcy's laughter, but they'd have to do.

"So—" he turned back to them and rubbed his hands together as at the consummation of a thorny business negotiation "—next week I'll be gone and you and Dulcy can begin to create your new family. All I ask is that you make Molly a big part of Dulcy's life." No one spoke. "Well, that's it." He strode toward the door. Zoe and Rick moved aside for him. "I'll leave you to explain to Dulcy. She doesn't need me."

Zoe intercepted him. She touched his sleeve. "Daddy, that's not true. Dulcy does need you. We all do. Don't go, please."

"You never called me Daddy before," he said.

"I didn't?" Zoe said. "I always think of you as Daddy."

"Come on, Zoe," Rick said gently. "Let's go find Dulcy. We can talk about the rest of it later. Right now, your father has some more unfinished business to take care of."

"But, Rick..."

"Zoe." There was the tiniest hint of warning in Rick's voice.

"Oh." Zoe followed him obediently. Logan stood aside and waited until they'd left the room.

"Why do you have to go to Mexico?" Molly asked softly. "You don't have to leave the country to let them become a family. You're part of that family."

He took a deep breath and turned to her. He tried to keep his voice level. He was afraid it would betray him. "Not because of them, Molly. I'm going to Mexico because of you." He leaned against the door and closed his eyes. "Do you think I could endure running into you at Sherry's or the grocery store or at Rick and Zoe's with Dulcy?"

"I'm sorry. The last thing I wanted was to contribute to your sense of failure." She sounded angry.

She, who understood so much about other people, understood so little about herself. Whatever it took, he had to show how desirable she was and how much he loved her.

He crossed the room in two strides, pulled her up from her chair and held her at arm's length. "I made those stupid demands because I didn't think you'd ever marry me for myself." He felt aware of the scent of her, the feel of her, the warmth of her in every fiber of his being. "I can't bear to know you're a dozen miles from me and not in my bed or my arms. That you're not my wife." He dropped his hands and turned away, thrusting his fists into his pockets. His palms burned where he'd touched her. He felt his shoulders sag and was suddenly unbelievably tired. "I'm tough, Molly," he said quietly, "but I'm sure as hell not that tough."

"Oh, my dear," she whispered.

He turned back to her and saw that she stood where he'd left her and that tears streamed down her cheeks. "Molly, how can you not know that I love you more than life itself?"

She laughed shakily and ran her hand across her cheek. "I suppose because you never mentioned it." Then she held out her arms to him.

They clung together fiercely as though each was trying to absorb the other. He drank in the scent of her hair, the remembered softness of her breast against his chest. He drew back. "Something's different. You don't fit the same. You're taller."

She laughed. "It's these damned high heels." She kicked them off.

"That's better," he said, and bent her head back to kiss the hollow of her throat, her ears, her eyes, her soft cheeks still wet with tears. When at last he found her sweet mouth and felt her lips part for him, he drank her kiss like the water of life and felt his soul bloom again.

After a long moment, he broke the kiss. "God, Molly, what am I going to do? I have to take that job. They're counting on me."

She laughed and hugged him harder. "That's the first time you've ever asked for input from me on any decision."

"I can't lose you again, my Molly." He kissed her again and realized that if he didn't watch it he'd lock that damned library door and make love to her on Sherry's hearth rug.

She must have realized it, too, and broke the kiss, gasping. "Whoa," she said.

"It's been too long." He nuzzled her neck. "I want you right here, right now."

"Well, you can't have me right here and now." She laughed. "I know Rick would approve, but I'm not too sure about Zoe. Sherry would want to coach from the sidelines and she takes yoga. I'd wind up at the chiropractor's."

"Zoe will get used to having a stepmother. She likes you." He heard Molly's breath catch in her throat and his heart turned over. "You will marry me, won't you?"

"When you get back from Mexico?"

"I can't wait that long. Now, today. Yesterday, if possible. If I have to dump the job, I will. I can't lose you for six months or six days. I'd get jungle rot and die."

They both heard the timid knock at the door and sprang apart as guiltily as teenagers caught necking on the porch swing. "Molly?" Sherry said. "Are you all right?"

"Sure, Sherry. Fine and dandy. Thanks for asking." Molly glanced down at the evidence of Logan's passion. "Uh, we'll be out in a minute." She giggled. "At the moment we're engaged."

"Engaged!" Sherry whooped and opened the door.

Molly stepped in front of Logan, who snorted in annoyance. "I didn't mean engaged-engaged. I meant we're busy."

"Oh. Sorry."

"It's all right, Sherry," Logan said. "Molly was quite correct. We are engaged. In every sense of the word." He bent his head to Molly. "We are, aren't we?"

She smiled up at him over her shoulder. "Yes. Yes, we are."

"MyMolly, MyMolly!" Dulcy shoved Sherry aside and raced to Molly.

"MyDulcy, MyDulcy!" Molly laughed and scooped the child up. Zoe and Rick followed. Zoe leaned back into the circle of Rick's arms.

Logan saw she'd never looked happier. He smiled at Rick who grinned back and winked at him.

"Rick and Zoe say we're gonna get pizza. Wanna come?" Dulcy asked Molly.

"Sure, kiddo. Soon as I find my shoes." She let Dulcy down, and the child raced to Rick and Zoe.

At the doorway she whirled. "Come *on*, Grandfather Logan! Me and Rick and Zoe and Sherry and Molly's hungry." She took Rick's hand and began to drag him to the front door.

Logan watched them. "I did the right thing, didn't I, Molly?"

She kissed him on the cheek. "Indeed you did, my dear. I'm so proud of you."

EPILOGUE

"DAMMIT, Molly, these Easter eggs look as though they'd been buried in a toxic-waste dump."

Molly glanced up from her sketch pad. Logan sat across the kitchen table. The sleeves of his plaid logger's shirt were rolled up over his elbows. His fingers, palms and wrists wore a rainbow of pastel colors. There was a blotch of hot pink on the end of his nose.

Molly laughed and reached an index finger across the table. She rubbed his nose.

"Stop that."

"You look as though you've grown your own clown nose. I'm only trying to remove a large pink blob. Sit still." She rubbed. "There. Better."

He grumbled, "I can't do this. I thought Dulcy and Elizabeth were going to dye these eggs. How did I get stuck with it?"

Molly set down her sketch pad and assessed the mess across the table. Small bowls held liquid dye in green, purple, gold, red and the hot pink that had wound up on Logan's nose. A carton of eggs, some pristinely white, some mottled, sat in front of the nearest bowl. "Don't grumble, darling. Elizabeth thinks she's too old for Easter eggs and Dulcy's lost interest. Besides, it will do you good."

"Heck of a job for a grown man."

"Logan, I can't believe you never dyed Easter eggs before. Not even when you were a child?"

"We collected our eggs from under the hens in the morning and ate them fried or scrambled as soon as possible." He looked sulky. "How come this one's black?" He looked down at the egg drying on paper towels in front of him.

"Because when you add all the colors together, you get black. Or sort of Oxford gray. I have to admit you're right. It does look nasty."

Dulcy put down her book, got down from the bar stool at the kitchen counter and came over to peer around Logan's shoulder. She ducked under his arm and climbed onto his lap. "That's okay, Grandfather Logan. I'll help you." She patted his hand consolingly. "See, you got to hold it like this." She took a fresh egg, inserted it carefully into the circular wire holder and dipped it precisely into the pink liquid. The dye reached halfway up the egg. "Then, see, you let it dry." She blew on the wet egg. "Then you turn it over and dip it in the yellow." She concentrated. Molly watched her over the top of the sketch pad. "You mustn't let the colors touch." She carefully placed the egg, still in its holder, to drain over an empty bowl. "There. When it's dry, we'll glue some ribbon where the colors meet. See?"

"And a little child shall lead them," Molly whispered. Logan growled at her.

Elizabeth, two inches taller and beginning to develop a hint of bosom and a narrow waist, stuck her head around the kitchen door. "Hey, Dul, I'm not grooming Maxie by myself. Not if you expect to ride."

"Okay, 'Lizabeth." She jumped off Logan's lap. "Grandfather Logan, you bring Rick down to see me ride when he gets here, okay? He doesn't get to see me ride Maxie much. I can even jump a little, can't I, 'Lizabeth?"

Elizabeth shrugged. "A little. Actually, Gram, she's getting pretty good, aren't you, kid? I think she'll be ready to ride short-stirrup classes in the May horse show."

Dulcy beamed.

"Elizabeth," Molly said, "'Dul' is not an attractive nickname."

"That's okay, MyMolly, I like it when she calls me that. She means it good, don't you, 'Lizabeth?"

"Yeah, kid, I guess so. Well, come on, for Pete's sake. They'll be here any minute and Maxie's been rolling in the mud."

"Okay, 'Lizabeth. I'm coming." Dulcy skipped out the back door.

"Dulcy, don't slam—"

The door crashed. "Oh, well," Molly said and caught her breath. She could hear Dulcy's laughter floating on the evening breeze as she ran down the hill with Elizabeth.

Molly closed her eyes, remembering how she had promised herself that one day she would hear Dulcy laugh. She'd heard that laugh often now, but it never failed to warm her heart.

Logan carried the dishes to the sink, poured the dye down the sink and ran water into the dishes. He sat at the bar, marked Dulcy's place in *Gulliver's Travels* and noted it was the section about the civilized horses.

Molly put the remaining eggs back into the refrigerator.

Logan caught her around the waist as she passed, and pulled her onto his lap. "Do you realize that ever since we got home from Mexico, those girls have been over here nearly nonstop. We've barely had a moment alone."

She nuzzled his neck. "Don't you count last night in bed? I do."

"At least we don't have to sleep in separate beds any longer when they're around. But they wear me out. Don't they ever wind down? And now we've got Zoe, Rick, Anne and Phil all coming for dinner."

"You love playing family patriarch, admit it."

He nuzzled her neck. "Do you want me to grow a long white beard and take a young concubine?"

"Beards scratch, and if you bring home a young concubine I'll kill you myself before you die of excess passion."

"You're the only concubine who brings out the passion in me."

"I'm not a concubine. Just a plain old wife."

"There is no 'plain' about you." He kissed her gently, then more deeply, his tongue reaching for the soft familiar ridges along the roof of her mouth. She relaxed in his arms and answered his tongue with hers. His hand crept from her waist to her breast.

She captured it and held it away from her. "Later. Don't forget we've got company coming."

"All right, witch. At any rate, I need to talk to you about something before the others get here."

She caught her breath. "That sounds serious."

"It is. I heard from my lawyer today. George Youngman has surfaced in North Carolina. Would you believe he wanted a reference?"

"I would believe anything of that snake. So they've arrested him?"

Logan shook his head. "They've decided not to prosecute. With Tiffany dead, there's no way he could be convicted."

"So he gets away with lying to you? Blackmailing Tiffany? Everything?" Molly pulled away and began to pace. "Just like that? He starts all over again?"

Logan chuckled. "Not quite. He got that little reference he asked for, but I doubt if he liked it much. He won't stay in North Carolina long. Or any place else we can trace him. There are too many people out for his blood."

"If you keep the pressure on, maybe sooner or later he'll get out of the private detective business and take up something he's fit for—snake-farming, maybe."

"Let it go, Molly. I can. Finally. Because it all turned out better than I could have hoped. Without Youngman I might never have met you." He leaned out to capture her hand and pulled her back into his arms.

She brushed a kiss against his forehead. "And Quentin's portrait would have been finished two months earlier. I don't think Mrs. Dillahunt has forgiven me yet."

He slid the tip of his tongue into the hollow at the base of her throat and mumbled.

Molly caught her breath. "What?"

He raised his head and grinned. "Mrs. Dillahunt can get a grip, as Elizabeth would say. It's time passion took precedence." The gate alarm sounded in confirmation.

Molly slid off Logan's lap and ran her fingers through her hair. She looked down at his lap and laughed. "At least my passion isn't so obvious."

He ran his finger across her swollen nipple. "Want to bet?" He smiled lovingly at her.

"Hey," Zoe and Rick called from the living room.

"Oh, damn." Molly smoothed her sweater down. "Hey, you two, we're in the kitchen," she called. "Dulcy wants Rick and Logan to go watch her ride Maxie. She's started jumping and she's very proud of herself."

"Just Rick?" asked Zoe.

"Us, too. We'll follow them down."

"I brought the salad." Zoe put a crystal bowl into the refrigerator with accustomed ease.

"Thanks. Would like you a soda or a glass of wine?"

Zoe shook her head. "Can I help with dinner?"

"You've already helped. Anne's bringing dessert. The asparagus is in the warming oven. Logan's grilling the chicken outside on the deck."

Zoe sat on the nearest bar stool and hooked her running shoes around the rungs. She smiled at Molly. "It's nice having you home again from Mexico. We all missed you. Dulcy especially."

"Six months was much too long to stay away from home, but it was either that, or sit here and wait until Logan finished industrializing the Yucatán."

"I'm not sure I could pick up and move to a strange country that way."

"Plus marry a strange man at the same time."

Zoe laughed. "Granted, my father can be very strange sometimes."

Molly answered her laugh. "That wasn't what I meant and you know it. It's amazing how those two girls have grown, isn't it?"

"Not only in size. Dulcy's so much surer of herself. Did she tell you she's been coming over with Elizabeth three afternoons a week to ride Maxie?"

"Elizabeth's really getting into this mentor-teacher thing, isn't she? That should keep them from each other's throats for another couple of years."

"Thank you for having them over so much since you've been home. As much as I love Dulcy, it is really nice to have Rick to myself occasionally."

"We're glad to have her."

"Is my father planning to stay around for a while?"

"He's worked out a deal with the company. He'll be gone no more than a month at a time and no more than three times a year. Age has its privileges. He's becoming the engineering guru—just nod in, fix the problems and come home again. Thank God for modems and fax machines."

"Are you going with him?"

"Depends on where he goes. If we're talking Greece or Argentina, I'm all for it. I may not be so anxious to follow him to Siberia. We were in Mexico long enough so that I could set up a decent workshop and get all my commissions finished. Logan owed me a new kiln, after all, for finding Dulcy in the first place. But I can't continue to do that. And I miss the animals, this place, the familiarity. Still, that doesn't mean we won't travel for pleasure. We're going to Alaska in June. We'd like to take Dulcy with us."

"And Elizabeth?"

"Elizabeth has other fish to fry. Horse shows, friends. She'd miss the malls. No, just Dulcy."

"Check with Rick, but I'm sure she can go. As a matter of fact, we all three had so much fun when we visited you in Mexico at Christmas that Rick and I were thinking of asking you to take Dulcy for a week so we can go to Cabo San Lucas."

"Good idea. But don't wait until June. You won't be able to fit into a bathing suit."

"Huh?"

"You're about three months along, right?"

"Molly! How did you know?"

Molly laughed. "You look as though someone lit up a halogen bulb inside you."

Zoe looked at her chest ruefully. "You're right. I'm blown up like a pair of balloons. None of my bras fit."

Molly laughed. "I wasn't talking about the size of your bosom. You glow."

"Oh." Zoe smiled. "Rick says he can't tell yet, but none of my skirts will button."

"When were you planning to tell Logan?"

"Tonight. We had our ultrasound today. It's a girl."

"Have you told Dulcy?"

"No." Zoe looked out the window. Logan and Rick leaned on the pasture fence while Elizabeth stood in the center of the small ring and watched Dulcy trot around her. "I'm scared to tell her, Molly. You saw her at Tiffany's memorial service—she didn't even cry. The three months after you left for Mexico were rough. The first time Rick and I took her to the cemetery to show her Tiffany's grave, I don't think she took it in. I know she didn't understand what relationship Jeremy and my mother were to her."

"But you said it's better now."

"Oh, yes. We take flowers for their graves, try to give her a sense of the people she came from. She's beginning to feel she belongs. I'm afraid she'll think we prefer our own baby to her. That won't happen."

"I know and so will she, although I don't put it past her to manipulate you with guilt to get her way. Just give her plenty of reassurance. She'll be fine, bar the normal jealousy and resentment that comes with any new baby." She patted Zoe's tummy. "You'd better tell her and Logan before you put on maternity dresses."

"Oh, Molly, I can't believe it. We tried too hard for so long to have a baby. It's as though Dulcy blessed us all. You and my father, my father and me, even Rick and my father are friends now. And I don't know what I'd do without Anne to help with carpool now that Dulcy's in kindergarten. And Elizabeth to baby-sit."

"Enjoy it while you can. In another year, Elizabeth won't give you the time of day. Make sure you keep in good with Sherry. Not only does she adore Dulcy, she has a pool."

"I'm going to need all the help I can get. Expanding the store to take over Daddy's old apartment, the construction, the dust. I don't know what I would have done if Daddy hadn't kept his office so he could supervise when he got back."

"You better get finished quick, my dear," Molly said, laughing. "He's already got the plans drawn up to build himself an office across from my workshop, complete with space for Jeremy's exercise equipment. It definitely does not fit into my guest room." She made a fist and raised her arm. "Although with him to coach me, I may get in shape for the first time in my life."

"A separate building? Why not build onto your workshop?"

Molly snorted. "I adore Logan, but I wouldn't share an office with him unless it was in a parallel universe."

The alarm rang again. A moment later Anne and Phil Crown came in. Anne held out a chocolate cake. "Here, Mom. Phil's got the ice cream."

"I THOUGHT tonight went really well, dear heart." Molly curled against Logan and nestled her head against his shoulder. "Just think how far we've come in seven months. We're turning into a real family."

"And I'm going to be a grandfather again," Logan said. "I'm not sure I've got the hang of it with Dulcy and Elizabeth yet."

"You're doing fine." She ran her index finger down his chest to his waist and below. He gasped as she began to caress him. She nibbled his shoulder. "So why don't we try something you do have the hang of?"

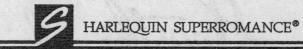

HARLEQUIN SUPERROMANCE®

ANOTHER MAN'S CHILD
by
Tara Taylor Quinn

Marcus Cartwright is rich and handsome. What's more, he's in love with his wife. And Lisa Cartwright adores her husband. *Their marriage, however, is falling apart.*

That's because Marcus can't give Lisa the baby they've always longed for.

So he's decided to give Lisa her freedom—to find and marry someone else. To have her *own* child.

It's a freedom Lisa doesn't want. But she can't convince Marcus of that.

So Lisa decides to take matters into her own hands. She decides to have a baby. And she's not going to tell Marcus until the artificial-insemination procedure is over....

But will Marcus be able to accept Another Man's Child?

Watch for *Another Man's Child* by Tara Taylor Quinn
Available in February 1997
wherever Harlequin books are sold.

Heartbreak RANCH

Four generations of independent women…
Four heartwarming, romantic stories of the West…
Four incredible authors…

Fern Michaels
Jill Marie Landis
Dorsey Kelley
Chelley Kitzmiller

Saddle up with Heartbreak Ranch, an outstanding
Western collection that will take you on a whirlwind
trip through four generations and the exciting,
romantic adventures of four strong women who
have inherited the ranch from Bella Duprey,
famed Barbary Coast madam.

Available in March,
wherever Harlequin books are sold.

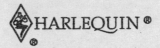

HARLEQUIN ®
®

HTBK

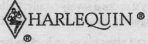

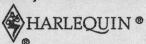

Harlequin and Silhouette celebrate
Black History Month with seven terrific titles,
featuring the all-new *Fever Rising*
by Maggie Ferguson
(Harlequin Intrigue #408) and
A Family Wedding by Angela Benson
(Silhouette Special Edition #1085)!

Also available are:
Looks Are Deceiving by Maggie Ferguson
Crime of Passion by Maggie Ferguson
Adam and Eva by Sandra Kitt
Unforgivable by Joyce McGill
Blood Sympathy by Reginald Hill

On sale in January at your favorite
Harlequin and Silhouette retail outlet.

Look us up on-line at: http://www.romance.net   BHM297